I0739626

Sidewalk Press

sidewalkpressbooks.com

THE GARDEN OF DEAD DREAMS

THE GARDEN OF DEAD DREAMS

ABBY QUILLEN

Sidewalk Press

sidewalkpressbooks.com

THE GARDEN OF DEAD DREAMS

Published by
Sidewalk Press
sidewalkpressbooks.com
sidewalkpress@gmail.com

Cover and interior design by Aaron Thomas

Publisher's Cataloging-in-Publication Data
Quillen, Abby.
    The Garden of Dead Dreams/Abby Quillen
      p.   cm.
    ISBN 978-0-9899822-3-8
      1. Authors—Fiction.   2. Female friendship—Fiction.
3. Missing persons—Fiction. 4. Japanese Americans—Fiction.
5. Northwest, Pacific—Fiction. 6. World War, 1939-1945—Fiction.
I. Title.
    813'.6—dc23

For Aaron.
Loop and Lil agree,
you're a sight to see.

Chapter One

❖

Etta Lawrence wasn't the only one who came to Roosevelt Lodge to become someone else.

That's why they'd all come.

Even after two months, Etta couldn't believe she was here, especially tonight. It was Director Edwin Hardin's birthday, and the forty students at the Buchanan Academy mingled in the great room waiting for him to descend the spiral stairs. The first fire of the season crackled in the granite hearth, which soared three stories to hold up the crisscross of fir ceiling beams. The reflection of flames flashed in the warbled iron-cased windows along the south wall, and in champagne flutes and eyeglasses.

The poets leaned on the grand piano, singing along as one of their brethren played Cole Porter songs. A group of aspiring novelists sipped drinks near the windows. An award-winning playwright chatted with a group of students near the stairs. It was exactly how Etta had imagined the academy when she'd first read Saul Bellow's quote blazing across the website: "Eleven months at the secluded Buchanan Academy transforms an amateur into a literary master."

Was it transforming them yet?

"He's coming," someone whispered. The pianist switched mid-song to the cheerful refrain of "Happy Birthday." The familiar lyrics tangled in Etta's throat with the sticky aftertaste of her champagne. She pressed onto her toes, hoping to catch a glimpse of the director on the stairs.

Edwin Hardin stepped in front of the fireplace wearing slacks, a vest, and a double-breasted jacket. His lanky frame swayed in front of the fire's glow. Someone handed him a champagne flute. He raised it, lifting his jowls into something resembling a smile, as the students clapped and cheered.

The director held up a withered hand. "Thank you, thank you. What a surprise." He cleared his throat. "But let us not waste time celebrating an old man whose best days have passed. Let us celebrate you—the future of American literature."

Etta recognized the phrase even before Hardin pointed his glass at the bronze plaque above the fire: *Roosevelt Lodge was constructed as a Works Progress Administration project in 1933. The legendary author Vincent Buchanan acquired it in 1958 to accommodate the Buchanan Academy, announcing: "The future of American literature will rise from Oregon's primeval forest like embers lifting off flames into the heavens."*

The director lowered his glass and leaned forward, his gaze sweeping the room. "It takes courage to leave your family and friends. It takes courage to dedicate yourself to your craft. To immigrate to this hallowed hall.

"You were selected from thousands. And you have just nine more months away from distractions and commitments. Away from the pressures to submit and sell. Tell me, are you chiseling the world into words?" He raised his glass again. "What will you make of yourselves? What will you become?"

The students launched into another round of "Happy Birthday" as Director Hardin stepped away from the fire.

Etta squeezed her eyes shut. She was only half aware when the song ended and her classmates' voices swelled into the spaces around her.

You were selected from thousands.

She'd been ecstatic when she'd received her acceptance letter praising her writing sample, a short story she'd published in the *Michigan Quarterly Review* six years ago.

But if Hardin knew about Etta's past, she wouldn't be here.

"Catching up on sleep?"

Etta opened her eyes, nearly sloshing champagne across her cashmere sweater. Her tension melted at the sight of Olivia Saxon's grin. She inhaled the swirl of lavender floating from her roommate.

"My roommate snores like a drunken lumberjack." Etta teased. "Keeps me awake."

"Very funny." Olivia narrowed her brown eyes and tucked her curtain of mahogany hair behind her ear. "Is it me, or is Mr. Hardin already sauced? I swear he slurred some of those words."

Etta glanced at the director teetering next to the hearth, a group of students clustered around him. "Well, isn't he, like, eighty?" Etta raised an eyebrow. "Surely he's earned a little sauce."

"Seventy-three." Jordan Waterhouse stepped to Olivia's side, a chunk of pale hair falling across one eye, and rested his hand on Olivia's back. "He was born the year Buchanan won the Pulitzer. Apparently you haven't had your one-on-one with the old man yet. Last year he mentioned that fact about five times during the longest twenty minutes of my life."

Etta laughed. "I thought it was a nice speech."

Jordan brushed the hair off his face. "You'd hope so. He gives the same one every year. Always leads with 'What a surprise.' That whole bit about chiseling ourselves into words was a tad grandiloquent, don't you think?"

Etta made a mental note to look up grandiloquent as Olivia turned her gaze to Jordan again. Were they going to kiss? Right here? As the student writer-in-residence, Jordan seemed to consider himself exempt from the regulation that forbade romantic relationships between students, which the students jokingly referred to as the "Carnal Code."

Last year Jordan had won the coveted Buchanan Prize, awarding him a second year at the academy sans the twenty-five thousand dollar price tag. Fevered calls from agents, editors, and literary magazines were sure to follow.

The Buchanan Prize was the real reason thousands of students competed to spend a soggy year studying at the isolated academy. It was why Etta had labored over her application for months, drained her savings account, and jammed everything she owned into a five-by-five storage unit. Of course, to win, she'd need to somehow write the most dazzling story of her writing career in the next seven days.

Hopefully the chef's assistant would serve the cake soon and the events committee would present the director with the rare first edition of Buchanan's *Rebellious Tides*, which they'd collected donations to buy. Then Etta could zip back to her cabin and write for a couple of hours before bed. She still hadn't crafted the opening yet . . . or the middle . . . or the end, despite upping her daily word count and employing all of the tactics that she'd honed over the years. She'd worked on a ten-page study of her main character, a forty-five-year-old magic shop owner, for two weeks before deciding he was duller than her droning Aunt Mary. Perhaps her main character should be younger. Or female. Or a toad.

Crash.

Etta spun toward the windows, stunned by the sound of breaking glass, even as silence fell across the room.

As she drew her gaze from the windows, the hair on her arms and the back of her neck pricked up. Why was everyone staring at her?

No, not at her. At Olivia.

Olivia had dropped her champagne flute. The director gasped, as he perhaps calculated the value of the shards of glass glittering around her ballet flats.

Vincent Buchanan's Federal Glass collection normally lined the china cabinets in the dining room like museum pieces— reminders of the author who founded the academy. But earlier tonight the events committee had dusted off the flutes, filled them with champagne and sparkling cider, and handed them out to the students, who'd run their wet fingers over the rims and compared the crystal's eerie songs.

The director let out a laugh—a deep, breathless chortle. Then he caught his breath and asked Candy, the chef's assistant, to retrieve a broom and mop.

When Candy appeared in the doorway a few minutes later with her cleaning implements, Etta and Olivia were the only ones still standing in the middle of the room. The rest of the students had flocked away from the broken glass. Olivia's slender fingers trembled, and Etta reached for Olivia's hand.

But Olivia was staring across the room.

"Excuse me."

Etta jumped at the sound of Candy behind her but followed her roommate's gaze, blinking into the shadows next to the double doors leading to the foyer.

She recognized Robert North instantly. She'd seen his picture on the back of *Portages: Poems from Life's Passages*. It shouldn't have been such a surprise. The students had been gossiping about the famous poet all week. The director tried to keep the logistics of impending author visits quiet, insisting it kept the students more focused on their writing. But somehow the students always found out.

Robert North was the most famous author to come so far. Not quite a celebrity like Nikki Giovanni or Ted Kooser, perhaps, but still a famous poet. The female students had been speculating about whether he'd be as attractive as the grainy photo on the back of *Portages*, and Etta had spent an embarrassing amount of time examining Olivia's copy. She'd even memorized the "About the Poet" passage beneath the photo: "Robert North became poet laureate of Maryland when he was twenty-eight years old . . ." Maybe that was because he'd become a poet laureate when he was the same age as Etta. And she was probably the oldest student at the academy by at least a couple years.

Robert North was thinner and more disheveled than in his picture. His blaze of black curls flamed out around the shadow of stubble on his chin. He looked like he'd stepped out of a J. Crew catalog, his hands barely tucked into the pockets of his crumpled black linen pants, his white dress shirt hanging loose, the first two buttons undone. Was he shaking his head at Olivia?

Or did Etta imagine that? A moment later Carl, the academy's chef, strode to the poet's side rolling an oversized suitcase and tipped his cowboy hat toward the stairs. Then Carl and Robert North disappeared behind the hearth.

"You okay?" Etta whispered as Olivia tugged her toward their classmates who were huddling in front of a banquet table along the east side of the room.

Olivia didn't seem to hear. She gazed at the staircase, where the chef and poet were now spiraling toward the third floor. It was the one part of the lodge off-limits to students. Vincent Buchanan had once resided in a third-floor suite photographed in a 1965 *LIFE Magazine* spread that hung framed on the west wall of the dining room. Now the director, his administrative assistant, the librarian, and the resident authors lodged in their own third-floor suites. The remaining rooms were reserved for visiting authors—like the poet.

On the landing, the chef and poet talked for a moment then the chef strode into the long hallway, rolling the suitcase behind him. Robert North leaned on the log railing, looking down on the great room. He looked miles away, his face hidden in the low light.

Olivia yanked her hand from Etta's and swirled around, darting into the flock of students who were now moving toward the middle of the room, talking and laughing.

Etta searched the crowd for her roommate's red skirt and glimpsed a flash of red on the other side of the hearth. Olivia? Etta made out her roommate's slender form flitting toward the double doors leading to the foyer.

Olivia stepped into the glow cast from the antique sconces, gripped one of the ornate iron handles, heaved the door open, and left.

Etta glanced back at the third floor landing. The poet had vanished.

Chapter Two

THE NEXT MORNING ROBERT NORTH HELD A GUEST LECTURE during the morning workshop. Ten minutes into the lunch hour, he still hovered over the walnut lectern in front of the classroom reading a poem from *Portages*. The chef had slipped Etta an extra cinnamon roll at breakfast, and Etta was salivating at the thought of the flaky layers stowed away in her bag.

Robert North cleared his throat and thrust his hand into the air. "Mother wanders the heavens like a nor'easter. Do not weep for her." He gazed at the ceiling, and a vein pulsed from his eyebrow to his hairline. Then he looked down and closed his book, flipping through his notes. Across the room someone coughed.

Etta glanced at Olivia, who was sitting at her desk near the back of the classroom. Etta's roommate hadn't returned to their cabin last night. It was a common pattern. Olivia had been sleeping at Jordan's most nights. But still, Etta had lain awake for a long time thinking about her roommate's quivering hands and hasty exit.

Now, under the glow of the track lights, Etta couldn't recall exactly what had seemed so troubling last night. That's what she hated most about her bouts of insomnia: the way the darkness worked like a magnifying glass, amplifying trifles into dilemmas.

"As I said, you'll keep hearing the banal phrase, write what you know. But what does it mean?"

Etta turned back to the front of the room.

A few hands floated up, but the poet's blue gaze drifted to the iron-cased windows. "I'll tell you what it doesn't mean: Don't make your characters slightly veiled versions of yourself. Christ almighty, don't bore your readers with lackluster details from your life."

His gaze swept the classroom. "No, what you must do is infuse your literature with your emotions. Heartbreak and anguish. Remorse and frustration. Tedium and jealousy. All of the sweet wretchedness of being human."

Etta nodded in agreement as the poet shoved his notes into his briefcase. He strutted down the center aisle toward the exit, avoiding eye contact with the students he passed.

As Etta's classmates rose and streamed out of the room, she meandered to Olivia's desk for their daily trek to the dining hall.

Olivia flung her black bag toward Etta. "Hold this." Olivia flipped through her notebook, pulling out papers, examining them, and stacking them on her desk. "I'm sure I have it." She leafed through the stack and then shoved it back into the notebook. "Did I leave it at Jor's?"

Olivia took her bag back, yanked it open, and pulled out one book and then another, piling them on her desk.

Etta plucked the small paper sack out of her own bag and shook the cinnamon roll onto her palm, trying to stop herself from cramming the whole thing in her mouth. "Can't you find whatever it is after lunch?"

Olivia flipped through one of the books on her desk. "I'm going to ask him to read my story."

Etta raised an eyebrow as she peeled off the outside layer of the roll. "Jordan?" She put it in her mouth and savored the sensation of the sugar dissolving into her tongue.

Olivia laughed. "Robert North."

Etta nearly choked on her bite. "Seriously?" According to the rules, visiting writers did not do critiques. The lodge was intended to be a retreat for visitors, a restful stop on a whirlwind book tour. And Robert North wasn't any visiting author. He'd mentioned twice during his lecture that *Portages* was on the short list for the National Book Critics Circle Award, and he'd recently been featured in an *Atlantic Monthly* article entitled, "Turbulent Troubadours."

Olivia hurled some papers into the air. "Thank God. I thought I was going to have to go through the pile on my desk. Hey, where did you get that? I want some."

Etta extended the roll toward Olivia. "We're not supposed to ask visiting authors to read our work."

"We're not supposed to take more than one cinnamon roll." Olivia giggled and pulled a chunk off the roll. "Master Chef Carl certainly does shower you with gifts," Olivia said, mimicking the chef's drawl.

Etta laughed. "It's just a cinnamon roll. Not an engagement ring."

Olivia lifted her hand, examining the ring Jordan had given her in the light. "I told you, it's a promise ring." Olivia dropped her hand. "Besides Carl's sweets taste a lot better. I'm just saying . . ."

"Don't . . . and don't look at me like that." Etta frowned. "I told you, Carl and I are friends. He's the only one out here with a radio. The only one who goes to town every week. I know, 'Creativity is the offspring of solitude,'" Etta repeated the motto of the Buchanan Academy. "But sometimes don't you want to hear the news, or just get a weather forecast?"

"Whoa, methinks the lady doth protest too much." Olivia giggled. "Has it occurred to you that I'm jealous because I'm not getting the cinnamon roll treatment?" Olivia stuffed another bite of the roll into her mouth and stacked her books back in her bag. She leapt to her feet. "Ready?"

Etta shook the remnants of the cinnamon roll into the wastebasket next to the door and followed Olivia down the stairs. As Olivia disappeared down the hallway, Etta lingered in the great room gazing at the oversized leather sofas across from the crackling fire. She stifled a yawn and imagined stretching out on the couch and reading *Portages*. Of course, she couldn't do that. With the shortened lunch hour, she'd have to shovel down her food and race to the library to dash off a critique of Chase Quinn's short story for the afternoon workshop.

Etta tried to breathe despite the tightness in her chest. She should be the one asking for help. Olivia had already won a contest. The students wrote a play during their first month at the academy, and the resident authors chose the best one to be produced for the Autumnal Equinox celebration. Olivia's play would be performed for the entire academy in a couple of nights. Etta, on the other hand, could barely thread two sentences together lately. She'd always dreamed of writing something that didn't help people escape reality, but held it up to the light and exposed the rawness and wonder of it in a way no one ever had.

But her bag contained the drivel she'd completed since she'd arrived at the academy—one awful play, two unfinished short stories, and the start of a very bad novel. None of it was all that interesting or marketable. The more she tried to write about important things, the more drab and insular her work became. Etta imagined all of it in the flames, the pages curling and blackening—the embers rising into the heavens.

Clamor resounded in the dining hall—conversation, laughter, glasses clinking, silverware scraping against porcelain. Etta made a beeline for her table. Vincent Buchanan had encouraged students to mix and mingle in the dining hall. As the brochure for the academy reported, meals allowed the novice writers to chat with literary luminaries and fellow apprentices. However, within a week, the students had formed cliques and started eating with the same people. Most of the resident and visiting authors rotated, sitting with different students at each meal.

Etta slid into her seat next to Poppy Everson and tried to mask her disappointment that Petra Atwell, everyone's least favorite resident author and literary luminary, sat across the table next to Jordan complaining about her tomato bisque.

Petra held up a piece of her sourdough bread. "Where's the damn mayo? What is this, Weight Watchers?"

Etta managed a smile and turned to Jordan. "Where's Liv?"

Etta's question evaporated into a burst of commotion at a nearby table. She bit into her turkey sandwich, and the sourdough melted into the roof of her mouth.

"Ms. Atwell, can I ask you a question?" Poppy asked.

"As long as it's not my age." Petra tapped her fingernails against her chin. "Or anything about marriage, divorce, money, or sex."

Poppy giggled.

Etta set down her sandwich and pulled her soup toward her. A heart. The chef had drizzled the white cream on her tomato bisque in the distinct form of a heart. Etta smiled and glanced at the stainless steel door that led to the kitchen. She plucked her spoon off the table.

"Does your dad still speak to you?" Poppy asked.

Etta dropped her spoon with a clank.

Petra Atwell's 1990 memoir *Wintersong* had shot to the top of the bestseller list, not exactly for its literary qualities. Petra had revealed the details of an incestuous relationship she'd had with her father during her teenage years. Gordon Atwell was a newly elected congressman in the United States House of Representatives when his daughter's tell-all hit the bookstores. The six-foot-five, two-hundred-and-fifty-pound representative stepped down from Congress, but only after falling to his knees in a press conference and bellowing that his daughter was a temptress. Neither of Petra's two subsequent memoirs had garnered the same attention as *Wintersong*.

Etta glanced at Jordan, sure he'd be shocked by Poppy's brazenness. But Jordan was gazing into the distance. Had he even heard Poppy's question?

Petra jabbed a burgundy-painted fingernail in Poppy's direction. "I'll tell you something about men. Whether it's your father, your lover, or your damned minister: they all think they're smarter than you until you prove them wrong. You can either write, or you can keep everyone happy. You can't do both." Petra fixed her dark eyes on Etta. "Isn't that right, Loretta?"

"It's Etta."

Petra didn't break her gaze.

"My name. It's Etta."

"Oh. Well, Etta, you can either write or you can please people. You can't do both. Isn't that so?"

Poppy raised one of her pencil-thin eyebrows and bit her bottom lip.

"I guess so," Etta murmured, shifting in her chair. She ladled a spoonful of soup into her mouth. When she looked up, Petra was thankfully distracted, picking the lettuce from her sandwich. For the first time, Etta wondered if the resident author might be attractive beneath her caked-on foundation and hair-sprayed, black-dyed bouffant, but she shifted her gaze away at the risk that the resident author might want to continue their conversation.

That's when she saw what Jordan was so fixated on.

Everyone called the long rectangular table across the west wall "Poet's Row," because the ten aspiring poets at the academy sat there gabbling about climbing rhyme scheme, iambic pentameter, quatrains, sestinas, polysyndeton, and other topics that made Etta want to take a nap.

There sat Olivia.

Jordan's girlfriend was huddled at the end of the table next to Robert North. Less than an inch of space separated their cheeks.

Chapter Three

◆

Later that afternoon, Etta slid into her seat gripping her critique of Chase Quinn's story, still warm from the laser printer. She admired her first sentence: "Ancient Soldier is a tale about torture. Unfortunately after a riveting opening, it rambles, becoming torturous to read." Not bad for a critique she'd dashed off over lunch.

Their first week at the academy, the students had gotten a week-long intensive in criticism. A famous *New Yorker* critic visited and made a plea for tough love in the literary community. He called on the students to "resurrect the disappearing art of professional criticism." At first Etta had struggled to say anything unfavorable—she'd been on the other side too many times—but she'd noticed a heightened ability to help others improve their work lately. Critiques came easily, snappy sentences zipping onto the page.

The classroom still buzzed with students talking. Walker Ryan was nowhere to be seen. The author's Monday critique sessions dissecting plot and story structure were her favorites. He liked to stop talking mid-sentence, point to a student, and say, "Tell me a story." If the student managed to spin a coherent tale, Walker boomed, "See, that's all it takes. A beginning, a middle, and an end." When Walker was in the room, Etta almost believed it was that easy, and once it had been. Lately, however . . .

Etta glanced toward the door just as Olivia raced through. Her angular cheekbones were flushed a deep red. She slid into her seat at the back of the room, leaned over, and shuffled through her bag.

"Forgive me for my tardiness." Robert North appeared in the doorway a second later. "I'll be filling Mr. Ryan's shoes this afternoon."

The visiting author strolled to the front of the room and dropped his soft leather briefcase on the oversized oak desk. He frowned. "Trying to in any case. The man has monster feet." He spread his hands wide in front of him, exaggerating the size of Walker's feet. A murmur of laughter rippled across the room. Robert North dropped his hands. "Seriously, he's a giant. A literary giant." The poet spun around and grabbed some papers from his bag.

"Ah, now, critiques. Isn't this the paradox of the writing academy?" He strolled halfway down the center aisle then swirled around, striding back to the desk. "We force you—the writer, the creator, the inventor—to become your own foe, the smiling mortician of your own well being: a critic. We can only guess at the world's oldest profession, but critiquing was invariably the second. The moment someone did anything, a detractor appeared to rip him to shreds.

"Back in 400 B.C., the Greek painter Zeuxis said, 'Criticism comes easier than craftsmanship.' I wish someone would explain that to Truman Scott of *Pen & Poet*, who called *Portages* . . ." Robert North plucked a scrap of glossy paper from his bag, and held it up to the light. "'North's most self-absorbed and listless verse yet.'" He crumbled the paper and threw it down. "Only a worthless critic can discount a lifetime of work with a blasé string of adjectives. Never forget, we are the noble ones. Reviewers cling like vultures to the peripheries of the literary world waiting for us to stumble so that they can tear at our flesh and lap up our blood. They are literary backwash."

Robert North rifled through his briefcase again, this time producing a silver thermos. He unscrewed the cap and took a drink. His forehead glistened. He set the thermos on the edge of the desk. "So how are we to become what we hate the most? How are hopeful new writers to tear apart their classmates' livelihood like that heartless bastard Truman Scott, who wields his pen like a machete? I'm afraid I don't have any answers. But let's get to it now, shall we? I suppose the residents have you form a circle or some New Age garbage like that. We'll skip the pretence today and get right to the assault." He picked up the papers from his desk and ran a hand through his waves. "'Ancient Soldier' by Chase Quinn. Who will read a critique before we divide into groups to mutilate this one?"

Etta slumped into her chair and stared at the papers on her desk, skimming the first sentence. Under the track lights, it looked considerably less constructive and more . . . savage. Why on earth had she been so cruel? It only got worse. She'd written that the story got "as tedious as spending a fortnight in a hanging cage," and that the "climax was as predictable as death resulting from an executioner's axe," phrases that had sounded decidedly more clever when she'd written them.

Etta snuck a glance at Chase Quinn sitting a few desks away. A tuft of coppery hair fell across his forehead. He wiped his palms against his slacks and leaned forward in his seat, his brown eyes shifting behind his thick square-framed glasses.

Where was Walker Ryan? Until today the four resident authors had always overseen the afternoon workshops, which were dedicated to the critiquing process. The Buchanan Academy was notorious for the grueling weeklong formal critique. The resident authors represented four different forms of writing: fiction, poetry, non-fiction, and screenplay. And the students focused on critiquing corresponding aspects of a story with each one. They dissected plot on Mondays with Walker, the novelist. They assessed character development with the memoirist Petra Atwell on Tuesdays. They analyzed dialogue with the playwright Winston Goss on Wednesdays. And they scrutinized language with the poet Opal Waters on Thursdays. On Fridays, the resident authors conducted the afternoon workshop together, and the students assessed the merits of a story in its entirety.

"Come on now, it may be a sadistic exercise." Robert North strode down the center aisle. "But you're joining the literary community. When you're not writing, you'll be criticizing other writers. Just ask Truman Scott, who incidentally was once a classmate of mine in this very room. Yes, take a look around. Your enemy may be sitting next to you. Of course, with friends in this business, who needs enemies?" Robert North's voice faded, and his blue gaze went to the back of the room again.

Etta glanced over her shoulder, and a chill zipped up her spine. Robert North and Olivia were staring at each other, and Olivia's dark eyes were glossy and bloodshot, her mouth curling down at the corners.

"Now will you kindly read your critique for us ... what's your name?" Etta swirled around and exhaled when she saw that Robert North was pointing at Pari Daswani, not her. Pari bounced to her feet and said her name for Robert North, the words rolling off her tongue in her Indian accent. The class had critiqued Pari's short story a few weeks before. It was set in New Delhi, and Etta's classmates had called it exotic and alluring, adjectives Etta was certain no one would ever use to describe her prose. Pari glided to the front of the room, her yellow and red printed skirt swishing behind her.

Etta flinched, and it took her several seconds to register that the door at the back of the classroom had slammed shut. She spun around. Olivia's desk was empty.

When the workshop ended, Etta stuffed Chase's critique in her notebook. Perhaps she would revise some of her more pointed remarks and give it to him during the evening mandatory writing session.

"Isn't that for me?"

Chase stood over her. His pale, freckled fingers reached toward Etta's notebook, and a messy pile of critiques stuck out from under his other arm.

"Oh right." Etta retrieved her critique and handed it over, averting her eyes from Chase's. Maybe he'd appreciate her honesty.

She slipped past a group of students talking in the doorway, hurried down the hallway past the framed oil portrait of Vincent Buchanan, and jogged down the spiral stairs. It was her favorite time of the day—the three hours Vincent Buchanan had appointed as "unstructured time," He'd encouraged the students to fill it with non-writing activities. The author had recommended that they spend at least part of it doing some form of physical exercise: walking along the nature trails near the lodge, playing tennis or badminton, working in the organic vegetable gardens, tending the orchids in the greenhouse. For the rest he recommended a non-literary creative activity. Some students drew, painted, worked with clay, and did other handicrafts in the art studio on the lower level of the Lodge. A few women knitted on the couches in the great room several days a week. Other students practiced musical instruments or sung in the old stables, which had been converted into a soundproof music studio years before. A dozen students spent their unstructured time in the theater rehearsing Olivia's play, which would be part of the autumnal equinox festivities on Wednesday.

"Loretta." The voice was shrill. Etta halted and gripped the handrail even though her foot was hovering above the last step.

"Did I scare you?" Petra Atwell sat on one of the couches, her dark eyes reflecting the fire. She held a paperback in one hand and a mug in the other. Etta stepped off the stairs. "No. It's just, I told you, that's not my name."

"Well it certainly gets your attention." Petra sipped from the mug. It looked out of place in her manicured hand—misshapen with a lopsided handle, like a child had made it. "I asked that Texan for a shot of Irish whiskey. I think he used a thimble." Petra's laugh sounded like two pieces of sandpaper scraping against each other. "Etta's not short for anything? Did your mother stammer? Sounds like a stutter, not a name."

Etta forced a tight smile and started toward the entryway.

"Don't tell me you're stupid enough to go on one of your little excursions today. Fog like this, you're liable to vanish out there."

Etta turned around. "How did you know?" She paused. She was going to ask Petra how she knew that Etta went running during her unstructured time. But it wasn't as though Etta's runs were a secret, even if she usually steered toward the lesser-traveled trails to the west of the Lodge to avoid seeing anyone.

"You'd be surprised at all the things you know when you pay attention." Petra rested the mug and the paperback on the arm of the couch and examined her fingernails. "Like your friend sitting with the poets today." Another gravelly laugh. "She a Robert North fan?"

Etta glanced toward the door. "He's helping her with a story."

Petra's laugh was louder this time. She ran a hand along her stiff curls, which didn't budge beneath her fingers. "Robert doesn't know shit about stories. The man writes lyric poems."

Etta blinked. For some reason that fact hadn't occurred to her before. "Well maybe he's helping her with her word choice." Etta avoided Petra's gaze, annoyed at how defensive her own voice sounded.

"Yes, well, I suppose she wouldn't be the first girl Robert helped with word choice. Frankly, I'm not sure it would be wise to take his advice."

"He writes beautiful poems," Etta said and then blushed, realizing Petra wasn't talking about writing.

"You should tell your friend to be careful." Petra lifted the paperback to block her face.

Heat flooded from Etta's body. Swirling red rose border. Gothic typeface. A half-clad, red-haired model. It's the last place Etta had imagined she'd see a Courtesan romance. At least she didn't recognize the cover art. She twirled around, made a beeline for the door, and pushed her way outside.

An ocean of fog swam before her.

Etta edged down the porch steps. She glimpsed a movement in front of her and halted.

"Is someone there?" The fog swallowed her voice.

She glanced behind her at the double doors to the lodge. She couldn't bear the thought of another conversation with Petra. She took hesitant steps forward, the bark underfoot reassuring her that she was on the trail.

The fog silenced the usual forest symphony: bluebird and thrush songs, woodpeckers drumming their beaks against hollow trees, squirrels jetting through the undergrowth. Etta could only hear her own footsteps and her breath moving in and out.

She rounded the bend and stepped into the clearing. The fog thinned slightly, and she made out the women's residences: two rows of ten small cabins facing each other. She jogged toward her cabin, digging in her pocket for the key.

Etta glimpsed the person sitting in the wooden chair next to the front door as she stepped onto the porch. She let out a sound halfway between a gasp and a scream and jumped backward even as she recognized him. She laughed. "Jeez Jordan, you scared me."

His blonde hair fell across his face as he shifted forward in his chair.

"Was that you on the trail ahead of me?" Her voice sounded unnaturally high-pitched, and she eked out a laugh as she poked at the lock with her key. "Where's Liv?"

"You tell me."

"You okay?" Etta pushed the door open, flicked on the light, and sighed at the usual disarray. Olivia's blankets and down comforter were twisted into a clump on the bed, her sweaters and jeans scattered in piles across the floor, her desk mounded with papers, empty soda cans, and a pair of socks. Etta stepped inside. "I'd invite you in, but you know the rules." Etta laughed. The "Carnal Code" forbade male and female students from socializing alone in cabins, but the students universally ignored that stipulation.

"Did you look in the greenhouse? She's been helping Poppy with the orchids." Etta sat down on her bed and glanced toward the door, expecting to see Jordan leaning on the doorframe. "Jor, I was kidding. You can come in." She waited. "Jordan?" She slipped her shoes off and padded to the porch.

The chair was empty.

Chapter Four

◆

THE NEXT MORNING OPAL WATERS LEANED ON THE DESK IN front of the classroom with her long legs stretched in front of her. She brushed a whitish-blonde lock behind her ear and scanned the room while Etta's classmates finished their writing warm-up. It was too early for anyone to look as composed as Opal did. Carl jestingly called Opal a food fascist, because of her list of dietary sensitivities and restrictions, but Opal's diet clearly had some merits. The poet had to be in her fifties, yet her blonde hair was silken, her ivory skin flushed and dewy. Hardly any lines etched the skin around her pale gray eyes.

Unlike the other resident authors, Opal rarely congregated with the students outside of class. She ate her meals with the director, his assistant, and the librarian. She never lounged in the great room in the evenings, or read in the library, or sunned herself at the swimming hole on hot summer afternoons. Some students speculated that the resident author thought herself too distinguished to associate with amateurs after she'd been presented with the Bobbitt National Prize for Poetry last year. But maybe she was just upset because she couldn't eat Carl's fried catfish fritters or New Braunfels bratwurst. That would put Etta in a bad mood.

"You've all written two pages now, correct?" Opal stood. "Tell me, were you inspired to write when you walked in the door this morning?"

Someone groaned. "No," boomed a voice behind Etta.

In the center of the room, Chase Quinn raised his hand and spoke before Opal called on him. "A lot of us write best at night. These morning writing exercises can be, you know, less productive for us . . ."

Opal fixed her pale gaze on him. "Am I wasting your time, Mr. Quinn?"

Chase shook his head and lowered his gaze to his notebook.

"Sir, I hate to disappoint you, but writing is not about inspiration. Writing is discipline. It is self-control."

Etta glanced at her notebook. She knew all about discipline. For years, she'd written one to two thousand words a day. At that pace, she'd be done with her story tomorrow. But lately it felt like the words were trapped somewhere just out of her reach, and the few she managed to wrest loose were maimed and limping.

Opal's gray gaze drifted to the windows. "Writing is the pestiferous gadfly that won't let you take a vacation or day off. It's what stops you from becoming a doctor or a lawyer, an executive with a corner office and a secretary. It's what strips you of friends, of children—of noise." She clenched her fists. "It won't let you enjoy anything for its own beauty—only for your next poem or story, for your own aspirations. For your own ego." She let her breath out at once and spun around.

Opal stacked her papers and inserted them into a manila folder. Then she gripped the folder, plucked her coffee cup from the desk, strode down the center aisle, and disappeared out the door.

Etta stared down at her tidy handwriting. She'd written two rambling pages about the weather. The wind had started blowing sometime late in the night, and Etta had written about the currents carrying the fog away, ethereal wisps of vapor fanning out above the trees and sweeping out to the Pacific Ocean. There was no point to it whatsoever, but Etta had written for twenty minutes in a row, a feat compared to her progress in the last couple of weeks.

"Writing is anguish," a voice came from the front of the room. Etta lifted her head. Mallory Chambers, one of the Poet's Row students, stood where Opal had a moment before, a smirk on his face. "It's worse than being on the rag or going through menopause. It's worse than when I told my mother I'm a raging dike. It's worse than when I realized that the few people who have read my dismal poems committed suicide straight after, because I make people miserable."

Mallory paused, and Etta felt a giggle rising in her belly. She didn't want to laugh, but Mallory was trying to make his baritone voice high-pitched, and he sounded more like a puberty-wracked teenager than like Opal. Etta stole a glance at Mallory's twin sister Hillary. Although the fraternal twins had deep-set dark eyes and short, muscular frames, Etta never would have guessed they were related if someone hadn't told her. Mallory wrote outlandish poems and loved to perform them for the class, whereas Hillary hardly spoke and hadn't let anyone read excerpts from her novel-in-progress. Rumor had it that Hillary was writing about a pair of siblings whose father murdered their mother when they were children and that it was at least somewhat autobiographical. Hillary stared at her notebook, her face hidden behind her brunette frizz.

Laughter rippled up from the back of the room. Mallory grinned and took an exaggerated bow. He lifted a hand and cleared his throat. "Writing is my anorexia and bul . . ." Mallory looked up. His face turned scarlet, and his gaze shot to the floor.

Etta spun around in her chair. Opal Waters leaned against the doorway, looking even slighter than usual, drooping and wan, like a dandelion just before the seeds scattered.

Before Etta could contemplate how much Opal had heard, the resident author was gone. Etta thought about rising and following after Opal to express her disagreement with Mallory's words. But she guessed comfort would be the last thing the resident author would want. Apparently the rest of the students felt the same way, because for a long moment, they all sat staring at the door.

Olivia was the first one to rise and stride out of the classroom.

Etta stuffed her notebook in her book bag and jumped up as her roommate disappeared out the door. Etta squeezed past a group of students converging in the aisle, sailed out the door, and jogged down the stairs to the second floor, hoping to catch up with her roommate. The morning mandatory writing hour would start in fifteen minutes.

Etta hadn't seen Olivia since yesterday morning. Both Olivia and Jordan had skipped dinner last night. Etta always felt jumpy when her friends missed required meals at the same time. If the director found out about their relationship, they could be disciplined, perhaps expelled. Or maybe not. As Poppy liked to point out, Jordan's father owned *The Drinking Gourd*, a literary magazine that regularly published short fiction and poetry by Buchanan alums, which seemed to gain Jordan special esteem at the academy. He was, for instance, the only student who didn't have to share his cabin with a roommate.

Etta heaved open the door to the library. A wall of warmth met her as she stepped inside. The old radiators under the window hissed and clicked. The reading lamps on the glossy myrtlewood tables in the middle of the room were off, and the librarian's office was dark. But sunlight flooded in through the row of narrow paned windows at the end of the room. Etta walked toward them, glancing up at the shelves that lined each wall.

Buchanan had collected a renowned private collection of literature about the American West. Last week Etta had discovered signed editions of Norman Mailer's *Executioner's Song* and Mary Austin's *Land of Little Rain*. She'd searched for *Desert Solitaire*, hoping to read Edward Abbey's famous 1969 inscription to Vincent Buchanan praising the Buchanan Academy as affirmation that the American novel would "defend itself against the ceaseless assault of commercialization." But the books weren't in alphabetical order, and if there was any sort of arrangement to them, Etta hadn't discovered it.

Etta gazed down on the expanse of grass and the green house, trying to detect movements through the glass roof. Was Olivia helping Poppy tend the cymbidiums? The director's orchids seemingly required more nurturing than a newborn. Poppy spent much of her unstructured time carting plants back and forth to the sink for watering and verifying that the humidity and light conditions were ideal.

The door creaked open. Etta swirled around and blinked, trying to adjust her eyes to the shadows.

"Hello there."

Etta recognized Carl's twang and stepped forward, blinking to make out his form.

After a minute the chef stepped to Etta's side. His brown eyes flashed golden in the light. "Your hair's on fire."

Etta touched her ponytail then dropped her hand and smiled. "Have you seen Olivia?"

"Matter of fact, I have." Carl nodded in the direction of the glass door to the archives room. "Saw her in there."

Etta swirled around and peered at the dark room next to the librarian's office. "In there? She wouldn't be in . . ." Etta let the sentence die on her lips and stared at the embossed words on the door: *Buchanan Research Room. By appointment only.* The librarian had given the students a brief tour of Buchanan's archives during orientation. What Etta remembered most was the smell—a pairing of dust and furniture polish.

"Why would Olivia be in there?"

"She was damn intent on reading something. Don't think she even saw me. Must have been about four thirty this morning."

Etta stepped toward the archives room. The collection contained editions of all Buchanan's novels and correspondence, including letters from presidents and other famous authors. Uriah Winston Mills, or "the major," as everyone called him, never smiled, and he'd looked even more grave than usual as he'd outlined the steps academic researchers took to gain access to the room. First they sent letters of intent to the director. If approved, they were given appointments, at which time Carl drove to Jackson to escort them to Roosevelt Lodge. Researchers were only allowed to take in a pencil and paper or a laptop and were chaperoned at all times. Etta imagined sitting in the cramped room under the librarian's gaze and shivered.

She glanced outside. "Was the major in there with her?" The tree branches swayed just slightly in the wind.

"Didn't see him," Carl said.

Etta squinted into the tinted glass on the door. She could only make out shadows, but she recalled the basic layout of the room: the narrow antique case down the center that displayed World War II memorabilia: a rifle, a uniform, propaganda posters; Buchanan's writing desk and chair and two leather armchairs in front of the tinted picture window; shelves of acid-free boxes and shiny Mylar-wrapped books; framed posters of the movies adapted from Buchanan's books. Etta had recognized Gary Cooper in one poster and Lauren Bacall and Humphrey Bogart in another.

Etta turned back to Carl. "What were you doing here so early?"

"Needed something to read while I waited for the bread to rise." Carl extended a book. The red cover was faded and Etta couldn't make out the title.

"I got your heart."

A moment of silence hung in the room, and then Carl grinned, the skin at the corner of his eyes pinching. "Well, shoot, Etta. I meant for Miss Atwell to get that."

"Hey, where's your hat?" Carl's golden brown hair had grown since the last time Etta had seen it. It fell across his forehead, making him look boyish, even though a few silvery strands glittered in the sunlight.

"Wasn't fixin' to run into anyone."

"You look better without it." Etta's cheeks flashed with heat when the words were out, and she dropped her gaze to Carl's feet. He wore a pair of Nikes in place of his usual work boots. "Do you run?"

"Only if something's chasing me." Carl laughed at his own joke. "Hardin wants me to cover the grounds today. I can drive the truck for some of it, but I reckon I'll be doing a fair bit of walking."

"Cover the grounds? Do you do that a lot?"

Carl shook his head. "Hardin's convinced someone's been hanging out near that old cemetery. Probably just a hiker, and I can't see what harm anyone could do to a bunch of old headstones. But that's not the way Hardin sees it. I told him I'd check it out."

Etta groaned. "Does this mean Candy's making lunch?"

"Don't worry, she can't destroy sandwiches. I don't think." Carl grinned. Candy, a student at Portland Culinary Academy, was at Roosevelt Lodge for a six-month apprenticeship, and she didn't seem to have yet learned there were spices other than salt.

"Where's this cemetery?"

"You mean to tell me you've never run that far?"

Etta smiled.

"It's up past the swimming hole, off the trail a ways. Used to be a little town up that way, even smaller than Jackson. Most of the graves are as old as things get in these parts. Vincent Buchanan's buried there, and I've heard there are a few other newer graves—a rancher who lived up the road a piece, his wife. You could come with me if ..." His voice drifted off as he realized that, of course, she couldn't go.

Outside, the tops of the trees shook. Etta's pulse fluttered against her wrists. Had they been talking for five minutes or fifteen? Had the mandatory writing session started? "I've got to go," Etta said, as she twisted around and hurried down the aisle between the tables.

She hefted the door open, turned and gazed at Carl's silhouette against the trees. Dust stippled the air around him. "Bye," she called.

An hour later as everyone else made their way down to the dining room for lunch, Etta exited the stairs on the second floor, padded down the hall, slipped inside the library, and closed the door behind her, inhaling the dry heat from the radiators. She made sure the major's office was dark before switching on the overhead lights. Then she crossed the room to the archives and gazed at the embossed letters on the door.

Etta twisted the brass doorknob. It didn't budge. She pressed her face close to the glass, blinking at the outlines of the display case and shelves, the shape of the armchairs in front of the windows.

She'd seen Major Mills and Opal Waters in the room on separate occasions. Once when Etta had stopped at the library to print a critique, the novelist Ralph Powell, who was visiting the lodge for a few days on his book tour, was sitting in one of the leather armchairs next to the major. But students? Students didn't go in the archives. Why did Olivia go in there at four thirty in the morning? How did she get in?

Etta squeezed her eyes shut. She'd been jealous of Olivia. She hated to even think of it, of that awful word "jealous" in reference to her own feelings. But it was true. Even before the resident authors had chosen Olivia's play to be produced, Etta had envied her roommate's silken hair and creamy complexion. She'd wasted many mornings peering into the cloudy mirror in their shared bathroom rubbing at the spatter of freckles on her cheeks and trying to comb her unruly nest just the right way to hide the mole on her neck. One morning she'd gone through half a tube of makeup trying to make the pearly scar next to her eye vanish, although she'd once considered the remnant of a gash she'd gotten while playing tackle football with her brothers as a badge of honor.

At some point in the last two months, though, Etta had stopped being jealous of Olivia. Maybe it was Olivia's wide grin or the way she gripped Etta's arm before revealing whatever piece of gossip she was dying to share. Or maybe it was the way Olivia pulled her crumpled T-shirts from the floor and smelled the armpits before putting them on. Or maybe it was the short story Olivia had written for her critique, which was dark and strange and impossible not to love—an edgy fairy tale written from the perspective of members of an extended family of pig farmers.

Of course, Etta knew it wasn't any of those things.

Olivia had cried, twice that Etta had heard, late at night as Etta lay staring at the ceiling. They were soft sobs, so low and sad that Etta couldn't bring herself to say anything to her new roommate. But, as it turned out, hearing a person weep in the night made it impossible to envy her in the morning.

Chapter Five

◆

ETTA STEPPED INTO THE DINING HALL A FEW MINUTES LATER. When she glimpsed Olivia sitting at their usual table next to Poppy, tension melted from her neck and shoulders. Olivia was so messy in most ways that her perfect posture always took Etta by surprise. Olivia's hair was coiled into a loose twist at the nape of her neck.

"Excuse me," a voice came from behind Etta.

Etta spun around and was standing face to face with Chase Quinn. "Hi Chase."

He said nothing.

Etta stepped out of his way, and he strode past her, his red hair disappearing into the swirl of people moving about the room. Etta remembered a few sentences from her critique of "Ancient Soldier," and a hollow ache spread through her stomach and into her chest. She wrapped her fingers around the doorframe. Why had she been so cruel?

Etta looked up, and Olivia was waving at her and grinning. Etta smiled and propelled herself toward their table. She plunked her book bag on the floor and winced at the scrape of her chair as she yanked it out.

Poppy blew on her beef stew—a medley of shredded meat, carrots, potatoes, and green beans—that might look appetizing, except that morning Carl had mentioned that he'd be covering the grounds again, leaving Candy to prepare lunch.

"Where's Jor?" Etta asked.

Olivia produced a slice of French bread from the basket on the center of the table and extended it to Etta. "Either the lid fell off Carl's salt shaker, or Candy's cooking today."

Etta groaned. She thought about telling Olivia and Poppy about Carl's whereabouts, but focused on unwrapping a pad of butter instead. "You don't know where Jor is?"

Olivia shook her head and tore a piece of bread off her slice. She rolled it between her palms, forming a ball.

Maybe he's mad at you for sitting with Robert North yesterday," Poppy said.

Etta opened her mouth to discount Poppy's comment. Did Poppy have a doctorate in saying the wrong thing to people? Then Etta thought of the way Jordan acted before he disappeared from their porch yesterday. "Are you and Jor fighting?"

"Of course not. Listen . . ." Olivia lowered her voice. "I'm about to burst. I have some gossip." Her dark eyes jetted back and forth. "But you have to swear on your lives that you won't tell anyone. Promise?"

"On our lives?" Poppy raised a thin eyebrow and grinned. "Wow, this must be good."

"It is," Olivia whispered and glanced behind her. She set the bread ball, which had taken on a grayish hue, next to her stew and leaned forward. "Do you promise?"

Etta nodded and inched her chair closer to the table. Olivia glanced over both shoulders again, and Etta reached for the glass of ice water in front of her. She was salivating, partly from hunger, but mostly from the suspense Olivia seemed to be reveling in creating. She took a gulp and plunked the glass down too hard. Water sloshed over the sides. Etta yanked on her napkin to mop up the puddle, and her spoon clattered to the floor. She closed her eyes. "Please just tell us, Liv."

Poppy shoved Jordan's spoon toward Etta. "By the time Jor gets here, his soup will be a big slimy salt lick anyway." She giggled. "A slippery stewsicle."

"That's disgusting," Etta said with a groan.

Poppy stuck her tongue out and bulged her eyes, pretending to lick a Popsicle. Etta laughed.

Olivia leaned forward. "So you guys have to promise you won't tell anyone . . ."

"Okay," Etta said.

"Because if you do . . ."

"You'll slaughter us in our sleep." Poppy giggled again.

Olivia narrowed her eyes at Poppy. "I'm serious."

Poppy managed to compose her face, although she looked as though she might dissolve at any second. "Sorry," she said. "We won't tell."

"It's about . . ." Olivia mouthed something Etta guessed was Opal.

"Opal?" Poppy asked. Olivia spun toward the table where Opal Waters ate. Opal wasn't there. The seat between Director Hardin and Major Mills was empty.

Olivia glared at Poppy and surveyed their surroundings again.

"Sorry," Poppy whispered.

Finally Olivia leaned back in and waved Etta and Poppy closer, until their faces were inches from each other's. "Opal is having an affair with someone at the academy . . ." The words all ran together and Etta couldn't make out the last few.

"Who with?" Etta whispered.

Olivia's eyes shifted from Etta to Poppy. "A student."

Poppy gasped. "Jordan?"

"What? No. Why would you say that?" Olivia frowned.

Poppy frowned too and looked down. "I don't know. I'm only guessing. I mean, because they're both gone right now."

Olivia reclined in her chair, her dark eyes glazing over. "I don't know who it is. Just that it's a student."

"How do you know any of this?" Etta took another gulp of water.

Olivia shrugged and took a bite of her stew, crinkling up her face as she swallowed.

"Everyone makes fun of Opal," Etta said, thinking of Mallory's lampoon of the poet. "Who would have an affair with her?"

"It's true," Olivia whispered. "Trust me."

"Then tell us who told you," Poppy said.

"If you must know . . ." Olivia's mouth spread into a forced smile, and she waved at someone behind Etta. Etta clenched her napkin in her hand. If someone distracted Olivia before she divulged her source, Etta felt capable of shouting at the person. But then Olivia returned her attention to Etta and Poppy. "Robert told me, and he has reason to know."

Later that afternoon, the windowpanes rattled as gusts of wind rolled through the clearing in front of Etta's cabin. She tugged her hat over her ears and zipped up her raincoat. She wasn't about to miss her run. She'd lived through her share of tornadoes back in Landon. Mother Nature wasn't going to deter her with a little wind.

She walked to the door, stepping over Olivia's navy Penn State sweatshirt, which was twisted with a T-shirt and a pair of wool socks, and reached for her key, which she'd set on Olivia's desk. She drew her hand back and stared at the desk. Gleaming on top of a stack of papers was the promise ring Jordan had given to Olivia.

Etta picked it up and rolled it in her hand, examining the tourmaline—the red center edged with green. Etta slipped it onto her finger. It felt heavy and loose. She held her hand in front of her and closed her eyes. She'd tried on her mother's plain gold wedding band once. Just as then, Etta tried to imagine the sensation of a ring settling a place for itself in her flesh, of the weight becoming so familiar it was invisible.

The ring's hexagonal setting was the only thing that exposed it as an antique. Jordan had boasted that his great grandfather had given it to his great grandmother over a century ago in Saint Petersburg, and that when his grandparents had fled Russia after World War II, his grandmother had worn it across the Atlantic to the west side of Chicago, where it was handed down through another generation of Jordan's family.

And here it was haphazardly placed next to Olivia's stacks of papers and strewn discs, beside her frog-shaped tape dispenser and a half-drunk can of flat diet soda—except Olivia must have left it deliberately. But why? Was she meeting with Robert North again?

Etta laughed. It was just like her to plot some sort of dramatic romantic tryst where there was none. Olivia was probably just working in the ceramics studio. Etta shook the engagement ring into her palm and set it back on Olivia's desk.

Etta left her cabin and ascended the hill to the east of the lodge, hunching her shoulders into the wind. As she descended into the cedar grove, she hummed to block out the low moaning of the wind, and thought about her story.

Back when she'd run along the Huron, characters introduced themselves to her; plots mapped themselves out; dialogue sprang forth. Now all Etta could think about was the eerie darkness that seemed to be settling over the forest, the incessant howling, and the gusts that pushed her back a half step for every step forward. Finally she spun around, abandoned her planned route along the south side of the grounds toward the cemetery Carl had told her about, and sprinted toward her cabin. She slowed to a stop on the lawn in front of Roosevelt Lodge, rested her elbows on her knees, and swallowed down gulps of air.

"Are you experiencing a myocardial attack?"

Etta yanked off her hat and stood. Her classmate Reed Morinsky stood a foot away staring at her, his thin lips folded downward. "Reed. Hello. I'm just, I was just, you know, running."

Reed pushed his wire-framed glasses onto his nose with his middle finger and gazed at her, as though trying to assess whether she was really all right.

"What are you doing out here?" Etta asked, hoping to break the silence.

"I'm rehearsing my lines." Reed said it in a matter-of-fact tone that suggested that Etta should have known what he was doing, which of course she did, since that's all Reed had been doing for more than a month.

"Oh right. How's the play coming along anyway?"

Reed shrugged. Like most of her classmates, Reed was a few years younger than Etta, but he was nearly a foot taller than her with a mop of thick blondish-brown hair. It was long in the back and fringed in the front. He'd been waiting in line last week to get his hair cut by Candy. In addition to a culinary student, she was a licensed hairdresser, much to the delight of the director. Most years he hired a hairdresser from Jackson to cut students' hair once a month. Candy's own hair was cut in a blunt cut with wispy bangs, a la Jane Jetson. Etta wasn't sure she wanted the intern anywhere near her head with a pair of scissors. Reed's haircut confirmed that determination.

"When is the play again?" Etta asked. She knew the answer to that too, but Reed's silence was a tad unnerving.

"Tomorrow."

"Right. The equinox party. Okay, well, better, you know, let you . . ."

"Did you hear the announcement?"

Etta took a step backward and glanced toward the Lodge. She'd run past the garden on her way back to her cabin. Maybe Carl would be out tending it.

"Hardin canceled the compulsory writing session this evening. Instead there will be an all-school meeting at seven— attendance mandatory."

Etta turned and squinted at Reed. "An all-school meeting. What's that?"

"I envisage it is as it sounds: a gathering which everyone is required to attend."

"Yes. Thank you, Reed. I mean, why, what about?"

"I thought perhaps you would know?"

Etta dropped her gaze to her hat. Her knuckles were white. She relaxed her fist.

"Hardin didn't say what it's about?"

"Only that it's of importance. And mandatory."

Etta nodded, twisted around, and ran along the south side of the lodge. She was past the garden before she realized that she hadn't said goodbye to Reed.

Etta arrived in the great room at five minutes before seven and hovered near the door. Most of the students had stayed at the lodge after dinner, and a number of them were draped across the sofas in front of the fire. The Poet's Row students were clustered near the windows, and the sound of their laughter occasionally erupted through the room. A couple of girls sat cross-legged on the floor playing cards. Outside the grayish afternoon was giving way to darkness, and the room glowed yellow with firelight and with the puddles of light from the rustic chandeliers. Someone had set up four rows of dining room chairs behind the couches.

"Hi Carl," Amanda Watson called from the sofa.

The chef strode in from the dining room. His cowboy hat was tipped forward, and he had a wooden chair in each arm. His cheeks were ruddy above his five o'clock shadow—perhaps chapped by the wind? He set the chairs down, and his face eased into his boyish grin. He tipped his hat at Amanda and winked.

Etta stepped back into the entry hall, rubbed her hands together, and ran them down the front of her wool sweater. Didn't Carl know what a snob Mandy Watson was? She'd written her entire novel in verse. Of course, he could tip his hat at whomever he pleased if he wanted to listen to Mandy prattle on about how a lot of people wrote novels and a lot of people wrote poetry, but she'd decided to try her hand at doing both at the same time.

"Hi Loretta. Whom are you hiding from?"

Etta spun around and met Petra Atwell's gaze. The resident author had on a knee-length wool cape, which matched her cherry-red lipstick. Her foundation was even more caked on than usual. She held an unlit cigarette between her claw like-fingers.

"It's Etta."

"Oh yes, how soon I forget. If it's a comfort, I had a hell of a time remembering my third husband's name. Always called the poor bastard Dick. That was number two's name. But come to think of it, Dick was a fitting name for number three too."

Etta managed a polite smile, and Petra stared at her for a long moment.

"I hate to break off such an edifying conversation . . ." Petra waved her cigarette in the air. "But I have a feeling I'll need this before our little get together. What I'd really like is a drink, but that Texan's so stingy with his whisky, I may as well have water." Petra reached for the iron door handle.

"Ms. Atwell?" Etta said.

Petra spun around, and her coat fanned out around her. She was so petite that for a moment she looked like a child, like Little Red Riding Hood. "Jesus, don't call me Ms. It makes me think of all that Gloria Steinem, 1970s crap. White ivy league Playboy bunnies liberating us from our bondage and all that shit."

Etta stared at her.

"You had a question?"

"Oh, yeah, do you know what this meeting is about?"

Petra shook her head. "I'm not in Edwin's inner circle, but the man canceled a compulsory writing session, so it must be paramount. Vince didn't cancel one in all the years he ran this place."

"You knew Vincent Buchanan?" By the time Etta's words were out, the heavy door had slammed closed behind Petra, and Etta was standing in the foyer alone.

The door creaked open again, and Etta stepped toward it. Maybe Petra had heard her question after all? Opal Waters stepped inside, and the smile froze on her lips when she saw Etta.

Etta stepped out of the way and tried to think of something to say, but words tangled on her tongue.

"Hello." Opal unbuttoned her apple green pea coat and thrust it toward Etta. Etta reached for it, gathering the wet wool in her arms, and frowned. Did the poet think Etta was a door person? Opal's heels clicked against the wood floor as she strode into the great room.

Where had Opal been? All of the visiting and resident authors had rooms on the fourth floor of the lodge. It wasn't exactly nice weather for a walk. The wind was still howling and tiny raindrops had started pelting from the sky.

Etta slung Opal's coat onto a bare hook and then glanced over her shoulder and slipped her fingers into one of the pea coat's satin-lined pockets. It was empty. She found the other pocket and slipped her hand inside. She fingered the contents: a key, a pen, a crumpled piece of paper.

Edwin Hardin's deep voice echoed into the foyer, and Etta yanked her hand from Opal's pocket. The meeting had begun. Etta pulled the crumpled piece of paper from Opal's pocket and stared at it. She considered returning it. Instead she walked to her own raincoat, pushed the piece of paper into her pocket, and raced into the great room.

Chapter Six

◆

Etta found the only vacant chair at the end of the back row, next to Chase Quinn.

"Hi Chase," she whispered.

He didn't turn.

She sat up in her chair, trying to see over Mallory Chambers' head, and scanned the room for Olivia. She hadn't seen her roommate all afternoon.

Director Hardin stood in front of the hearth. His stately voice always made what he said sound significant, except Etta had no idea what he was talking about. She must have missed something, because he wasn't making any sense.

"Chase," she whispered and then tapped on his arm.

Chase glared at her.

"Sorry, can you tell me, did I miss something?"

Chase rolled his eyes and shrugged, turning his gaze back to the director.

Etta stopped herself from sticking out her tongue at the back of his coppery head. Instead she tried to focus on what Hardin was saying, no matter how little sense it made.

"Carry on with your scholarly activities. Do not hesitate to wander the grounds, but please travel in pairs and groups." Hardin's eyes wandered toward the ceiling. "Galen was always unstable, but he had good times and bad. He could be coherent. However, by the time he was admitted into the Oregon State Hospital . . ." A tremble seemed to ascend through Hardin's body then his head quivered, and he let out a sigh. "He was delusional—dangerous."

A gasp came from somewhere in the crowd, and Etta felt her own heart thumping against her chest.

Hardin's eyes softened. "Now, let's not panic, students. We are not certain that Galen has been trespassing. We were notified of his release from the hospital five months ago. Since then, we've been more vigilant than usual about securing the property, and we have reason to suspect someone has been camping near the west boundary. I must emphasize again: Galen was not released because he is better, but because the state claims it can no longer afford to care for those with his condition, with the budget cuts and whatnot." Hardin's eyes seemed to get lost on something behind the students. "Roosevelt Lodge was Galen's home for a short while, and we expect he may return. Please do not under any circumstances speak to strangers, and report anything out of the ordinary immediately." He looked at the ceiling. "Any questions?"

In front of Etta, Mallory Chambers bolted to his feet. "Are you telling us, sir, that there's a madman on the loose?"

A darkness seemed to pass over the director's eyes. "Mr. Chambers, name calling is unnecessary. However, yes, Galen should be considered . . . unstable."

A hand rose in the center of the room. Etta couldn't hear the speaker. "Please stand and repeat your question." Hardin's voice seemed to be wearing down, as though he'd already grown tired of answering questions.

Maura Wilkins' black curls rose above the rest of the heads. "Sir, what about the party tomorrow? We've been working hard on the play, rehearsing every day, will this interfere . . ." Her voice trailed off.

Hardin wrinkled his forehead. "The equinox party will go on as planned. That reminds me, if there are no other questions,

I have an announcement." He rifled through his pocket and pulled out a card. "Yes, yes, our chefs will need some help with food preparation. I know many of you have agreed to help with decorations or will be preparing for the dramatic production, but can any of you assist our chefs on tomorrow afternoon?"

A hand rose in the front of the crowd.

Etta straightened her spine and tried to see over all the heads, the rows of hair—straight, curly, a bald spot. Amanda Watson? Was it Mandy? She would be eager to spend the day flirting with Carl. Without thinking Etta thrust her hand into the air, and Hardin nodded in her direction.

"Okay, Ms. Saxon, and whoever that is back there. Two should be sufficient." He slipped the card back in his jacket and continued shuffling through his pocket.

The director pulled cards from his pocket, glanced at them, and slid them back in, dropping his hand to his side. "I thought I had . . . in any event, if there are no further questions, I will call this meeting to an end with a reminder for everyone to be vigilant. If anything strikes you as out of place in any way, it is imperative that you report to me immediately."

Edwin Hardin stepped away from the hearth and made a beeline for the staircase. The room swelled with a cacophony of voices. Olivia had volunteered? Etta slumped against the back of her chair. Liv liked to cook? Etta could hardly prepare a ham sandwich and had once started a fire while boiling eggs. At home she ate as many dinners as possible at a restaurant or out of a take-out box. Of course, how hard could party food be? Anyone could arrange carrots and celery on a platter.

"I suppose you will be curtailing your solo runs."

Etta jerked her head toward Chase, but he was no longer in his chair. Reed Morinsky stood in front of Etta gazing at her through his wire spectacles.

"Oh, hello Reed."

There was a red lump on the end of Reed's long nose that Etta hadn't noticed earlier. Etta shifted her eyes away, and glimpsed Carl leaning on the doorway to the dining room. Robert North glided up beside him. Robert North gestured as he talked to the chef. Carl laughed.

"Is that satisfactory?"

Etta turned back to Reed, who was staring at her expectantly. Had he asked her a question? Etta nodded.

"Excellent. Shall we start Wednesday?

"Wednesday?"

"It's the day after the equinox. We will not have any classes in observance of the end of the first quarter. And the dramatic production will be over, so I shall have more time for other pursuits. I should alert you, however, my cross-country team in high school called me Cockroach. Of course, you should not concern yourself about falling behind; I shall not leave your side, with Galen roaming the woods."

"Cockroach?" Etta giggled. "They called you a cockroach?"

"Yes. Cockroaches hold the record for the fastest land insect. The Periplaneta americana has been clocked running four point nine feet a second."

Etta tried to stifle her laugh and managed another nod.

Reed grinned, revealing his gapped front teeth. Etta's eyes went again to the red spot on the end of his nose. "I must excuse myself," he said. "I'm assisting the major with the cataloging project, and I have a thousand words to compose tonight to reach my daily quota."

Etta nodded, but the mention of writing made her feel short of breath. The equinox party was tomorrow. And then she had five days until her critique.

Reed threaded around the groups of students clustered in front of the staircase. None of them said hello or seemed to notice him pass. Did Reed have any friends at the academy? Etta couldn't remember seeing him with anyone. What would it hurt to go running with him?

Pari and Hillary stood talking at the foot of the staircase. Hillary's pale face looked even more washed out than usual, her eyes watery. Etta should have asked Reed to fill her in on what she'd missed at the beginning of Hardin's speech.

Carl. Etta could ask Carl. She swirled toward the doorway to the dining room. But the chef and Robert North were gone. Carl had probably returned to the kitchen.

Etta made a beeline for the dining room. As she stepped inside, she halted, blinking to adjust her eyes to the darkness. She wound around a few tables then froze.

A voice eased from under the kitchen door—shrill and high-pitched. A woman. And she sounded angry. But Etta couldn't make out her words. Etta stepped toward the door, wincing at the squeak of her hiking boots against the wood floor.

"This is dangerous. I don't think you understand how much trouble . . ." This voice was male. He didn't sound angry. More pleading. Scared. Etta took another step toward the kitchen. A thin line of light sliced the darkness below the swinging door.

"Leave me alone." The woman's voice dissolved into sobs.

"Wait. Listen. Listen to me. This isn't . . ." The man's voice was louder. Closer. Etta realized what was about to happen, and she shot into the shadows next to the kitchen door, leaning into the wall. The door swung open and hit her foot. It flapped closed, and Etta stifled a gasp as Olivia glided across the dining room.

Etta held her breath as the door swung open again and swished shut. Robert North crossed the room, steps behind Olivia.

Etta pushed the weight of her down comforter off, exposing herself to the cold air for as long as she could stand it. Then she buried herself in her comforter's warmth again. The outline of Olivia's empty bed was lumpy, strewn with clothes and books. Olivia's conversation with Robert North earlier was tangled and hazy in Etta's mind, as though she'd dreamt the entire incident. Had Olivia pronounced her love for Robert North? Or had

Robert North said he loved Liv? No, there was no mention of love, only danger.

Etta sat up. The thought of turning on her lamp and looking at her watch filled her with relief.

Ten forty-one.

Forty minutes since she'd looked last.

Etta slipped out of bed, padded across the room, and sat down on Olivia's bed next to the twisted-up comforter and Olivia's lime wool sweater. Both smelled of Liv's lavender-scented oil.

Etta would walk to Reed's cabin and ask him to unlock the archives room for her. If he was working with Major Mills in the library, he'd probably know where the key was.

It was a crazy idea, walking to the men's cabins in the middle of the night, waking someone she hardly knew. But once it had flitted across Etta's mind several minutes—or was it hours?—ago, she couldn't let it go. Maybe it wasn't such a crazy idea. Crazy would be staying all alone in this messy cabin, sitting awake in this suffocating room.

Before Etta could talk herself out of it, she slid off of Liv's bed and marched across the room to her dresser. She yanked her rain pants over her flannel pajama bottoms, laced on her running shoes, and slipped her rain jacket off the hook in her closet. She grabbed her key off of Liv's desk, nearly knocking over the can of Diet Coke that still sat there. Then she crossed the room and stepped outside.

All of the cabins were dark. Etta descended the stairs and took a couple steps into the clearing. Something rustled. Etta spun toward it, squinting at the outline of her cabin and the trees towering behind it. For the first time since she'd overheard Olivia and Robert North's fight, she thought of the director's speech.

An unstable man camping in the forest? It seemed funny all at once, like something from a novel, except it was too preposterous for serious fiction. Etta had lived alone for years and had never been scared of ghosts or serial killers, or walking alone at night. She'd worked as a volunteer ranger in Isle Royale

National Park for a couple of summers during college, and she'd savored the long nights, the creak of the trees, the sound of Lake Superior lapping onto the shore.

Another rustle.

Etta sprinted to her cabin and jabbed at the lock with her key. She collapsed against the door for a few minutes. Then she walked to Olivia's bed and slumped against the clump of pillows. Something jabbed her arm and she untangled it from the twisted blankets. A book. A black paperback Penguin edition of Vincent Buchanan's *The Western Defense.*

"Introduction by T. Clarence Johnson," read the small white letters along the bottom.

Of course, it had been required reading at Taylor High School. But it was one of the few reading assignments she hadn't finished. The battle scenes were so tedious. Etta flipped the book open to the introduction and nearly dropped the book. Someone had scrawled a word across the bottom of the page. Etta steadied her hands as she stared at it. "Murderer."

She lifted her gaze and read T. Clarence Johnson's introduction:

More than any other novel in the history of American literature, Vincent Buchanan's The Western Defense *begs the question: can a work of fiction change the course of history?*

When Viking Press released the novel in January of 1943, the author had already written three novels, won a Pulitzer Prize, and been hailed by critics around the world. His soaring status in the literary community gained him unprecedented access to high officials in the U.S. Armed Forces and Defense Department to pen what would become his magnum opus.

The Western Defense *poses a hypothetical question that was not far from any American's imagination at the time: What if Japan carried out an attack on the West Coast of the United States in the winter of 1944, striking three metropolitan areas in a single night? Buchanan's answer was unapologetic: Americans would wage the most Herculean response the world had ever seen—and they would triumph.*

Within weeks of its publication, The Western Defense *was credited with increasing the morale of American soldiers in the Pacific and Europe and bolstering the willingness of the men and women on the home front to sacrifice for the war effort. Franklin Roosevelt called Vincent Buchanan "a modern day Paul Revere"—a nickname that would later become the author's epitaph.*

"This novel may have saved the world," Harry Truman reportedly proclaimed a year and a half later, after the Japanese surrendered.

The Western Defense *also has its critics. Opponents of the Japanese Internment argue that Buchanan's book is a loosely veiled justification for Executive Order 9066, which authorized the military to round up Japanese Americans on the West Coast in 1942 and relocate them to inland camps. Some even decried The* Western Defense *as propaganda, conjecturing that the Office of War Information commissioned Buchanan to write it. In 1945, when the Pulitzer Prize Committee named* The Western Defense *as their distinguished work of fiction by an American author, a handful of editorialists across the country denounced the choice.*

Half a decade later, at the close of the nineteen hundreds, among the balloon drops and Y2K hysteria, the historian Nicholas Bryce opened yet a new chapter of controversy when he revealed on ABC's Great People of the Twentieth Century *that Harry Truman read* The Western Defense *during the summer of 1945 just before the blasts in Hiroshima and Nagasaki echoed across the world. The same week* Time Magazine *named Buchanan's novel the most influential book of the century.*

Nearly all readers and critics agree, however, that The Western Defense *is a work of literary genius, which stands without peers for its vivid characters, emotional depth and breathtaking detail. Despite the controversies surrounding his best-known book, Vincent Buchanan's legacy as America's most-celebrated author and patriot lives on.*

Etta pulled the book closer and stared at the word "murderer." Was it Olivia's handwriting? She flipped through the rest of the book. Forty pages of critical commentary by two different scholars then the text of the novel. No more handwritten comments.

She closed the novel and flipped it over. The picture on the back was of a young Buchanan. He looked to be in his mid-thirties. His black hair was buzzed on the sides and wavy at the top, and he had a sober look on his angular face.

Etta carried the book to her own bed. She took off her shoes and rain clothes, crawled under the comforter, and flipped past the commentary to the first chapter. She pulled the book close to make out the small font and read one of the most famous first lines in American literature: "One hundred and seventy million cubic miles of churning salt water separated good from evil in November of 1944 . . ."

Etta couldn't put the book down. The characters jumped off the page—a young mother who survived the L.A. bombing and decided to walk with her children to Mexico, a group of generals at the Pentagon who planned the U.S. counterattack, a soldier in San Francisco who drove tanks down Haight Street and set up enforcements on both sides of the Golden Gate Bridge. Sometimes she backtracked and read aloud, listening to the haunting melody of Buchanan's language resonating through the room. At some point Etta dropped the book on her nightstand and flicked off her light.

She awoke later and turned toward a sound on the other side of the room. Olivia's silken hair was splayed across her pillow.

Chapter Seven

◆

ETTA AWOKE ON THE EQUINOX TO THE SOUND OF RAINDROPS rolling across the roof. She sat up. It had been a dream, of course. She'd been in San Francisco and felt the earth shake with Vincent Buchanan's bombs. A blinding light had flooded the sky, fluorescent white. A blast followed —earsplitting and silent at the same time. Etta was in a cable car, teetering up a hill, sitting across from her mother, who was old and growing older every second, her gray hair turning white, dissolving to ashes, her skin brittle, splintering apart as she spoke. Everyone was scattering, running, yelling. But Etta could only stare at her mother's arms. Blue veins laced her translucent flesh, as though a spider was spinning webs beneath her skin.

Etta clicked on her lamp and blinked back the yellow light. Her cellular phone was tucked away in her desk drawer, where it had been for two months. It didn't get reception on the grounds, which wasn't a problem because no one would be trying to reach her.

Etta had called her father from the administration office a few weeks after she'd arrived. But she'd waited until it was after eight in Michigan and called his office phone at Temple Christian College, hoping even he wouldn't be at work so late. She'd left a

49

curt message, explaining that she'd be unreachable except in an emergency and had recited the academy's phone number.

Now Etta felt desperate to hear her mother's voice, not the razor that had sliced her ear the last few times they'd spoken, but the one that used to sing hymns to Etta and her brothers when they drove to Grand Rapids on Sunday mornings. It was the only thing Etta had liked about church—hearing her mother sing.

A memory tugged at the corners of Etta's brain. She'd heard Olivia's voice sometime in the night. A male voice too. Was it another dream? No, she remembered seeing her roommate there. But now Olivia was gone. Her bed was hastily made, the white comforter pulled across the narrow mattress.

Etta reached for *The Western Defense*. Today was a holiday at the academy. There would be no mandatory writing sessions. No morning workshop. No lectures. Everyone was preparing for the festivities that evening.

Several hours later, Etta finished the last page, closed the book, and stared again at the grainy black and white photo of Buchanan. The empty sensation that accompanied finishing a book settled over her. Then she remembered what had made her read it in the first place. She flipped to the introduction again and stared at the word "murderer." What did it mean?

She would ask Olivia today. They would be together all day, preparing food. She'd ask Olivia about visiting the archives, about Jordan, about Robert North.

Etta rounded the bend, and Roosevelt Lodge came into view, the windows glowing yellow in the rainy haze. Etta was nearly to the porch when she glimpsed Chase Quinn in front of the wooden doors, his coppery hair tufting out from beneath a black skullcap. He was talking to somebody, his arms flying up from his sides as he gestured.

Chase swayed, and Etta glimpsed the sleeve of Petra Atwell's red coat and the glowing embers of her cigarette extending from one of her talons. A puff of smoke clouded around Chase and rose into the porch light.

Etta swirled around and hurried back into the trees. She couldn't face Chase and Petra right now. She'd take the shortcut through the forest to the men's cabins and then take the trail from there to the theater entrance.

Etta stepped into the clearing outside the men's cabins, and her eyes went to Jordan's door. The porch light was on, a ghostly blue beam in the haze. Was Olivia there? Etta had only been over to Jordan's cabin twice, both times with Olivia, but she moved toward the light. Maybe she and Olivia could walk to the kitchen together; they could talk. Etta knocked on the door and waited. No answer. She knocked again, and then pulled her hood off, wiping beads of water from her eyebrows and the tip of her nose.

"Jordan?"

She waited.

"Olivia?"

Etta stared at the doorknob. Jordan didn't lock his door so that Olivia could come and go as she pleased. Etta brought her hand to the doorknob and twisted, pushing the door open a crack. "You here, Jor?"

The curtains were drawn. It took Etta's eyes a minute to adjust to the shadows. Then a chill rose through her. Jordan's bed was neatly made. The dressers were bare. The cabin looked vacant, except for Jordan's 1939 Remington typewriter, which sat on his desk. "Would Fitzgerald have used Microsoft Word?" Jordan had asked Etta over lunch one day. Etta didn't see why he wouldn't have if it had been available, but she hadn't challenged Jordan on it.

"Jor," Etta called again. She stepped into the cabin and the floorboards gave a little under her weight. She pressed the door closed behind her and looked around, searching for any signs her roommate had been there. Then she saw Olivia's name. For a moment it felt like she'd conjured it. But there it was, *Olivia*, on a small yellow sticky note affixed to the top of a stack of papers next to Jordan's typewriter. Etta stepped closer, leaning over the chair to make out the rest of the words.

In your haste to break our engagement, you forgot "your" story.

Etta almost reached over to pluck the sticky note off the paper so that she could see the notebook paper beneath it. But she yanked her hand back. She was dripping wet. Beads of water were rolling off her coat onto the floor.

The pages beneath the sticky note were yellowing at the edges, and someone had written across the pages in jagged all-caps letters, The felt-tip pen had bled in spots and blacked in parts of some of the letters. Something about the way the words crowded into the margins made Etta want to draw her eyes away. It certainly wasn't Olivia's handwriting.

After Etta slammed Jordan's door shut, ran down the path, and pulled the heavy theater door open to the sound of Maura Wilkins' girlish voice echoing from the stage, Etta finally absorbed the words on the sticky note: *In your haste to break our engagement . . .*

Flute music drifted from the kitchen. Etta stopped outside and ran her hands through her hair, trying to shake some of the water out. The flute faded, and was replaced by a synthesized drumbeat. Then chanting female voices. Was Carl listening to New Age music? Etta pushed the kitchen door open.

Candy stood behind a stainless steel table in the center of the room, her blonde hair and bangs flattened beneath a hair net. Pots and pans hung on a rack several feet above her, like oversized wind chimes. She punched her fists into a ball of dough, her eyes closed.

"Hello," Etta called.

Candy didn't seem to hear, which wasn't surprising with the chanting vibrating through the room. Etta walked to the table and watched Candy flip the dough over and form it into a ball. Her eyelids sparkled with a swath of silver eye shadow, which extended to her tweezed eyebrows and onto her temples. It looked a little like the Elmer's glue and glitter projects kids concocted in grade school. A high-pitched hum was coming from somewhere behind her nose—more of a whine than a chant.

The song ended, but the breathy high-pitched hum still emanated from Candy's nose. Her head circled lazily. She flicked her eyes open, and Etta stepped backward.

Candy frowned. "We're out of biscuits, and the coffee's long gone." She rounded the ball of dough with her chubby fingers and then dropped it and punched both fists into it, flattening it onto the table.

"Is Carl here?"

Candy pretended to look under the table. "Hey Carl, take off your invisibility cloak."

Etta smiled. "Do you know where he is?"

Candy shrugged. "If you must know, he and the director were in here for like a half hour whispering back and forth about something then the hillbilly says he has to go somewhere and he doesn't know when he'll be back, and now I'm stuck making all the food for the biggest party of the year." She rolled her eyes. "He promised some stupid girls are supposed to come help, but did they even bother to show up?"

"I'm one." Etta smiled. "I'm Etta."

Candy said something, but a gong reverberated through the room then another and another. They grew louder and louder.

"Can we turn that down?" Etta shouted.

"It's Peas Lite," Candy shouted back.

Etta tried to make the words make sense. Then she spotted the stereo on a shelf across the room and made a beeline to it, grasping for the knob. The gong faded to a more humane volume. The top CD on a pile next to the stereo said Peace Light. Etta glanced through the rest of the pile. *Jewels of Silence,*

Transformation Trance, *Music for Healing*, and six or seven CD's by someone named Jimmie Dale Gilmore. Etta slid one of the Jimmie Dale Gilmore CDs from the middle of the pile.

"Be glad the hillbilly's not here, or we'd be listening to that. 'The chef gets to pick the music,' he says. Just my luck I have to work for a hillbilly."

Etta set the CD on top of the others. "Carl doesn't like New Age music?"

"He calls it Sew-age music."

Etta laughed and studied a framed photo of a woman propped next to the stereo. The woman was young, mid-twenties perhaps. Her reddish brown hair fell below her shoulders, and she was squinting into the camera like the sun was in her eyes.

"Let me guess, you're wondering if the hillbilly has a girlfriend."

"No," Etta said, even though that's exactly what she'd been thinking.

Candy grinned. "You wouldn't be the first one. You are a pathetic bunch of girls out here, stuck in this forest with that weird chastity code, all hot and heavy for the hillbilly. You should see the ladies at the grocery store in Hicksville Jackson fawn over him. 'Can I help you, Carl?' 'Let me get that, Carl.' It's disgusting. I wouldn't worry too much about the girl in the photo though. She's dead."

Etta's face filled with heat. Dead? She opened her mouth to ask what happened to the pretty woman, but decided against it. She glanced at the door. Where was Olivia? "So, do you want me to cut up vegetables or something?"

Candy dropped the dough ball onto the table. "We're going to need five quiches—two vegetarian, two with bacon and sausage, and one with smoked salmon. The ingredients are in here." She wiped her hands on her apron and started across the room.

"Quiches?"

Candy spun around, her hair hardly moving beneath the hair net. "Don't tell me you don't know what quiche is?" The air hissed between her teeth as she exhaled.

"Of course I do."

"Thank God. It would be just my luck if the hillbilly sent me someone who doesn't even know how to cook. Don't wait for a hand-written invitation. Follow me." Candy pulled open the door to the walk-in refrigerator.

Etta trailed behind the intern.

Four hours later, Etta's T-shirt and jeans were coated with flour, her upper back was stiff, and she never wanted to hear another chime, gong, or synthesizer for the rest of her life. But as she scanned the steel table holding her five quiches, in addition to the crab cakes; bacon-wrapped scallops; salad; five loaves of bread; and two layered cakes that Candy had somehow prepared in the same amount of time, she felt more pride than she'd felt about her writing in a long time. She had an impulse to put her arm around Candy, and the words *thank you for letting me help* bubbled into her throat. But Candy was smacking her gum and staring at the food with a dullness that made Etta swallow her words.

As Etta walked down the trail to her cabin, she started to feel giddy at the idea of a party: music, cocktails, and fancy clothes. She'd never liked parties much, but seeing all the food laid out made the idea of people and conversation seem electric.

Etta stepped into the clearing as a screen door slapped shut. It took her a minute to register that it was the door to her own cabin. Olivia's voice flooded into the clearing. Etta stood staring at her porch. Her first instinct was to close her eyes and pretend she wasn't seeing what she was seeing. But there they were, Carl and Olivia, coming out of Etta's cabin, standing just inches from each other, staring at Etta.

Silence spread across the clearing. Carl drawled a hello. He'd hardly said her name when she heard her own voice, loud, sharp, and angry: "Where the hell were you guys today?"

She felt her body twisting. She ran into the trees, her feet somehow finding the trail, and she didn't stop until she couldn't take another step. The firs loomed around her, blocking out much of the dusky afternoon light, and the sound of her breath filled her ears, short spasms of air in and out.

She heard her name. Olivia was jogging toward her, her long hair wet and crushed to the sides of her face. "Etta. Please. Wait."

By the time Olivia caught her, Etta was laughing. She leaned over and grabbed her knees with her hands. The laughter wouldn't stop gurgling up. Etta had written so many scenes just like this. Of course in one of Etta's books, it would have been Carl who raced up the trail, his shirt wet and clinging to his muscular chest, his drawling voice calling out Etta's name.

"Etta, please it's not how it looked." Olivia heaved the words out.

Etta tried to swallow her laughter.

"I know how it must have looked. But . . ."

Olivia looked almost gaunt as she folded her arms across her chest; skeletal fingers clutching bone-thin arms.

"He's going door to door. Warning everyone to be careful, to walk to the lodge in pairs and all that." Olivia didn't make eye contact. Shadows filled the hollows beneath her eyes.

"Are you okay?"

"Out of shape. You run fast, girl." Finally Olivia met Etta's gaze. "Please say you're not mad at me."

Now it was Etta who couldn't make eye contact. She dropped her eyes at the hollow spot in Olivia's neck. Olivia was just so pretty, so flirtatious. When Etta had seen Carl, she'd just assumed . . . But when she met Olivia's gaze again, she realized she'd been mistaken. "I'm sorry, Liv." Etta stepped toward Olivia and put her arms around her, surprised at how small and fragile her roommate felt in her embrace. When Etta dropped her arms, she took a step backward. "It's just, you guys didn't come today. I had to make all the food . . ."

"The party." Olivia's voice was sharp. She spun around and started down the trail. "The play. We can't be late."

Etta watched Olivia's form disappearing around the bend.

The play.

Olivia's play.

Etta had almost forgotten.

Chapter Eight

❖

SOMEONE HAD HUNG JAPANESE LANTERNS FROM THE TREES, lighting the path to the lodge. But even with the hazy light, the trail was difficult to negotiate in high heels. It didn't help that Olivia and Poppy were striding toward Roosevelt Lodge at a stallion's pace or that the umbrella Poppy was supposed to be holding over all three of them kept swaying so that Etta's cheek got sprayed with the pools of water collecting on top. Etta grabbed the end of her dress. The red satin feathered across her legs, sending a tingle up her spine. As they rounded the curve to the Lodge, cello music floated through the trees. A man's baritone voice and a woman's throaty laugh buzzed through the drizzle like an electric current.

At the base of the stairs, Poppy collapsed the umbrella and shook it out. Paper lanterns hung from the porch's eaves, illuminated spheres in the darkness that made the slanting slivers of rain shimmer silver. One of the doors to the Lodge swung closed, and Etta was standing alone.

She teetered up the stairs into the porch light's yellow glow and unzipped her raincoat, wincing at the rush of cool air that flooded across her neck. The cello music emanated from the seams of the Lodge—a haunting melody that seemed too somber for a party.

"Ah Loretta—an expert at masquerade." Etta jerked her head up and stepped backward. Petra Atwell's face danced with shadows from a swinging lantern, the embers of her cigarette glowing red. The bodice of her black floor-length dress plunged low in the front, revealing surprisingly ample cleavage for such a petite woman. She held a squat glass, and it caught the porch light—two translucent ice cubes floating in clear liquid. Next to her, Walker Ryan's lanky frame emerged from the shadows and dwarfed Petra. It must have been their voices Etta had heard in the trees. Etta inhaled the sweet hickory of Walker's cigar and smiled at her favorite resident author.

Etta opened her mouth to correct Petra on her name then she realized what Petra had said. "Excuse me?"

Walker pulled the cigar from his mouth and swirled it between his thumb and index finger. "Ignore her. She was just elucidating her rather cynical view of human social behavior for me."

"Trust me, I have far more cynical views than this. I merely contend that it's plain deceit to dress in a costume and pretend to be witty when one is as boring as a *Save the Children* telethon." She glared at Etta. "Don't look like a bruised peach, Loretta. I'm not talking about you . . . per se. All parties breed liars. These unbearable literary soirees are the worst. Miserable bores who spend their days hypnotized by laptop screens masquerading as stars and starlets. Putting on airs, pretending to be someone you're not. It's pathetic. Wouldn't you agree, Loretta?"

Etta held Petra's gaze for a moment, and then Walker's booming laugh broke the silence. "Petra, you are as charming as a viper. Let this young woman enjoy her night." He stubbed his cigar out in an ashtray that was resting on the handrail. "Can I escort you inside?" Etta nodded, pulling her gaze from Petra as Walker opened the door for her. She stepped inside just as the cello melody ended on a low note. A round of muffled applause followed.

The sconces in the foyer were low, casting a warm glow on the oak walls. Etta let Walker take her raincoat and hang it on a hook next to the door. The door to the great room swung open, and a cacophony of voices poured into the small space. Reed stepped into the foyer, came to a halt and looked Etta up and down. "Wow." He pushed his wire frames up with his middle finger.

"Well, hello Mr. Morinsky," Walker said. "Will your performance be starting soon?"

"Yes, Mr. Ryan." Reed's voice cracked. He cleared his throat. "The curtain will rise in forty minutes." His squinty eyes shifted from Walker to Etta. He had on brown corduroys and a worn tweed blazer with leather patches on the elbows in place of his usual khakis and starched shirt. A layer of foundation glistened on his forehead and nose, and blusher colored his cheeks.

Walker laughed, a booming echo. "I'm looking forward to it. Winston is one hell of a director. Julia and I saw his first Broadway show—must have been twenty-six years ago. He makes magic on the stage. If he'd move to Hollywood, I'd think about going to the show again." He looked from Reed to Etta, and then smiled. "Break a leg, son. I need to figure out where I left my drink."

Walker pulled the door open and stepped into the great room. Reed's eyes shifted back and forth behind his glasses.

"Are you nervous?" Etta asked.

Reed rubbed his hands together. "Yes. I suffer from severe glossophobia prior to every performance."

"What-a-phobia?"

"Glossophobia. The fear of speaking in public. It afflicts seventy-five percent of people."

Etta nodded. "Oh, right. Well, just picture us all naked."

Beads of sweat formed on Reed's brow, and Etta wished she could take back the sentence. "I mean, I've heard that can work," she mumbled.

"Yes, I have heard of that tactic as well. However in my case it would be a detriment. Regrettably, I'm also afflicted by gymnophobia."

Etta glanced over her shoulder at the door to the great room. "A fear of gyms?"

His forehead was now slick with sweat. "Gymnos is Greek for nudity."

Etta stifled a smile. "Oh. Well, picture us all wearing fur coats then."

Reed pushed his glasses up with his middle finger and smiled, revealing the gap between his front teeth. Etta wondered if his makeup would roll right off his face.

"I must go through my voice exercises now. I hope you enjoy the performance." The front door swished closed behind him sending a draft of cool air sliding across Etta's arms.

A cello chord echoed through the room as Etta walked toward the hearth. A spray of sparks rose from the flames, which jumped in the fireplace as though someone had just teased them with an iron prod. Except Etta was the only one standing anywhere near the fire.

Everyone else stood around the cello player sitting in front of the windows. It was Rodney Patterson. His thin black hair was combed in long stripes across his forehead. It should not have surprised Etta to see Rodney. His somber short story had been as haunting as his cello notes. But he'd never seemed like someone who'd be comfortable performing in front of a crowd. Etta wasn't sure if she'd ever heard his voice. Now he was sitting on the edge of a wooden chair, his lanky body bent over the cello. He rocked as he bowed the instrument's strings, his eyes fluttering open and closed as the notes climbed up and down octaves, faster and faster. The effect was so raw that Etta couldn't draw her eyes away. Rodney looked as though he was possessed by something, as did the people clustered around him. Two women stood just on the edge of the circle of light, dressed in silk. They had their backs to Etta, but their faces were reflected in a windowpane. Lorna and

Lydia. Their bodies swayed in tandem with the flicks of Rodney's slender wrist.

"As they say back home, that dress could charm the heart of a rusty lizard."

Etta spun around. Carl grinned and lifted his wine glass.

"You cut your hair."

Carl ran his free hand along his newly buzzed head. His face looked even more wind-chapped than the last time she'd seen him. He had on a black tailored suit jacket and a green tie, and he looked so different than usual that she couldn't help but stare for a minute. Finally she shifted her gaze back to Rodney. His fingers flew up and down the neck of the cello as he jerked the bow across the strings. The song ended as abruptly as it started, and the room fell silent.

Then clapping and whistling erupted, and someone—Mallory Chambers?—whooped Rodney's name.

Carl's breath feathered across Etta's hair. "How are we supposed to dance to that? Think he takes requests?"

Etta smiled. She was about to suggest the musician whose CD's she'd seen in the kitchen, but she couldn't remember his name. Jimmie Dave something? Rodney started another song, and Etta watched, mesmerized by the slow movement of the bow drifting up and down.

"I was hopin' to talk to you . . . about earlier" Carl's voice was just above a whisper.

Etta remembered all at once—Olivia and Carl on the porch, her own angry voice echoing into the clearing. Heat rushed into her cheeks. She waved her hand in the air to try to dismiss what he'd said. "Are you hungry?" She spun around and moved toward the long table between the fireplace and the windows. Carl strode after her. The table was covered in white tablecloths, with a candelabra in the center. The flames cast flickering shadows across the piles of plates, the tray of silver, the bottles of wine and the glasses, and the glistening food platters.

Carl handed her an empty plate, and his hand brushed against hers. She moved down the table, picking a few things from the appetizers: a slice of watermelon, a strawberry, and two crab cakes. She glanced at the three quiches on display, but they looked a little too familiar to be appetizing.

Carl deposited a wedge of the smoked salmon quiche onto his plate. The thought of Carl eating something she'd cooked, along with the ache that had started to resonate from the arches of her feet from her high heels made Etta feel unsteady.

Rodney finished his song, and rose, resting his cello on its stand. The room swirled with people.

"Dry Riesling will enhance the sweetness of the crab, bringing out its delicate flavor, like a lemon slice would."

Etta reached for the wine glass Carl was extending to her. "I usually avoid California vintages like a long tail cat around rockin' chairs, but this one's pretty good." Carl plucked his plate off the table and moved toward a table near the wall. Etta teetered after him, taking a gulp of wine and savoring the sweetness of it at the back of her throat.

Several of the myrtlewood tables from the dining room had been pushed together and covered in white tablecloths. The center was lined with tea candles and a dusting of glitter, which made Etta think of a high school dance. Carl sat down and Etta set her plate across from him, relieved at the release of pressure on her toes and arches when she sat down. She scanned the room for Olivia and Poppy, trying to recognize faces in the crowd.

Two people were sitting at the other end of the long table. Jordan? Yes, his whitish blond hair caught the candlelight. Etta searched for his eyes and tried to smile at him, but he was intent on someone sitting across the table. Chase Quinn?

"You okay?"

Etta's gaze leapt to the voice. Carl was sawing at the quiche with his fork.

"Sorry, did you say something?"

He looked up, his face lit up by the tea candles. "Yeah, I was hopin' to talk to you . . ." He dropped the fork with a clank onto the edge of his plate.

"Is it that bad?"

Carl blinked and glanced down at the quiche. "I reckon that depends."

"On what?"

"On whether you prepared this fine dish."

Etta laughed, all at once feeling the wine buzzing through her empty stomach. She wrapped her fingers around the stem of the glass. "If it's horrible, you should just tell me."

He grinned, his eyes pinching at the corners. "It's delicious . . . 'cept the crust might be a smidgen tough."

"A smidgen." Etta laughed. "What exactly is a smidgen?"

Carl frowned. "Ever tasted sheet rock?"

Etta laughed so hard that it took her a minute to register that Olivia was at her side, crouching between her and Carl. Olivia gripped Etta's arm. Her fingers were freezing, and Etta winced, automatically jerking away. Her glass teetered, and Carl's hand shot across the table to settle it.

"Liv, hi."

Olivia was hissing into her ear, but Etta couldn't make out any words. She searched for Olivia's eyes. They were wet, glossy. Had Olivia been crying? Etta glanced at Carl.

"Are you okay?" The words sliced through whatever Olivia was whispering.

Olivia looked over her shoulder, and then snapped her eyes back to Etta. "Please come. Now."

Etta glanced at Carl. "We were . . ."

"We're going to miss the play."

Her words were so sharp that Etta felt herself wince again. "Liv, I'm sure they'll make an announcement."

Olivia stared at Carl. "Can my friend come with me to watch the play I wrote? Is that okay with you, or do you want to keep her in this corner all night?" Her words were icy.

Carl set his wine glass down, his gaze shifting from Olivia to Etta and then down to his plate. "I was just leavin'. Got to go check on some things." He slid off the bench and strolled past Olivia, leaving his plate and glass on the table.

"Let's go," Olivia hissed. Etta let her roommate pull her to her feet. She gripped Olivia's hand and followed her through the crowd and into the dark hallway that led to the dining room. She tried to seek out Carl in the fluttering shadows. But she only saw Jordan and Chase Quinn. Their gazes seemed to be following her down the hallway. Then Etta was sure Jordan had leapt to his feet and was following them. But it must have been her imagination, because Olivia and Etta's footsteps were the only ones echoing in the darkness.

Etta didn't have to ask where they were going. She knew the hallway led to the theater, which was a relief, because something about the ragged way Olivia was breathing made Etta not want to ask any questions.

Chapter Nine

◈

SMOKE ROLLED OUT FROM BENEATH THE BLUE VELVET CURTAIN and rose into the stage lights. Etta tried to pull her hand from Olivia's. Her first instinct was to spin around and grab at the door handle. But then she inhaled the dusty smell of the theater. It didn't smell like smoke. It must be a dry-ice machine. Etta's feet and calves ached, and she was tempted to lean down and slip the high heels off. Instead she let Olivia pull her forward. Strands of Olivia's hair had fallen from her hairdo, and they swung back and forth as she hurried down the narrow center aisle, her head flicking from one side of the room to the other. They had their pick of seats; the theater was empty.

Buchanan had supposedly salvaged the seating from a theater in downtown Portland that had closed in the fifties, but they were in pristine condition. They were polished maple with spring cushions covered in royal blue velvet, and they had built-in ashtrays on the arm rests and brass fedora holders beneath.

A door squeaked open, and a tumble of laughter vaulted into the theater. Etta turned to see who it was. "Pay attention" Olivia snapped, grabbing her hand. "Where will he sit?"

Etta's face filled with fire. Who, she almost asked, but she couldn't bring herself to say anything. Olivia looked so frantic, angry.

"The first row." Olivia's fingers squeezed Etta's palm. Etta tried to tug her hand away, but Olivia had a good grip. Olivia led Etta to the space between the front row and the stage.

"We have to be able to see him." Olivia's head flew back and forth. Voices drifted in. The seats in the middle of the room started to fill up. "Etta," Olivia snapped again.

"What?" Etta snapped back this time.

"Where's he going to sit?"

"Who? Who are you talking about?"

"Olivia." A deep voice came from the stage, and both Olivia and Etta spun around. The fake smoke swirled just in front of them. Winston Goss, the resident author directing the play, was standing over them, his legs hidden by the fog of dry ice. His torso seemed to float. "Oh thank goodness you're early. I panicked when I realized I hadn't saved you a front row seat." He grinned, and Etta realized she'd perhaps never seen him smile. Winston was not unfriendly. He just usually seemed too consumed in thought to be genial. "I can't wait for you to see what a marvelous script you've written. It's just, it's, you know . . . I think there's too much smoke. You wouldn't believe how much dry ice I had delivered." He exhaled, wiping at his forehead. "I think I'm more nervous with this one than with my bigger productions, because it's just so original, so unconventional. I hope you like what we've done with it."

Etta moved to the seat next to the narrow staircase leading to the stage. She slumped into the chair, only half listening to Olivia and Winston talk. A couple of people filed into the seats at the end of the row and others crowded into the row behind her. The play Etta had finally hammered out at the last minute for the contest was admittedly mediocre, perhaps worse than mediocre, but Winston had covered her pages with red ink. Her dialogue was forced. Her stage directions were too complicated. Her characters were unbelievable. On the last page, he'd written: "You should strive to entertain the audience, not firebomb them with your ideals." It was only Etta's first month at the academy, and it wasn't as though she was a playwright or anything. It seemed to her that Winston had been a tad tough on her.

The house lights dimmed, Etta lifted her gaze to the stage. Olivia's face was flushed, her glossy eyes darting back and forth. She looked nervous. No, terrified. All at once, Etta wanted to hug her roommate. So what if Winston was ebullient with his praise for Olivia and thought Etta's play was horrible? Olivia deserved it.

From the stage, Winston scanned the room from behind his tiny wire-framed glasses and raised a hand. Olivia ambled to the seat next to Etta and dropped into it and then pushed herself forward and hovered on the edge, fixating on something across the aisle.

"Welcome to the thirty-eighth annual fall equinox dramatic production at the Buchanan Academy. Tonight we celebrate the equinox." Winston rose a hand, quieting the applause that followed. "A day where darkness and light are equal—a day of balance, of equity, of harmony. I can't help but think of Vincent Buchanan's deep reverence for this day, for the change of seasons, for creativity, for art. I was honored to teach here for several years when Vincent was here, and this night, like everything else here, is a reflection of him, of his belief in the extraordinary potential of young writers. The first time I came to the academy, to this lodge, to this small theater, he told me about this contest and insisted that the quality of the equinox play always surprised him. I was skeptical." A few people in the room laughed. "I read plenty of plays, hundreds a year, and I can usually tell if the writer is an amateur in the first scene. But this year, wow, this year, I can truly say, I was . . . This one . . . I will let it speak for itself. Please give Olivia Saxon your applause. Stand up, Olivia. She deserves it and so much more."

The room exploded, whistles and shouts rising from the back. Olivia stood, her attention still on something on the other side of the aisle. Etta leaned forward to see what she was staring at, but the only people sitting across the aisle were Director Hardin, Major Mills, and Opal Waters. Olivia sat down as

Winston disappeared into the smoke. The stage lights went out, the curtain rolled open, and blue light filled the stage.

Etta was so transfixed by the performance that she forgot she was in the theater until Olivia's elbow nudged her forearm. "Can you see him?"

It was a climactic moment, and Etta didn't want to pull her attention away from the stage. For the first time in more than an hour, she remembered that it was Reed on the stage, not Hans Gretelstein, his character.

Hans was a troublemaker, a muckraker, a journalist who thrived on routing out scandals. The setting was obviously the academy, although it was never stated as such and there was far more blue smoke than Etta had ever seen at Roosevelt Lodge. But it was obvious: a college in the forest, a group of students draped across desks carrying on with pretentious, long-winded conversations that inevitably concluded with someone declaring that his own writing was magnificent. With each conversation, Etta felt laughter surging through her and rippling across the audience behind her, building on itself into something contagious and almost out of control. The character of "Poet," much like Robert North, found a way to draw every conversation back to the artistic merits of his recently-published poetry collection.

Hans Gretelstein divulged secrets about his classmates in his stories. At first they were small. He exposed a plagiarist. An affair. An accounting scandal in the administration building. But now he had written, "The Exposé," which contained a secret so threatening to the academy that his classmates started plotting his demise. They would lead Hans out into the forest, deep into the trees, so far that he could never find his way back. That's what they did, except Hans brought his scandalous stories with him and scattered the pages as they led him away. And then he followed his stories right back to the academy. His classmates led him out into the forest again, but this time all he had to scatter behind him was his poetry.

"Can you see Hardin?" Olivia hissed.

Etta glanced at Olivia, and then returned her gaze to the stage. Reed, or Hans, walked through the jagged paper-mache trees, his face pale in the blue light, smoke clouding around his waist. He looked scared, and he was far from the school now. His poems were confusing him, taking him down the wrong paths. "Poetry. Damn poetry. Nuances. Digressions. Pretensions. Meandering. Impossible to follow." Hans slumped against a tree.

"What's he doing?" Olivia hissed. She was sitting on the edge of her seat, leaning forward, clutching onto one of the curling arm rests. "You can see him better. He's on the far end."

Etta could just barely make out Hardin's long legs stretched out in front of him. His face was hidden in the shadows. "I'm sure he likes it. It's really great," she whispered.

"Does he look like he likes it?"

"Truth . . ." Hans' voice echoed through the theater. Hans had his exposé with him. He had brought it into the forest. Why hadn't he scattered its pages instead of his poetry? Etta scowled at the back of Olivia's head for distracting her from such an important moment. Hans fell to the ground, his face drawn, his eyes moist. Was he going to cry? He dug into the soil and set the exposé in a shallow grave, covering it with fistfuls of dirt. "You can bury me. But truth is immortal."

The royal blue curtain jerked shut, and for several seconds the theater was silent. Hans'—or Reed's—gaze was so pained, so haunting in the moment just before the curtain closed that Etta squeezed her eyes shut. The house lights blinked on. The applause was deafening—whistles and hollers. Everyone seemed to stand at once, except for Etta. She pushed herself to the edge of her chair, but she couldn't bring herself to her feet. She felt like the wind had been knocked from her. Did Hans die?

The curtain jerked open, and the actors were standing in a long line, Reed in the center.

Olivia stepped in front of Etta, blocking her view. Etta reached for Olivia's arm, and Olivia spun around. Her eyes were watery, and her expression made Etta drop her hand.

Olivia strode past Etta and climbed the steps onto the stage. She glided to the center and stood in front of the actors, who were now holding hands and bowing in synchrony, thrusting their hands into the air and swooping down, their knuckles almost grazing the stage. The applause intensified with Olivia's presence. Someone shouted Olivia's name. The actors came up from their bows and a couple of them dropped their hands. The applause began to die down.

Olivia lifted her hand with a jerky motion and then dropped it. She stared at Director Hardin, and the director, standing now, stared back.

A hole spread through Etta's stomach as silence eased through the room.

Etta heard a rustle and spun toward the staircase next to her. Robert North ascended the steps two at a time and made a beeline to the center of the stage. He stepped up beside Olivia. His beard had grown in—a swath of darkness creeping up his face. He put his hand on the small of Olivia's back.

Someone coughed behind Etta, and the sound echoed through the room, amplifying the silence.

Robert North cleared his throat. "What a play," he finally said. "Congratulations are due to Olivia. She has performed no easy feat. Someone once said that writers are either recluses or delinquents, or both. That's no easy group to engage. So bravo. At the end of tonight's festivities, don't forget to travel back to the cabins in groups."

Robert stepped toward Olivia. But she stepped forward. "What did you think?" Her words sliced the air.

The director's voice wasn't loud, but it catapulted through the silence. "I think I need a smoke. Nothing caps off the equinox like a Don Carlos. Do you have a light, Petra? I need a light." Hardin strode toward the aisle, his shoulders thrown back. He looked relaxed. Had Etta only imagined the moment of hostility passing between him and Olivia?

Then Etta glimpsed the director's expression. The coldness in his blue eyes made her gasp for breath.

Chapter Ten

◆

ETTA SAT UP IN HER BED. OLIVIA WAS IN A STRAIGHT JACKET with her arms folded behind her back, her mouth had been bound with duct tape. It dissolved into glitter when she spoke, coating her lips and dripping onto her dress.

It was a dream. Etta rolled her head around, cringing at the ripple of pops in her neck. Sunlight flooded through the filmy curtains. How could it be morning? Etta had just shut her eyes. Etta's gaze drifted to Olivia's bed. The red T-shirt and black sports bra that Olivia had been wearing before the play were strewn across her pillows; her jeans with the red embroidery on the back pockets were crumpled next to the bed.

The last time she'd seen Olivia, she was on the stage next to Robert North, the velvet curtain jerking shut in front of them. Etta had waited in her seat for her roommate to emerge from behind the curtain, sitting there until everyone had filed out of the theater. Finally Etta had returned to the great room, circling the room for more than an hour looking for Olivia. Then Etta had joined a group of girls walking back to the cabins, hoping Olivia would already be tucked into bed. Of course, she wasn't. So Etta had sat up most of the night waiting for her roommate. Where did she sleep? Not at Jordan's . . . *In your haste to break our engagement . . .*

It took Etta awhile to realize what was different. The rain had stopped. The silence was almost unsettling. Etta stood and winced at the pangs in her calf muscles, remembering the high heels. She hobbled in a circle, trying to work the tightness out.

Carl's truck. It had awoken her sometime in the early morning hours. The coughing and wheezing of the engine had echoed through the night's silence. Or had that been a dream?

Etta pulled on a pair of running pants and a T-shirt and splashed some cold water on her face. At first she thought that the pipes were knocking, but when she turned off the faucet, the noise continued. Was someone at the door? In all of Etta's months at the academy, nobody had knocked on the door this early. Not one person.

Etta unlocked the door and opened it a crack.

Reed grinned. He wore an elastic sweat band around his forehead, which made his blonde mullet feather out around his face. "You remembered our appointment for this morning?"

Etta swung the door open. Reed's long-sleeved crimson T-shirt said Reed College in white letters, and he wore white shorts that exposed long, muscular thighs and white tube socks that were pulled nearly to his knees.

Etta dropped her gaze to Reed's vintage nylon running shoes, which were actually kind of cool. She vaguely recalled a conversation with Reed about running, but couldn't recall when it had been or what exactly had been said.

"Um, yeah," she finally said. "Are you ready?" Behind him, narrow slits of sunshine striped the clearing. The chill in the air reminded Etta of Michigan. She imagined her favorite running trail in Ann Arbor would be ablaze in orange and red by now.

"Can I ask a favor of you before we leave?"

Etta nodded.

"I know it is in violation of the code, and I would not ask if it were not critical. However, I am in need of your facilities."

Etta squinted at him for a moment, not just because the word facilities struck her as odd. She also cringed at the idea of inviting someone to use such a messy bathroom. She'd declared a mental truce of sorts with Olivia's housecleaning, even growing used to the pile of laundry crammed behind the door and the lotions and perfumes that teetered on the sink. But inviting a stranger in was a different matter. Etta fought the impulse to rush ahead of him to clean. She waved him inside.

While he used the bathroom, Etta gobbled down an energy bar from the dwindling stash in her desk drawer.

Reed emerged and made a beeline to the door. When he got to the porch, he peered inside. "We'll forget that happened."

Etta laughed. "You can come in."

Reed shook his head. "I would not think of compromising the regulations or your honor any further than I have already."

Etta laughed. "My honor? What if there was a giant beetle over there. A gargantuan beetle. As big as my fist. Would you come in and kill it for me?"

The color drained from Reed's face. "Is there a beetle?"

"This is hypothetical."

Reed let out a breath. "Well, regrettably, I would not be able to help you in the aforesaid circumstance. I am afflicted with entomophobia."

"Fear of beetles?"

Reed nodded. "Fear of insects and terrestrial invertebrates."

"Okay, well, what if it was a fire? Would you help me put it out? Or do you have fire phobia too?"

He stared at her for a long moment. "Wouldn't it be more appropriate for you to leave the premises if there were a fire than for me to enter?"

Etta laughed. "I guess so."

"Did you enjoy the performance last night?" Reed asked.

The figure in the doorway was Hans all at once, not Reed, and Etta squeezed her eyes shut at the memory of Hans' anguished expression as the curtain closed. "It was awful," Etta murmured.

When Etta opened her eyes, Reed looked as though she'd slapped him. "Oh my gosh, I'm sorry. I meant, it was awful what happened in the play—so sad. You were amazing. Really impressive."

"Really?"

Etta nodded. "Did you see Olivia after the play?"

Reed shook his head. His hair feathered across the headband. "Not after she left with Hardin."

Etta's throat constricted. "But Hardin left with Petra. To smoke a cigar."

Reed shrugged. "Oh, I thought I saw him exit the theater with Olivia through the side door. Perhaps I was mistaken."

"Yeah, you must have been." Etta felt claustrophobic all at once. She grabbed her key off her desk, slipped past Reed, and yanked the door shut behind them, jiggling the doorknob to make sure it was locked.

When Etta crested the hill behind her cabin, the sound of Reed's footsteps behind her, she realized she hadn't deposited her key in her usual hiding place under the porch steps. She gripped it more tightly, the jagged metal gouging into her palm, and quickened her pace.

Etta was so lost in her own thoughts—swirling images of the play, Olivia on the stage, the director's expression as he stepped into the aisle—that she didn't see the figure up ahead of her on the trail at first. She halted and fell forward, jerking her foot in front of her just in time to catch her weight. She gazed at the man's ruddy cheeks and gray stubble for what felt like forever, but might have only been a few seconds. Then she spun around and heard the sound of Reed's name being forced from her lungs, so guttural that her throat stung from the force of it. She sprinted down the steep grade, her eyes glued to the ruts and rocks in front of her, the gnarled roots, the puddles. How long had it been since she'd heard Reed's footsteps behind her?

She rounded a corner and leapt to the edge of the trail to avoid colliding with Reed. He brought his hands up to protect his face and then dropped them. His hair was drenched with sweat—stringy strands pressed to the head band.

"I saw him." Etta clutched Reed's hand, which was large and limp in hers, his palm slick. She yanked Reed behind her up the hill. She couldn't tell if the sound of the ragged breathing was coming from her or from him.

When they got to where she'd seen the man standing, she dropped Reed's hand. She felt dizzy and hunched forward, clutching her knees with her hands. When she felt steady, she pushed herself up and gazed in every direction.

"Was it Galen?"

"Galen?" The name sounded strange on her tongue. The forest was a sea of shadows, thick curling undergrowth, moss-coated tree trunks. Had she really seen someone? She wasn't sure of anything now.

Etta and Reed walked back to Etta's cabin. By the time they reached the clearing in front of the women's cabins, Etta was convinced she'd had a hallucination brought on by lack of sleep. Reed wasn't so sure.

"Did he have a weapon?"

"How many times do I have to tell you? It was nothing."

"But you thought you saw a beard? Certainly Galen would have a beard, living in the forest as he does."

Etta took a step backward, away from Reed. "Please drop it." The tone of her voice was sharp, and now Reed looked both dubious and bruised. Etta tried to smile.

"Can I tell you something?" Reed asked.

Etta squinted.

"Your shirt's on inside out."

Etta looked down. Her T-shirt wasn't just inside out, it was backward, the tag sticking out under her chin. They both laughed.

A note hung on Etta's door, folded in half and stuck on with a piece of masking tape. The white paper looked almost fluorescent against the dark paint. Etta peeled the tape off the splintery wood, cringing at the sound it made. Her mind went to love letters—calligraphy, poems, envelopes sealed with kisses. She unfolded the paper and laughed. It was the opposite of a love letter —a form letter, if one line of print could be called a letter at all. Someone had written the date and Etta's name on two blank lines at the top of the page. Beneath it was a type-written sentence: *Your presence is requested in the office of Director Edwin Hardin at:* Beneath it someone had scrawled *13:00.*

It was obviously from Teddy. The director's assistant was obsessed with military time and the metric system. According to Carl he'd spent his first year at the academy campaigning, with actual signs and posters, for all official correspondence and business to be done in military time and metric units. Hardin had finally given Teddy an ultimatum—the campaign or his job. So Teddy had stopped wallpapering the great room and the dining room with posters. Nonetheless, he managed to include a time or measurement in his correspondence, often at the expense of logic.

Etta pushed her key into the lock and turned, but it didn't budge. She pulled it out and tried again. She knocked, but apparently Olivia wasn't home yet. She leaned over and studied the lock then sat down on the chair next to the door and blinked back the sunlight.

Maybe her lock had gotten jammed somehow. She tried it three more times and then ducked behind her cabin, stripped off her shirt, put it on the correct way, and walked to the lodge.

Chapter Eleven

◆

"It's thirteen-twelve. You were summoned for thirteen-hundred." Teddy must have sensed Etta's presence as she'd stepped through the doorway, because his gaze didn't budge from his monitor. His fingers flew across his keyboard.

"You have to work today? I thought everyone had the day off."

"I work when I'm needed."

"Oh, that sucks."

Teddy narrowed his hazel eyes at Etta. His black curls were slicked down with a greasy hair product. "No, it's my job. Wait over there, please." Teddy gestured toward two red upholstered chairs that sat on each side of the window near the closed door to the director's office.

Etta plunked down in the furthest chair from the director's office and wiped her hands on her jeans. She'd heard that Hardin met with each student at least once a semester to check in. That's all this was, she told herself. But her hands trembled. She grabbed a *Poets & Scribes* from the pile on the small wooden table between the chairs, and flipped through one, gazing at the photos.

"Sir. Etta Lawrence is here. Shall I send her in?" Teddy squeezed the phone between his ear and shoulder, still typing. Then he rolled his chair away from his computer and lowered his voice. "Yes sir. I know you said that, sir. But it's more convenient for me to use the telephone." Teddy was silent again. "Yes, I understand that we're virtually in the same room." More silence. "I will, sir."

The door next to Etta swung open, and Director Hardin's long figure filled the doorway. He smiled, his jowls lifting slightly. "Come in."

Poets & Scribes slipped onto the rug twice before Etta managed to get it back on the table and follow Hardin into his office. She sat down in one of two upholstered chairs in front of his desk. Director Hardin sat in the leather chair behind his desk and leaned back, drumming his fingers on the arms of the chair. His office was exactly the place Etta would expect the director of a prestigious writing academy to work—wood floors, floor-to-ceiling bookshelves, antique stained-glass lamps—the kind of office Etta had always thought her father should have as president of a university, instead of the windowless box he worked in, which was furnished with just a desk and two wooden chairs. Of course, decorations, books even, would be too impious for Temple Christian College. Etta glanced at the framed black and white photograph of Vincent Buchanan that hung on the wall between two long windows and tried to imagine him in this office, sitting at this desk.

"Thank you for coming, Ms. Lawrence."

"Etta."

Hardin nodded and leaned forward, folding his hands over a pile of file folders on his desk. "I apologize for bothering you on a Sunday. I would not think to interrupt your writing unless it was of the utmost importance."

A buzz zipped up Etta's spine, a numbness spreading between her ears. It was happening. The worst thing possible. He knew about her past. She glanced at the door. She could stand, make an excuse, and flee the room. But then what? She turned back to the director. What would she say? She tried to string together sentences in her head, but they swirled together into the humming buzz.

"Well, Etta, it's due time we meet again. If only it could be under better circumstances. I'm afraid I have some news regarding Ms. Saxon. She was your roommate, yes?"

A calmness rushed through Etta. This wasn't about her. Then she processed his words: *was. Was your roommate.* A roar burst into her head, like air rushing out of a balloon, only louder.

Hardin's eyes shifted back and forth behind his wire-framed spectacles. "Ms. Saxon has left the academy and will not be returning. I hate to trouble you with anything that will interfere with your writing. However, I'm hoping you can gather Ms. Saxon's things so that we can ship them to her mother's house in New York. Carl will retrieve them tomorrow afternoon. Is that too soon?"

Etta stared at him and tried to shake her head, but she couldn't tell if she'd managed it.

"I appreciate your assistance. If you find it necessary to be absent from classes tomorrow for this purpose, just leave a message with Teddy. I will excuse you."

Etta nodded, although she hadn't known that attendance was kept in any formal way. She'd never had a reason to miss a class. The silence spread out between them, heavy and suffocating, and finally Etta stood and stepped toward the door. Then she spun around. "Why did she leave?" Her voice sounded strangely far away.

Hardin straightened the folders on his desk. Etta glimpsed the label on the top one—Saxon, Olivia—and a shiver rippled through her. "Oh yes, of course. I suspected you might ask that question. Your roommate is ill and needs some rest."

Etta's eyes drifted to the windows, and she thought of Olivia standing on the stage next to Robert North, her dark eyes shifty and watery. Of course, Hardin didn't mean Olivia was sick in the traditional way, that she had a cold or the flu or a migraine. But what did he mean? "Will she be okay?"

Hardin's hand wavered above his desk, trembling. "I wish this were the first time I'd seen this sort of thing. Some young people can't handle the pressure of the academy, the solitude, the expectations. I am convinced that only students already inclined toward instability fall victim to their demons here." He lowered his voice. "Or perhaps that's what I tell myself."

"But her play was so amazing," Etta murmured. She couldn't take her eyes off the director's hand. The tremor seemed to have taken on a life of its own, betraying his still face and poised posture. Hardin clutched the edge of the desk, his fingers still twitching.

The director stood and strode around his desk. Before Etta knew what was happening, her cheek was crushed against the pocket of his suit jacket and the slightly sweet, spicy scent of his cologne enveloped her. He pulled away. "I know this must be difficult for you. Roommates tend to grow quite close here."

Etta gazed at him, then reached for the doorknob. She thought about telling him about her run with Reed, the trick of the light. Instead she murmured, "My lock's jammed. I can't get into my cabin."

"It is standard procedure for us to change the locks when a student departs. Carl attended to it this morning. Teddy has your new key."

When Etta got back to her cabin, she pulled her iPod out of her desk drawer and scrolled through artists, found *Bob Dylan's Greatest Hits*, and pushed play. She turned the volume louder than usual and lay back on her bed.

Olivia had hated Bob Dylan, because his crooning reminded her of her mom's "crazy years." Etta had assumed Olivia was referring to her mom being a hippie. Now Etta repeated the words, "crazy years." Crazy years? As in psychotic? She squeezed her eyes shut, trying to remember everything Olivia had told her about her mom.

I'm the product of a one-night-stand. My mom slept with her literature professor.

Do you know your father?

My mom got stoned and forgot to tell him about me. She dropped out of college and moved to a commune outside of Taos. We lived in a teepee until I was three.

Etta squeezed her eyes shut then pushed herself off the bed. She mumbled the lyrics of "Blowing in the Wind" and slid the broken-down boxes from beneath Olivia's bed. She found her tape in the closet, and put together some boxes then threw things in haphazardly, mixing books, clothes, and blankets in the same box. The scent of lavender clung to everything. When she was done, she sat on her bed and scanned the bare floor, the empty desk, and the stripped mattress. An exhausted satisfaction settled over her for a minute, like it always did when she finished a big cleaning project. It was the same sort of feeling she got from a long run.

Then tears burned down her cheeks. In the last several months, the constant loneliness that had for so long been a part of her life had dissipated. She'd thought it went away because applying to the academy had been the right thing to do, moving across the country, becoming somebody other than the person her parents detested. But now she knew it was Olivia.

The next morning Etta slid into her seat behind Maura. Most of her classmates were already in their seats. One of the Poet's Row students was on his feet, telling the others a story, gesturing, his voice booming through the room. Outside red and orange speckled the undergrowth beneath the trees. Etta turned to a blank page in her notebook.

She'd considered missing class, since Hardin had offered to excuse her, but what would she do? Sit in her room all day surrounded by boxes of Olivia's stuff? A noise came from the back of the room and Etta turned.

Director Hardin stood just inside the doorway with Walker Ryan. They were both imposing men, and they were at eye level with each other. The director had his hand on Walker's arm, and his skin looked ashen against Walker's canary yellow jacket. Walker shook his head.

Etta scanned the room, her gaze bouncing from Pari and Lorna to Lydia and Hillary to Jordan, Poppy, Chase, and Katie. They didn't know about Olivia yet. Etta had assumed the announcement would be made at Sunday dinner. Unable to bear the thought of it, she'd skipped dinner and relied on the stash of food in their mini refrigerator, most of which had been gleaned from care packages Olivia's aunt had sent. They arrived each month brimming with crackers, nuts and seeds, and jars of homemade granola, applesauce, and dried fruit, always with a handwritten note addressed to both of them, although Etta had never met her: *Dear Olivia and Etta . . .*

Director Hardin moved to the front of the room. His gait seemed more tentative than usual. Etta registered that he was standing behind the podium, heard some random words in his baritone voice. Olivia's name. And she had a vague sense of other things floating from his mouth: "troubled," "imbalance," "breakdown." But what Etta was most aware of was the sensation of eyes probing her. Maura's hair fluttered across the back of her chair, her gaze locking with Etta's.

Outside the sun was hovering just above the treetops. Etta stared at it until she couldn't stand the brightness and had to squeeze her eyes shut. She only opened her eyes again when silence descended across the room.

"Sir, I think Olivia was plagiarizing." It was Jordan. His voice was devoid of inflection, like he was reading aloud from a text.

Etta found herself searching for air at the same time that the room seemed to collectively exhale.

Chapter Twelve

◆

"**I** KNEW THAT PLAY WAS TOO GOOD TO BE WRITTEN BY A GIRL." A grin spread across Mallory Chambers' round face. "Kidding, kidding. But really, who'd our golden girl crib off of? Marlow or Shakespeare?"

Maura's hand shot into the air. "Does this mean that the runner-up should have won the contest, because Winston told me I was the runner-up?" Maura went on, but Etta lost track of the words. All she could concentrate on was the strange quality of Maura's voice—shrill and whiny.

Pari stood and spoke when Maura finished, her dark eyes surveying the room. "Perhaps everyone should take a lie detector test."

"Or maybe we should put a gallows in the basement. We can torture cheaters—lock 'em down there without food," Mallory interrupted.

The director looked dazed as he gazed at the back of the room, his white hair a tousle of flyaway strands.

"I'm only saying, another student could have been writing Olivia's material. There may be another offender," Pari said.

"Her writing was dark," someone at the back of the room murmured. "For such a sweet person."

"And weird," someone else said, much louder. "Remember that missionary pig farmer? One word—creepy."

"I don't see what that proves." It was Chase Quinn, and the sharpness of his voice surprised Etta. He was sitting sideways in his chair, his back to Etta. "If she had a breakdown, she is clearly disturbed. Perhaps she has some kind of multiple personality syndrome."

"The question is, if she didn't write those stories, who did?" It was Pari again.

"Maybe it was Galen," someone called out

Etta's pen bounced onto the floor with a clatter.

"Aha! Yes, the mad man as our golden girl's ventriloquist," Mallory called out.

"All right now, that's enough." Hardin's voice sounded fatigued, and Mallory's laughter overwhelmed it.

Hillary Chambers' slender arm floated into the air. "According to the "Academic Integrity Code" in the handbook, accusations of plagiarism must be written, and they must be followed by a formal hearing. Until those two things happen, this sort of speculation is improper."

The director gazed at the back of the room, his eyes motionless behind his glasses. Etta expected him to say something, at least to acknowledge Hillary's words with a nod. But it was Walker Ryan who spoke, resting his long fingers on the director's shoulder.

"Let's not waste all this imagination on chin-wagging. Let's get down to the business of storytelling. Raise your hand if you're one of the few poor souls who will be critiqued in the next month." Etta hoisted her arm, as did three other students.

"Good, good. Listen, here's the thing, it might not seem like it, but you're the lucky ones. Your classmates know how to critique now. They know how to excavate your challenges." He brought his hand down and hit the podium with it. "Now, I've had my suspicions that a few of you brought old work, stuff you've workshopped before. Listen, that's not the point, the point is to challenge ourselves, to get better. We want fresh stories. Not something you wrote last year. Prove it's current. Drop references, make me a character, make the lodge your setting, whatever. Show us it's new. Remember, this is your debut, your unveiling. Make it count." Walker waved his hand through the air again. "Why doesn't someone tell us a story right now?" His index finger descended on Katie Randolph.

Katie's eyelashes fluttered.

"You have five minutes to come up with one," Walker said. "The rest of you, write a five minute story starting with the sentence 'Since I saw you last . . .'" See where those words take you." He put his hand on Hardin's back and guided him down the aisle toward the door, whispering to him as they walked. Etta stared at the blank sheet of paper in front of her and tried to stop her hands from trembling.

"Jordan, stop!" Etta jogged to catch her friend, who was striding down the trail east of the Lodge. By the time Jordan spun around, Etta was only inches from him. Jordan swiped a long blonde lock from in front of his eye. Etta had always been mesmerized by the blue color of Jordan's eyes—a deep turquoise, like she imagined the Caribbean would look. "Why?" The word tumbled out of Etta's mouth, although she wasn't sure what to follow it with.

Jordan took a step backward. "Why what? Why did my girlfriend dump me? Good fucking question, Etta. Maybe you can tell me." He pressed his lips into a tight line.

Etta frowned and searched for words, but she couldn't find any.

Jordan slapped his bare forearm and flicked a limp insect off of it. It left a speck of red on his tanned skin. "Tell me Etta, do you think Zelda loved Scott?"

"Who?" Etta whispered, meeting his gaze.

"Fitzgerald. Zelda Fitzgerald. Do you think she loved him?"

Etta stared at him. "I don't know."

"Well, that's just great. Do you think Daisy loved Gatsby?"

"Jor, why . . ."

"Why did I tell on her? I don't know. She didn't write that creepy shit. I don't know who did, but it wasn't Olivia."

"Well, did you have to make a public announcement?" Etta glanced behind her, realizing how loud their voices were. She lowered her voice. "Couldn't you have told Hardin in private?"

Jordan laughed, but it was a harsh sound, almost a cough. "Jilted lovers are desperate creatures, Etta. We can't be trusted. Just ask Tom Buchanan." Jordan spun around. His blonde hair whipped around his head.

Before Etta could think of a reply, he was gone.

Etta reversed direction and hurried back toward the Lodge. The morning writing session started in less than five minutes. But Etta turned down a slender path that looked like it may be a shortcut to the women's cabins. At least it led in the right direction. She broke into a jog. The air was cool on her arms beneath her sweater. She quickened her pace, her gaze glued to the narrow slit of dirt. Then she heard something behind her and whirled around. A deer stood several yards away, staring at her, as surprised by the encounter as she was.

Etta laughed. "Galen," she whispered. She could barely catch her breath. "Are you Galen?"

Etta was in such a hurry to get inside her cabin that she didn't see the bundle until her foot was hovering just above it. She smelled the buttery richness of Carl's biscuits, even before she unwrapped the napkin. She unscrewed the lid of the stainless steel thermos next to it: Carl's chicken soup.

Etta sat cross-legged on her floor, devoured the three biscuits, and drank the chicken soup straight from the thermos, hardly breathing between gulps. She picked every crumb off of the napkin then she moved toward the largest of the boxes she'd packed the day before. She emptied it, strewing its contents onto the floor then moved to the next box, and the next until the room was piled with Olivia's things again. She filled the boxes again, but this time she pulled out every scrap of paper—every notebook, binder, letter, and book—and stacked them in a separate box.

Perhaps Etta had known all along that Olivia didn't write the dark fairy tales, that someone as flirtatious and girly as Olivia, someone who knitted pink hats and wore purple nail polish on her toes and listened to old Sarah McLachlan songs over and over again and gushed about how sweet her boyfriend was, did not produce such a bleak story and play. They were dark, but hilarious. Etta had sat for a long time after she'd read the story, not knowing whether to laugh or cry, a sensation she liked. The precariousness of it made her almost dizzy. And she liked the stories themselves. They were well-written. Witty. Ironic. Things Etta always wanted her novels to be described as. Instead Etta's classmates and teachers would scoff off her entire body of work as saccharine drivel for overweight housewives—if they knew about it.

But Etta had known that she and Olivia had more in common than Olivia's work suggested, known it the way you know when someone's watching you from across a crowded room. Etta stared at the piles of Olivia's notebooks, the pink and purple folders, and the peach cloth-bound journal. But who did write Olivia's story and play?

Etta pulled the box of papers toward her and flipped through some loose letters from Olivia's aunt. She'd drawn line illustrations of wildflowers and goats and her farmhouse along the edges. They were beautiful, but revealed little.

Etta flipped through a notebook. Olivia had started a letter to someone named Sam, which wasn't revealing in any way. The rest of the notebook was filled with blank pages.

Etta blew a strand of hair off her forehead and set the notebook on the floor next to the box. She pulled some books from the box and scanned the covers. *To Kill a Mockingbird, The Bean Trees, The Poisonwood Bible.* She stacked them back in the box and pulled out another notebook. It was filled with doodles. Etta put it back and pulled out a manila envelope with a round brown stain on the lower corner. She unfastened it, and a pile of thin papers slid out.

It was a story, typed on a typewriter. Jordan's typewriter?

"Cherry Blossom" by M.K. Lowther.

Etta read until a rumbling interrupted her thoughts. Was it Carl's truck? She glanced at the story, surprised that she'd already read four pages. It was riveting. She flipped back to the first page again, and read the first line: *I was only a child when I knew that America would become a sore that would ooze and fester until it bled.*

In the story, Peter Morrison, a twenty-year old from Seattle, discouraged by what he sees happening in the United States after the Stock Market Crash of 1929, travels to Japan. He visits Kyoto, the Katsura River, Mount Arashiyama, Nijo Castle, and the Golden Pavilion, and wanders around in a frenzy of bicycles, cars, trucks, streetcars, and rickshaws that weave through the wide streets. He starts watching "a merchant's daughter with a porcelain face and a head of ebony silk" in a marketplace each afternoon, and finally works up the courage to ask her name. She whispers, "Yumi," and then disappears into the crowd.

The truck was louder. Etta lifted her gaze from the paper. Was it pulling into the clearing in front of her cabin? Etta dropped the papers onto the floor and pushed herself to her feet as the truck's engine died outside. She bent down, gripped the sides of the tattered box she'd filled with Olivia's papers and pushed all of her weight into it, sliding it across the floor into her closet. She slammed the door shut.

Etta threw the front door open just as Carl raised his fist to knock. He took a step backward.

"What are you doing here?" Etta asked then realized how rude she sounded. "I mean, thanks," she tried to say, but her voice betrayed her. She cleared her throat. "Thanks for the soup."

"Haven't seen you in the dining hall. Didn't want you to starve."

Etta looked over her shoulder at the boxes of Olivia's things and tried to swallow. Most of them were overflowing; a red sweater sleeve hung over the side of one.

"Did Hardin tell you I was coming?"

She turned back to Carl. *Taste of Austin*, the white letters on his black T-shirt read. "Oh right." Etta stepped backward to let him inside. He strode past her to the center of the room. She followed him. "I tried to pack Liv's stuff, but I . . ." She let the words die.

"You all right?" Carl's voice was almost a whisper. He rested his hand on her back, and a prickle of heat raced up Etta's spine.

Carl wrapped his other arm around her and pressed her cheek to his chest. She breathed in the clean scent of his T-shirt, like towels dried on a clothesline. His heartbeat pulsed against her cheek. His breath tangled in her hair. They stood like that for a long time then Carl pulled away. Etta reached for his hand. He leaned over and his lips feathered across hers, his tongue flicking against her teeth. Etta's pulse quickened, swelling into her chest and wrists. Their lips didn't fit together at first then they shifted.

Carl tugged on her shoulders, and Etta pressed herself closer, letting her body sink against his.

Then Carl stepped backward, and an ocean of space swelled between them.

"Hi," he said.

Etta hung suspended in air, floating. She searched for Carl's eyes. But he was looking at something behind her. She whirled around.

Robert North leaned on the door frame, his arms folded across his chest. He smiled then pushed his weight off the doorway and sauntered into the room.

Chapter Thirteen

◆

"AH, LOVE, THE WISDOM OF THE FOOL AND THE FOLLY OF THE wise." Robert North crouched and lifted a crumpled button-down shirt from the top of a box, stared at it then dropped it back on the pile. He rose to his feet. "Of course, I'm just a washed up old poet. What would I know about love?"

Etta's cheeks filled with heat.

"Thought I might be able to lend a hand." He moved to another box, crouched, and ruffled through it. He pulled out Olivia's digital clock and set it back in the box. "Is this all of her things?"

Etta nodded, stealing a glance at her closet.

Robert North laughed. "You have your own cabin now." He held up a cord, which Etta guessed went to Olivia's laptop. "Just like me," he mumbled.

"Don't you have a room in the lodge?" Etta felt dizzy. She'd stared at Robert North's photo so many times, and now he was just inches from her. But all she really wanted was for him to leave her and Carl alone again.

He pulled a taper candle from a box and stared at it, twirling it between his fingers. "Oh yes, even we visitors get a room—a desk, an adequate view, a bathroom down the hall. Buchanan didn't want to make things too comfortable for the drifters, of course. But I've never envied the poor bastard residents with their fancy suites, stuck in the drizzle for a year. I'll only be here a few more days. It's hunger that feeds the artist's soul, not a paycheck." He laughed and the skin around his eyes pinched into their familiar creases. "Hate to break it to you, but that's the only lesson you need, and you didn't have to pay twenty-five thousand dollars to frolic in Buchanan's little Writerland to learn it. Spend every second of your life hungry—esurient."

"Esurient," Etta repeated. She had no idea what it meant, but she liked the sound of it on her lips. A poet's word. Robert North didn't look like he'd ever been hungry. He looked like he'd always had money and good looks and talent. A boarding school education. A mother who played bridge at a country club. A father who yachted. Fans who spent hours staring at his picture.

"Maybe they like teaching." It was Carl's voice, husky and twanging. Etta had almost forgotten he was in the room, and her pulse hammered into her chest at the memory of his breath in her hair, his lips on hers.

Robert North laughed again, but this time it was like an afterthought. "Oh right, that's why people do the things they do. They enjoy them. Silly me." He dropped the candle into the box, and picked up a framed black-and-white photo that Etta had found in one of Olivia's desk drawers. She had long dark hair and dark eyes like Olivia's. Olivia's mother?

A sound came from Robert North's mouth. Etta stepped closer. Had he said something?

Carl stepped between them and strode toward a box next to the door, his gait long and relaxed. "I reckon I should get started here if I want to make it to Jackson and back before the sun sets." He knelt, clutched the bottom of a box, and heaved it to his chest.

"Can I keep you company?" Robert North didn't lift his gaze from the photo. "On the drive."

"All right." Carl stepped outside, his figure long in the doorway. "Long as I can pick the music."

"As long we can stop at that dark joint on the way back for some whisky and companionship." He looked up and his dark eyes flashed with sunlight as he met Etta's gaze. "Not everyone's lucky enough to find love out here."

Etta's cheeks flashed with heat again. Robert North dropped his gaze to the floor. He was staring at the story by M.K. Lowther, which was splayed across the floor next to Etta's bed. "Mat," he whispered. "Where did you get this?" He reached for the papers.

"I've got to go." Etta lunged toward the papers and plucked them off the floor, hugging them to her chest as she retrieved her bag from next to the door. They felt delicate crushed against her bare arm, tenuous.

Etta jogged down the stairs and around the truck. Halfway across the clearing, she spun around and called goodbye to Carl, who was sliding a box into the pickup bed. She wasn't sure if he heard.

"Mat," Etta said aloud as she rounded the curve toward the lodge. No, not mat. Matt. Etta broke into a jog. M. must stand for Matt. But who was Matt Lowther?

The air in the great room was cool, and it sparkled with beams of sunlight and dust particles. Etta stood next to the fireplace in the same spot where she'd stood listening to the raspy moans of Rodney's cello two nights before. Everything from the equinox party was gone now—the long tables, the confetti, the streamers, the balloons. Perhaps she'd dreamt the party, the entire macabre night, invented it as she would a novel. Except if that were the case, Olivia would be sitting upstairs in the classroom. And she wasn't. She was . . . where? At a hospital? At her mother's house?

Etta crossed the room and dropped into one of the oversized chairs that faced the windows. She smoothed the papers in her lap and glared at them. The story was a distraction. Was it really going to tell her anything about Olivia plagiarizing or about where Olivia was or why she'd left? Etta should be writing the story for her critique. She remembered Olivia's eyes two nights ago—so watery—Olivia, beautiful Olivia—Where was she now?—and Carl, Carl's lips, his breath in her hair, the salty taste of his mouth.

Robert North obviously knew who Matt Lowther was, and there was something about the way he'd looked at the story that made Etta shiver. Maybe M.K. Lowther was famous. But why hadn't Etta heard of him? She couldn't stop herself from reading, starting from the beginning again, the first two words: "Cherry Blossom," by M.K. Lowther.

"Ah, a truant."

Etta was so immersed in M.K. Lowther's world that it took her a moment to realize someone was speaking, and a few more seconds to raise her head. Petra Atwell stood clutching her misshapen mug in her crimson-tipped claws. She pursed her waxy lips, blowing on whatever was in the cup. A puff of steam floated up and disappeared in front of her.

Etta rose to her feet, and the papers slipped from her lap, fanned out, and slid in all directions. A few of them disappeared beneath Etta's chair and she stooped to retrieve them, sitting back on her heels to steady herself. She peered up at Petra, who was smiling down at her. The resident author had a smudge of lipstick on one of her teeth.

"Jesus, you scared me," Etta said.

"Thank you, but you don't need to call me Jesus. So you've decided you're too good a writer to bother with pesky lessons and workshops?"

Etta shook her head. "No, I . . ." She glanced down at the papers and leaned forward to scoop them up. "I . . ." She let the sentence die in the air between them and concentrated on stacking the thin pages into a pile.

"Well, you certainly are good at creating fiction, I'll give you that," Petra said.

Etta felt some of the heat drain from her face. Petra was staring out the window, her expression concealed somewhere beneath her layers of makeup. "What do you mean by that?"

"You don't like compliments, do you Loretta?"

"Etta."

"Oh, yes. My mistake."

Silence hung in the room. Petra blew on her drink again, an audible hiss, and the aroma of her coffee wafted to Etta's nose, a burnt smell. "You're right, you know? Most of it is a waste of time. You can't teach talent. It's the only forgivable thing we get from our parents. It almost makes the emotional baggage endurable."

Etta had the sensation something was crawling up her neck. She knew nothing was there, but she lifted her hand and rested her fingers on her collarbone.

"So your friend couldn't handle the pressure. She always seemed more interested in flirting than writing, wouldn't you say?"

"She was . . ." Etta almost said a great writer, but then thought of Jordan's words: a plagiarizer. Heat flashed through her face. "No, I, I wouldn't say," she finally stammered, but only because she didn't want to leave another sentence hanging in the space between her and Petra. Olivia was a flirt, but she was the kind who didn't differentiate between men or women, friends or enemies. Olivia turned her charms on everyone in her presence; she drew people in, flattered them, and made them love her.

"Tell me something. Why did you come here?" Petra wasn't asking; she was demanding an answer.

Etta had a well-rehearsed answer for that question, but she shifted her gaze to the windows, surprised that the afternoon light was growing dusky, the trees a thick swath of shadows against the whitish gray sky. Were Carl and Robert North on their way to Jackson already or still in Etta's cabin? Etta had no sense of how much time had passed since she'd spoken to them. She'd read the story through once then half-way through again. Had she been sitting an hour? Two?

"Look at that," Petra said.

Etta glanced at her, trying to keep her expression even, and then she followed Petra's gaze to the trees. She didn't want to appear too interested in anything Petra found worthwhile.

"I thought I saw a fox," Petra said. She smiled at Etta and spun around, her long skirt feathering out around her. Her footsteps hardly made a sound as she crossed the room. Etta didn't bother to look out the window; she knew exactly what Petra had meant. A fox. Loretta Ann Fox.

Etta frowned and stared at her lap. Petra knew. And if Petra knew, who else knew? They weren't going to award the Buchanan Prize to Loretta Ann Fox.

Etta smoothed the papers on her lap, trying to put Petra out of her mind. She read the first line of the page that had ended up on top of the pile. It was the last page, the final scene of the story where Peter Morrison and Yumi meet up again in an unnamed American city, which seems a lot like San Francisco. The couple know they can't be together. A war between the U.S. and Japan is inevitable. Peter no longer feels safe in Kyoto. Yumi is scared to live in the United States. So they spend one final night together. *Their encounter was fevered and brief. In a hotel room on South Market Street, Yumi showed him that it is impermanence that gives the monotony of breathing its radiance.*

Beneath the typed text, the author had signed *M.K. Lowther, October 1985, Oregon* in fading ink. Etta ran her finger over the loose, cursive letters. She wanted to lose herself in the story again, wanted to become the story. To disappear in it.

Although Etta visited the library often, she'd never had a reason to knock on Uriah Winston Mills' office door, or step into "Major Mills' Quarters," as the embossed plaque beside the librarian's door read. His office was a closet-sized room next to the archives room. The window in the door revealed his barren desk and shelves to everyone who visited the library, but he usually wasn't there. Students weren't required to check books out in the traditional way; they just had to leave placeholders with their names where they withdrew books.

The major, as students referred to him, was tall and wiry, over six feet, Etta would guess, although she was too short to be a good judge of height. His head was nearly hairless except for a stripe of gray bristles near the nape of his neck. His angular cheeks and bulbous nose were a permanent crimson, which Etta thought may have been the result of too many years in the sun. Jordan was convinced that he drank too much. Mallory Chambers, found it endlessly humorous to compare him to the prim stereotype of a librarian. "If Major Bookworm had more hair, do you think he'd pull it into a bun?"

As his nickname suggested, Major Mills had been a military librarian. When Etta had met him at orientation, she'd asked, in a moment of nervous babbling, if soldiers were allowed to check out books on the front lines. She'd gathered from his curt reply that he was not someone who tolerated stupid questions. Thus, when she sat down at the computer, located the catalog icon, double-clicked on it, and the message *Ask a librarian for assistance* popped onto the screen, she had to muster a lot of courage to walk to the major's office door and gently tap.

The librarian's face was illuminated by the green banker's lamp on the corner of his desk. He looked up from some papers and eyed Etta over the wire-framed spectacles on the end of his nose, which looked too delicate for his weathered face. He frowned. Was that Etta's cue to come in? She swallowed down a breath, twisted the brass doorknob, and prodded the door open enough to squeeze through, wincing at the squeak of the hinges.

A wall of cologne met her. Etta's eyes watered. She heard a rattling and was startled to see that it was the papers in her hand. She shoved the story behind her back. The major frowned at her.

"I'm sorry to bother you. I'm looking for anything by an author. Matt Lowther. Or, um, M.K. Lowther."

Etta watched the major's reaction and wished she could grab her words from the air.

Chapter Fourteen

◆

Major Mills took his spectacles off, folded them, and slid them into the breast pocket of his white short-sleeved shirt. The outline of his glasses showed through the thin material. He leaned back in his chair. His expression became unreadable as silence settled between them. Maybe Etta had imagined the flash of anger.

Her eyes and nose were running. She wiped her eyes with her sleeve. "The catalog isn't working, so I just wondered if maybe, I'm looking for books by an author named M.K. Lowther, Matt Lowther I think . . . I'm just curious. Maybe he's written a novel?" She hated the chirpy quality of her voice when she was nervous. She wiped at her eyes again.

Major Mills stared at her. A thin scar, which Etta had never noticed before, ran from his right eye to his ear. It was all she could look at.

"Just curious?"

Etta nodded. The acrid air filled her throat. She coughed and wiped at her eyes with her sleeve.

"You'd do well to invest your time in more worthwhile reading pursuits. The classics, for instance." He rocked from side to side. His movement cast a fan of shadows on the empty bookshelves behind him.

"I don't know." Etta regretted the words as she watched the major's cold eyes draw close together. "I mean yes, the classics are good and important and all, but there are other worthwhile books too."

The major drummed his fingers on the arms of his chair. "Most books aren't worth the paper they're written on."

"I don't . . ." Etta swallowed her words, realizing she was only being defensive about her own writing. Besides her head felt too loose and watery from the cologne to carry on a debate with anyone, especially Uriah Winston Mills, whose thin lips turned down in a scowl when he wasn't talking. She wiped at her eyes again.

Major Mills continued his lecture about the classics. Etta glanced out the window behind her at the last slants of sunlight coming into the library and lost track of what he was saying. How long would she need to stand there politely nodding before she left? "*The Western Defense* is the only book anyone needs. We could burn the rest. "

"I don't know." Etta regretted the words instantly, mostly because of the major's sharp intake of air, but also because she felt strange and light headed, with all of her orifices full of cologne. Why was she arguing with him? "I mean, it's a good novel, great really." Etta's voice was rising, building into the annoying girlish chatter again. She glanced over her shoulder into the shadows in the library.

"What's your name?" The radiators clicked under the windows in the library. "Just curious," the major said in falsetto, mimicking Etta's use of the same words a few minutes before. She mumbled her name and reached for the door knob.

"Ms. Lawrence, I can see you're pleased with yourself. You think you're smart and just curious. Listen, those old guys going to bingo games at vets' clubs on Friday nights, the ones who ride on parade floats on the Fourth of July, they're the ones who shot without asking questions. The curious ones are rotting in the jungle."

Etta gave the major a tight-lipped smile as she did when she disagreed with someone but didn't feel comfortable saying so or when she suspected someone may be mentally ill. She wasn't sure which category the major fit into at that moment, but she knew that she wanted to leave. She stared at the major's angular face, his porous nose, his silken scar. He rolled his chair toward his desk, picked up a file folder sitting atop a pile of papers, and turned it over, resting his hands on it.

Etta spun around, pushed the door open, and raced through the library, gulping in the stale, dusty air.

She ran down the spiral staircase then stopped and watched the reflection of the great room in the windows across from her. A fire had been lit in the hearth. A few students sat on the couch in front of it. She could only see the backs of their heads in the reflection. Their voices swirled to her, slow and distorted, as though she were under water. Somebody else sat reading in a chair facing the window. A wave of nausea hit her when she saw her own reflection. She looked small and pallid, like a ghost.

Either her eyes had deceived her or the type-written label on the major's file folder had said, "Lowther, Matthew."

Etta skipped dinner, went to her cabin, and tried to put the pages of M.K. Lowther's story back in order. She sat down at her desk and skimmed the story again. Olivia had a typed manuscript by someone named M.K. Lowther. Someone Robert North knew of. Someone the librarian had a file folder on and was rude when questioned about. Etta stared at his signature on the last page of the manuscript. *M.K. Lowther, October 1985, Oregon.* She tucked the pages into the bottom drawer of her desk and crossed the room. Olivia's side of the room was empty except for five red plastic clothes hangers that were scattered across the bare mattress. They looked bright and garish.

Etta slid her closet door open and waved her hand around in the darkness. The string for the overhead light bulb feathered across her fingers, and she yanked on it. White light illuminated the shadows.

Air rushed from her chest. She dropped to her knees. The box with Olivia's papers—it was gone. A single sheet of white paper lay on the floor where the box had been. Etta swiped it off the floor then released it. It fluttered to the ground, but Etta could still see the words. They swam off the page then snapped into focus. *You're in trouble. Go home.* She stared at them for so long that they didn't make sense. Home. What was home? She plucked it the paper off the floor and crumpled it. Then she smoothed it and stared at the words again.

Go home.

"I don't have a home." Etta folded the paper into a square, pushed herself to her feet, and squeezed it into her pocket. She spun around and stared at the place where Robert North had stood rifling through Olivia's things. How dare he open her closet? Her heartbeat hammered in her ears. She grabbed her rain jacket and threw her door open, flinching at the icy air that flooded into the room.

When she pulled open the door of Roosevelt Lodge, she was met by the muffled commotion of dinner time—voices, laughter, dishes clinking. A pungent scent hung in the air. It smelled like Candy's spaghetti. The thought of the intern's briny tomato sauce made Etta's stomach turn sour.

She made a beeline to the staircase and jogged up the spiral steps until she was on the third floor landing, standing face-to-face with an oil portrait of Vincent Buchanan. It was like the one outside of the classroom on the second-floor landing, except it hung in the shadows, lit only by a beaded lamp on a round table nearby.

Etta stepped closer, trying to make out Buchanan's features. He was older than in most of the portraits in the Lodge. His once-black hair was white. His boyish face had become jowly. Even in his old age, though, Buchanan's eyes were youthful—dark and shiny.

How dare Robert North open her closet, go through her stuff, and tell her to go home? "I don't have a home," Etta wanted to shout at him. She peeled her gaze from the portrait and spun around. She'd never been on the third floor before. The ceiling was low and two dimly-lit narrow hallways stretched out perpendicular to each other. Etta's heartbeat pulsed in her ears.

She moved down one of the halls. Wall sconces—orange light bulbs shaped like candle flames—lit circles on the plush burgundy carpet. If she did find Robert North, the damned prodigy poet, she'd yell at him. What right did he have to take her things—or Olivia's things, but what did that matter? They certainly weren't his things. Or maybe Etta would just slip the stupid note under his door. You go home, Robert.

The carpet swallowed Etta's footsteps. She stared at the dark brown doors, each with small shiny gold numbers. It hadn't occurred to her that she'd have no way of knowing which room was his. She stopped halfway down the corridor. Maybe it wasn't a good idea anyway. She could keep the note and show the director, tell him that Robert North—a man who was supposed to teach, to encourage, to mentor—had told Etta to pack up and leave her dreams behind.

Etta heard a voice. It was so familiar that Etta moved toward it without thinking. She was almost to the narrow window at the end of the hallway when she realized whose voice she'd been drawn toward. She froze. She was standing between the last two doors—numbers six and seven—and Jordan Waterhouse sounded as though he was standing right next to her.

The door for room number six flung open, and Etta stood face-to-face with Olivia's ex-boyfriend. Jordan looked over his shoulder, a strand of his blonde hair falling across his cheek. Etta followed his gaze and met Opal Waters' pale, gray eyes.

"Oh." Etta glanced down the hall. "I was . . ."

"What? What are you doing?" Jordan's voice was sharp. Etta took another step backward. She gestured toward herself and tried to think of something to say, but all Etta could do was stare into the aquamarine eyes of one of the only people at the academy she had considered a close friend just a week before.

"You're the one who followed me up here, Etta. The one who seems to be following me everywhere I go. Are you spying on me?"

"Jor, no. I was . . ." Etta's words died in her throat. She could feel Opal's gray eyes on her. The author's quarters were off limits to students. Buchanan had designated the third floor as a writer's retreat, a refuge for authors to live and work separate from their lecturing and teaching duties.

"If you must know what I'm doing at every second, why don't you just ask me?"

Etta tried to shake her head, but she felt paralyzed.

"My father asked if I would give Opal a copy of his latest collection. I didn't want to make an ordeal of it with everyone around, so I came up here to leave it next to her door. Opal heard me in the hallway, and insisted on writing Dad a thank-you note while I waited. Is that okay with you, Etta?" He thrust a pink envelope toward Etta, but Etta's gaze went to Opal's room instead. It was awash in soft, yellow light. A gossamer curtain encircled a four-poster bed. Behind it, an open laptop sat perched in the middle of a downy white comforter. Had Jordan interrupted Opal while she was composing one of her painstaking poems?

"Just stop following me. You're creeping me out." Jordan brushed past Etta. His hair flapped across his collar as he glided toward the stairwell. It didn't occur to Etta until he was at the other end of the hall that he was a student too, and thus just as prohibited from trespassing on the third floor as she was. Of course rules had never seemed to concern Jordan much.

A sound made Etta jerk her head back to the room. Opal was just a foot away. She rested her slim fingers on the side of the door, and for a moment Etta was sure Opal was going to push the door closed, but the poet stood gazing at Etta. Her blonde hair was loose, and it was the first time Etta had seen her silky whitish locks, kinky from being in a twist all day, hanging around her slender face. "I think he's upset about Olivia," Etta whispered.

Opal's gray gaze didn't falter. "Of course. We all are," Opal's voice sounded exactly as it did in class—dignified, reserved, and distant. "She had so much talent. For her to throw it away—it's a tragedy."

"Jordan thinks she was plagiarizing."

Opal's pupils dilated instantly, as though she was hearing the news for the first time, and guilt washed through Etta. Why had she said it? Had she been jealous of Opal's compliment? She wished she could take the words back. "That's a rather serious charge." Opal said. "Do you agree with him?"

"No." Etta glanced down the hall. "I don't know."

"Well, I don't think it wise to spend time worrying about another writer's work. It's best to focus on one's own, and I'm glad you're here, because I've been meaning to talk to you about yours. You're up for critique soon. Isn't that right?"

Etta nodded and tried to smile although she wasn't sure she managed it.

"Can I give you some advice? I've been teaching at the Buchanan Academy on and off for nearly thirty years. Do you know that within a week, I can usually predict who will be a writer and who won't? Some students are just hungry for it. Do you think you are?"

Etta stared at her. Was that advice? "I guess so."

"The first critique is your unveiling, your debut. I don't . . "

"You predicted I would fail?" Etta interrupted.

Opal stared at her. The poet's lips formed a taut smile. "Oh my. It's not that easy to hurt your feelings, is it? Sensitivity is not an author's ally, which brings me to my advice." Opal stepped closer to Etta, and Etta noticed the poet's long nearly invisible whitish-blonde eyelashes for the first time. "Don't kid yourself if you think the literary world is different from any other business. It's a paternalistic boy's club run by a bunch of ass-slapping, locker room buffoons. To succeed at this game as a woman, no matter how brilliant or lackluster your prose is, you must discard every distraction from your life—hurt feelings and romantic amusements and, in your case, worrying about your roommate, who obviously couldn't hack it here, plagiarizer or not. You'll find out, it requires a ruthless amount of focus for a woman to succeed. If you don't have it, you may as well go home."

After Opal said good night and closed the door between them, Etta mouthed the words, "Go home" and pulled the note from her pocket. She unfolded the crumpled paper and reread the words. *You're in trouble. Go home.* For the first time, in the faint light from the candle-shaped sconce behind her, the words looked like a threat. Etta folded the paper and stuffed it in her jacket pocket, her fingers feathering against another crumpled piece of paper there.

She stood in the hallway, reading the words on it a number of times, but couldn't make sense of them. *All of us back together again. Except one. Where is he? Something else I've wondered— Did my father love you, or were you just another geisha?*

Then Etta recalled the sensation of her fingers sliding into the satin-lined pocket of Opal's pea coat so many days ago.

Chapter Fifteen

◆

MAURA LEFT POPPY'S CABIN FIRST. HER THICK, BROWN HAIR was pulled into a bun at the crown of her head, and it bobbled as she walked. She was nearly past Etta's cabin when she glanced up and brought her blue mitten to her mouth.

"I didn't mean to scare you." Etta's breath clouded in front of her. She burrowed her hands further into the pockets of her down coat. "Where's Poppy?"

"In the shower." Maura dropped her hand. "Why haven't you been in class?"

Etta pulled her hand from her pocket and ran it through her hair. Should she tell Maura she'd been hiding out in her cabin for two days, grazing from her dwindling food stash, and mostly lying on her bed, staring at the ceiling? She'd tried to work on a story for her critique, but hadn't gotten far. She kept coming back to the same questions. Where was Olivia? Why hadn't she said goodbye? Why had she been acting so strange for the weeks before she left? What had happened between Olivia and Jordan? Who was Matthew Lowther? How was he connected to Olivia, to Robert North, to Major Mills?

What Etta hadn't given much thought to in the last few days was her appearance. And she could tell from the expression on Maura's face that she looked disheveled. She pushed her hand back into her pocket to warm her fingers.

"You must be nervous about your critique?"

Etta shook her head, but a wave of panic rose through her and locked around her throat like a vice. She glanced at Poppy's cabin. Class would start in less than thirty minutes, and Poppy never missed her morning cup of sugar and coffee.

"Did you hear about Isabella Peña?"

"No. Is she in jail?" The controversial author had been the main story on WXYZ out of Detroit the weekend before Etta left for Oregon. They showed the same author photo repeatedly of Peña leaning against a tree and gazing at the camera. Peña, a Mexican-American activist and the author of several literary novels, had supposedly stabbed a man with a ball-point pen at a book-signing in Cleveland. The victim, a lineman in an auto manufacturing plant, had apparently waited in line for over an hour at a signing in a San Francisco bookstore, slid his copy of Peña's new novel *The Long Struggle* across the table, and whispered that the U.S. needed machine gunners on its southern border. The last Etta had heard, the victim had recovered but was considering filing assault charges against Peña.

Maura shook her head. "No. She's coming here tonight."

Etta laughed. Except Maura didn't look like she was joking.

"It hasn't been formally announced yet, but Winston told us. The press is hounding her, and she's decided to retreat here for a few weeks."

"Yeah, I guess you get some attention when you attack someone." Etta heard a sound and spun around. Poppy was on her porch locking her door. Etta jumped up, murmured goodbye to Maura, and jogged across the clearing, trying to keep her hands in her pockets as she moved.

"Oh good, Poppy. I need your help." The words came out in a breathless rush.

Poppy took her time turning around. "Where have you been? Please tell me you're not having a mental breakdown too."

"Will you do me a favor?"

Poppy pulled her striped pink and green stocking cap over her ears, which matched her pink corduroy jacket. She grinned, revealing her two straight rows of small teeth. "You want me to tell Carl you're in love with him?"

Etta rolled her eyes. "No," Etta said, but then thought of Carl's kiss and her cheeks filled with heat.

Poppy smoothed her skirt, which fell just above her knobby knees. The soles of her leather boots clomped against the stairs as she descended. She stopped on the last step and scanned Etta. "Bad news . . . a mattress exploded on your head."

Etta frowned and smoothed her hair. She'd heard lots of variations of the mattress spring joke. "Will you give this to Reed Morinsky for me? Please." She thrust a note toward Poppy.

Poppy scrunched her forehead, making her eyes look even buggier. "I don't talk to Reed."

"Then just give him the note."

"Oh no, Etta," Poppy glanced around in an exaggerated way. "You and Reed aren't, you know?"

Etta's fingers were starting to stiffen from the cold. "No, we're not 'you know.' Please Poppy, can you just do this for me? It's important. He's probably in the dining room right now."

"Jeez. Don't have an aneurysm." Poppy took the note from Etta and curled it into her mitten. "Can I read it?"

"No," Etta snapped. "I mean, please don't. Just make sure he gets it, okay? And please tell anyone who asks I'm sick." Before Poppy could answer, Etta spun around and hurried across the clearing to her cabin.

Etta sat cross-legged on her bed and read M.K. Lowther's story one more time. Then she crouched on her hands and knees and scoured under Olivia's bed—for what, she wasn't sure, since all she found was a layer of dust and an elastic hair band. Finally she yanked on a sweat shirt and some leggings, locked her cabin, and sprinted up the hill behind the cabin, pumping her arms as hard as she could, trying to forget the director's advice to travel in pairs. She focused on the crunch of the leaves underfoot, crispy after several days without rain.

At the top of the hill, she chose a narrow path that meandered along the north side of the grounds and ran at a fast clip. Some orange and yellow leaves still clung to the undergrowth, but most of the branches were bare and skeletal. After the first mile, Etta started to feel better, and by the time she reached her cabin again, sweating and out of breath, she felt almost like herself again.

She climbed the stairs, stepped onto the porch and jumped backward. A manila envelope was propped against the door. Etta picked it up, and a chill rose through her. Her hands started to tremble. Olivia's name was written across it in capital letters. It wasn't the first time Etta had found an envelope like it. She'd come home to one after a run a couple of months ago, propped against the door exactly where this one was. That time she'd deposited it on top of the clutter on Olivia's desk. But who didn't know that Olivia was gone? Was it a joke?

Etta went inside and closed the door behind her. She unclasped the metal tongs and slid the papers into her hand. Etta's hands shook and déjà vu flooded through her. It looked just like the story she'd seen next to Jordan's typewriter—the same handwriting, all-caps, the words crowded into margins.

Etta felt breathless. She walked to her desk, pulled open the bottom drawer, and rifled through it until she found the note. *Imagine, so many of us back together again. Except one of us. Where is he, Opal? Another thing I've wondered over the years—did my father love you, or were you just another geisha?* The handwriting was less frenzied, but all caps, with the same jagged a's and e's. The same person had written them.

Etta's footsteps echoed through the theater. The light switch she'd flicked on in the wing illuminated only the house lights; the stage was still dark. The velvet curtains hung motionless, framing the stage in swaths of black. Etta moved toward the spot where Olivia had been standing with Robert North as the curtain closed before them. She almost thought she smelled the residue of Olivia's lavender oil, but she knew she must be imagining it.

A row of spot lights flickered on. Footsteps echoed onto the stage. As usual, Reed's khakis were pulled up high, revealing white crew socks and leather penny loafers, and his wire-framed glasses sat slightly askew on his face. "Please do not be offended if I stand over here. Impetigo is highly contagious." Reed's voice echoed through the theater.

Etta instinctively brought her finger up to shush him. "What are you talking about?" she whispered.

"Poppy informed me of your ailment."

Etta cocked her head then brought her hand to her mouth. "Oh no, please tell me she didn't tell everyone I have—what is it ... impe ...?"

"I am afraid I am highly susceptible to germs." Reed pushed his glasses up with his index finger then brought his other hand up to cover his mouth, muffling his speech slightly. "I was born six weeks early and lived in an incubator for my first three months. My immune system never fully recovered."

"Reed I don't have ... what is it?"

"Impetigo. A skin infection characterized by small blisters."

"Gross."

"You should not be ashamed. Major Mills is a trained medic. He said impetigo is curable, although I suspect he will need to assess your case. Perhaps they will bring in a doctor from Jackson."

Etta shuddered. "Please tell me you didn't ask Major Mills to examine my skin."

"Your condition can be treated."

"I don't have a condition. Stop covering your mouth. Hasn't Poppy ever heard of a cold or the flu? Impetigo, really?"

Reed lifted his hand from his mouth, but it hovered just in front of his face. "If you are not ill, what reason would you have to be absent from class?"

Etta glanced out at the rows of velvet seats. "It . . . it's complicated. First you have to promise what we say in here is a hundred percent confidential, that you won't tell anyone, especially the major or Hardin, especially not Hardin, or Winston or Walker, or Opal or Petra, or Poppy—definitely not Poppy." Etta took a few steps toward Reed and lowered her voice. "Promise?"

Reed dropped his hand. His blue eyes flitted back and forth behind his glasses, and worry lines crossed his forehead. He nodded.

"Okay. So here's the thing." Etta glanced behind her. "I think there's something . . . I . . . Olivia's gone . . . weird things . . . Olivia knew something, or got herself in trouble, or I don't know. I need some records from the archives."

A sound echoed across the stage, Etta jerked her head in its direction and peered into the dark stage wing. Her heart slammed against her chest. Reed took a step away from the sound, squinted, and covered his face with his hands.

Etta sighed. "Hello?" she called. She detected a movement in the shadows.

"Jeez, do you have night vision or something?" Poppy padded onto the stage wearing her striped socks. She was carrying her boots.

"Impetigo, really? Impetigo? Was that the all you could think of? How about a cold, a migraine, a stomachache . . . a fever?"

Poppy rolled her eyes. "So, you were saying—you need some records from the archives . . ."

Etta crossed her arms and tried to swallow down some of the heat that was flooding into her face. "I asked you not to read the note."

Poppy shrugged and coiled a strand of her blonde hair around her finger. Her eyeballs drifted up. "Come on, Etta, I'm so bored out here in this stupid forest. What are we supposed to write about out here?—sitting in a classroom staring at the back of Chase Quinn's head, the flight patterns of moths? If you guys are going to go do something cool, there's no way you're leaving me out."

Reed rubbed his hands together and stared at the floor. He looked like an insect. Maybe it would be good to have someone else to help her too. "What do you think, Reed? Do you want Poppy's help?"

Reed's blue eyes were glossy, and Etta realized that he hadn't exactly agreed to help her. "You have not fully explained the mission," Reed finally said.

Etta waved both Poppy and Reed closer until they were standing within inches of each other, so close that Etta could smell Poppy's shampoo. "Okay, it's going to sound crazy. Everything I tell you needs to stay amongst us." She glared at Poppy.

Etta reached into her book bag and pulled out M.K. Lowther's story, the manila envelope that had been left on her porch earlier, and the note from Opal's pocket. She handed the pile of papers to Reed. "I'm not sure how, but I think all of this is connected to someone named Matthew Lowther." Etta explained what she knew, and Reed's watery gaze met hers. To Etta's relief, the worry lines had eased somewhat from his forehead.

"You said you're helping transfer library records?"

Reed nodded.

"Do you have access to the archives?"

Reed shook his head and stared at the pile of papers. "Students do not have access to the archives. However, you would not find this in there anyway."

Etta stepped closer to Reed. He was squinting at the back side of one of the yellowed "Cherry Blossom" pages. He handed it to Etta. Someone had jotted a fading row of letters and numbers in the middle of the page: BL UB271.J3S4 P.98.

Reed pushed up his glasses. "This is an LOC number, which means this book is part of the original collection. A librarian from the University of Oregon cataloged Buchanan's books when the academy opened in 1958. The academy converted to a local cataloging system in the eighties."

"LOC?" Etta whispered.

"Library of Congress. I think UB stands for military. I would guess it's part of Buchanan's research collection—the materials he used to write his stories and novels. They're in the basement."

"Can you find it?"

Reed shrugged. "Maybe. They're in boxes, but I think they're mostly in order."

"What I was really hoping to find is class rosters. I think Matthew Lowther might have been a student here in 1985. Would there be a class roster in the archives?"

Reed shook his head. "Student records are kept in the administrative office. I can ask Theodore if there's such a list."

Etta thought about it. "It's better that nobody knows we want this. If we can get this without Teddy knowing, that would be safer."

"You are not suggesting theft?" Reed whispered. "Theft is in violation of the academy regulations."

"I'll do it," Poppy interrupted. "I've always wondered what Teddy keeps in his desk. What do you want to bet he has piles of love letters to Hardin in there, or maybe vials of bat saliva . . . or rodent hearts?" She giggled.

Etta made a face. "I think Reed should do it."

"Oh come on. I'll sneak into the office at lunch. No one will even see me."

Etta narrowed her eyes at Poppy. "Fine, but please don't get caught. Can we meet at my cabin during unstructured time today?"

They nodded. Reed handed Etta the pile of papers and she stuffed them in her bag, shoved her hands into the pockets of her down coat, and took a few steps toward the wing of the stage. Then she spun around and mumbled, "Thanks."

Reed pushed his glasses up and smiled, revealing his too-far-apart teeth. Poppy twirled her blonde hair around her finger and chewed on her bottom lip.

Prickles rose through Etta's legs. *You're in trouble. Go home.* Was she putting Reed and Poppy in danger? She pushed the thought away. "Thank you both."

Chapter Sixteen

◆

Etta salivated at the thought of Carl's cooking—green chili, biscuits, tortillas glistening with butter, coffee with cream. She pushed open the stainless steel kitchen door. In front of her, a column of steam rose from a pot on the stove top.

"Etta."

Etta registered the familiar voice before she saw Amanda Watson's turned-up nose and flip of dark hair. "Amanda."

Amanda took a step away from Carl, who was standing behind the stainless steel table husking a cob of corn. They'd been standing close. Very close. Etta's eyes watered and her cheeks filled with heat. She coughed. She gripped the edge of the table as the cough turned into a hack.

Carl pulled the stringy remainders of husk from a corncob, snapped the top off, and threw it over his shoulder. It plunked into the pot of water on the stove. He strolled to the sink, poured a glass of water, and slid it across the table to Etta. "You okay?"

Etta nodded and wiped at her eyes with the back of her hand.

"Mandy was just telling me things might get exciting around here soon, with Ms. Peña on her way."

Etta could feel Mandy's eyes on her. "Sorry to hear about your . . . condition." Mandy cleared her throat. "I hope you'll be back in class next week. You're up for critique, right?"

Carl raised an eyebrow at Etta as he pulled the husk off another piece of corn. "You been under the weather?"

Etta shook her head. "Just a little cold."

A fold appeared on Mandy's ivory forehead. "Oh, I thought you had a skin . . ."

"You misunderstood," Etta interrupted. "I mean, you must have."

Mandy blinked. "Oh. Then you're coming to the reading tonight?"

Mandy combed her fingers through her smooth, glossy bob, which curled under her pointed chin.

Etta brought her hand up and smoothed her nest of coils. "Tonight?

"Isabella Peña will be reading from *The Long Struggle* at eight o'clock. Hopefully no one will get injured." She laughed at her own joke, and then glanced at her watch. "Oh goodness, I've got to run. You know how Petra is about tardiness. This morning Mallory was a couple minutes late. She said he was just like her second husband and asked if he had trouble with impotence as well. You should have seen his face." Mandy giggled again, a dainty titter of a laugh, and her cheeks flushed. "See you at lunch, Carl." She met Etta's eyes and then strolled past her. "Hope you feel better," she murmured. The words disappeared into silence as the door flapped closed.

Carl threw a husked piece of corn in the water and reached for another, breaking off the end. His hair was growing out, and it stuck out in tufts all over his head. "I reckon we should talk."

The kiss. That's the last thing Etta wanted to talk about right now with hunger gnawing at her stomach. Vapor rose from the pot behind Carl, clouded into the air, and then dissipated. "I'm sort of in a rush. Can we talk later?"

Another corncob plunked into the boiling water. "Why did you stop by if you're in a hurry?"

"I was hoping maybe I could get something to eat." Etta smiled.

Carl set a piece of corn on the table and frowned. "You been avoidin' me?"

Etta shook her head, as Carl scraped the pile of husks into a bucket beneath the table. "Haven't seen you in the dining hall, and you haven't stopped by for awhile."

"It looks like you've had Mandy to keep you company." Etta wished she could take back the words the second they were out.

"What's that supposed to mean?"

Etta glanced behind her at the door. She felt almost light-headed.

"Where have you been?"

Pressure swelled behind Etta's eyes. "I've been . . . since Olivia . . . I can't really talk about it right now . . . "

"What about Olivia?" His words were sharp.

Etta dropped her gaze at the floor. "It's complicated."

"Try me."

Etta opened her mouth, but nothing came out. What could she tell him? That she'd found a story by someone named Matthew Lowther, and she was sure it had something to do with Olivia leaving? That Olivia had been plagiarizing? That someone was threatening Etta? Or that maybe none of those things were true? Maybe she was distracting herself from writing a story for her critique, which was only a few days away. A story that could win her the Buchanan Prize. And she'd written nothing. Not one word.

"Fine. I'll talk." Carl picked up the piece of corn, pulled the rest of the husk off in one stroke, snapped the top off, and threw the cob into the pot. He grabbed another piece. "You ever noticed how everyone here has way too much in common—Andover or Philips Exeter then Harvard or Yale. Brown, if they're the rebellious types. They all think a trust fund is going to change them into Vincent Buchanan. It's absurd." He dropped his hand onto the table, and Etta winced at the clang it made. "When I

first met you at the bus station in Jackson, you seemed different . .
." Carl's words trailed off, and silence engulfed the room.

Is Mandy different?" Etta asked and regretted it instantly

Carl gazed at her then picked up another piece of corn. "I reckon she might be."

Etta spun around and pushed against the door. She hardly felt her feet against the ground until she was outside. The sun hung low in the sky, just above the trees to the south of the lodge. Etta's breath clouded in front of her. The sweat on her forehead evaporated in the cold, leaving behind a grimy film. She burrowed her hands in her pockets and walked toward her cabin as fast as she could, trying to ignore the hunger. She would go back to her cabin and write her story.

A note hung on Etta's door. Etta pulled it off then fumbled and nearly dropped it. Her fingers were too frozen to cooperate.

Your presence is requested in Director Hardin's office today at: 15:00.

Etta crumpled the paper and glimpsed something shiny next to her foot. She crouched and her fingers went to it before she recognized it. She picked it up and stared at it in her palm. Olivia's promise ring. The white gold and tourmaline.

A shiver rose through her, and she glanced behind her. It hadn't been there before. She would have noticed it. She clutched it in her palm and stood, unlocked her door, and stepped inside.

Everything looked to be in order. Her bed was made, her desk and dresser and the row of books on the shelf above her desk were neat and tidy. Etta slid the ring onto her thumb, crossed the room, and peered into the bathroom. It was exactly as she'd left it—the shower curtain half-way open, her toothbrush on the edge of the sink next to a tube of toothpaste. Why did she have the feeling someone had been there?

She traversed the room and sat down at her desk. Her notebook was open to a fresh, white page. Etta's stomach twisted with hunger and panic. Her classmates would be merciless during her critique, because that's how she'd been on theirs. Why?

Etta picked up her pen and stared at the paper. She squeezed her eyes shut. The stories that once flooded from her were gone. She rested her head on her arm. She wanted to cry, but she couldn't even do that.

Etta swung open her door. Reed and Poppy stood on the porch. Poppy rolled her eyes. "Tell him, Etta. Pea coats are for girls, right?"

Reed stepped forward and handed Etta a pile of books. He was wearing a black double-breasted pea coat over his wool sweater. Etta shook her head. "I don't think so."

Poppy rolled her eyes again. "Well, I know so. They're not the most fashionable choice for either gender, but they have all right lines, they can be slimming, and I suppose they could be appropriate for a variety of casual or semi-formal affairs . . . if you're female."

"Pea jacket is the preferred term in naval circles, and this one was issued by the United States Navy to my grandfather, Morton Randolph Morinsky in 1941."

"Well, apparently your grandfather was something of a cross dresser," Poppy said.

Etta laughed. "It's a nice coat, Reed."

"Thank you. You look nice too."

Poppy rolled her eyes and clomped into the room. Etta set the books on her desk.

"Please forgive me. I could not recall the exact number. I brought everything that started with UB."

Etta nodded, and Reed stepped inside, closing the door behind him.

Poppy plunked onto Etta's bed and flung her book bag off. She unlaced her boots and they clunked onto the floor. Her eyes went to Olivia's deserted side of the room. "I like what you've done with the place. You should be an interior decorator." Poppy grinned at Etta.

"Very funny. I've been a little busy."

"Yes, of course, with your critique impending. Are you finished with your story?" Reed crossed the room and sat down on Olivia's bare mattress.

Etta sighed.

Reed's face lined with worry. "It is easy to succumb to the pressure before a critique. Might I make a suggestion?"

Etta looked away.

"I accelerated my usual daily quota of one thousand words to two thousand in the weeks preceding my critique, which greatly boosted my productivity."

"Or you could ask your boyfriend to make you a drink. Nothing like a Long Island Ice Tea to take away the jitters." Poppy giggled.

"Carl isn't my boyfriend."

"When my grandmother found out I would be attending the Buchanan Academy, she made me take an oath that I'd abstain from alcohol." Reed sat down on Olivia's bed and crossed his legs. "She feared I would find myself dead in a pool of my own vomit."

Poppy giggled.

Reed pushed up his glasses. "Chaucer, Camus, Faulkner, Fitzgerald, Capote, Chandler, Poe, Dylan Thomas. Think about it, as an aspiring author, you are staring down the barrel of a loaded rifle and spirits are the trigger. "

"Wouldn't alcohol be the rifle and writing be the trigger?" Etta asked.

Reed narrowed his eyes as if considering it, and then pushed his glasses up again.

"I think you both need an appletini," Poppy leaned forward. "So I have news."

Etta snapped her gaze to Poppy. "Did you find it?"

"We have more important matters to discuss. You'll never believe what I found in Teddy's desk."

Etta crossed the room and sat down on the bed next to Poppy. "Did you get the roster? Can I see it?"

"It's important that we understand the implications of my discovery." Poppy pulled her bag onto her lap and unclasped it, then dropped a book on the bed. Etta gasped.

Swirling red rose border. Gothic typeface. Red-haired model. Etta searched for the author's name. Magenta Black.

Magenta Black was one of the most prolific of the Courtesan girls. At least she'd clearly been clever enough to write under a pen name.

"No one will know it's you, honey," Marla Epstein had told Etta. "It sounds like a nom de plume, and you've got a name I can sell." Etta was twenty-three when she published her first Courtesan romance, *Dissatisfaction*. She hadn't learned to argue with Marla yet.

She'd met Marla when she was temping at Morgan, Kane, and Associates. She'd mentioned to one of her co-workers that she was working on a novel, and within minutes everyone in the office knew. A few days later, a paralegal stopped Etta in the elevator and offered her sister-in-law Marla's contact information. She insisted Marla was an approachable, friendly New York literary agent.

When Etta finally built up the courage to contact Marla, she discovered Marla was not an agent, nor was she friendly. She was an editor for the Courtesan Intrigue imprint. Marla e-mailed Etta the guidelines. Etta blushed thinking about writing all of the sex scenes, which Marla assured her must be "hot," but then Marla not so casually mentioned how much money she'd make for writing four Courtesans a year. It wasn't grand, but it was more than Etta made schlepping papers at Morgan, Kane, and Associates.

So Etta had set aside the meandering literary novel she'd been working on for a year and the short stories she'd intended to submit to literary publications. She studied the guidelines Marla sent, read every Courtesan Intrigue she could get her hands on, and eventually wrote *Dissatisfaction*—"The story of a woman pushed to her limits and the man she had to have."

Fourteen Courtesans later, Marla had let Etta out of her contract, but Courtesan would own her birth name, Loretta Ann Fox, for the next ten years.

"Right, Etta?"

Etta jerked her head up.

"Which passages do you think Teddy reads to Hardin over their morning coffee breaks?" Poppy grabbed the book out of Etta's hand, opened it, and flipped through some pages, grinning. "He had, like, five of these in his desk."

"I don't understand. Why would Theodore read to the director?" Reed looked perplexed.

Poppy giggled. "Because Teddy's in love with him, silly. Haven't you noticed that your friend follows Hardin around like a lost kitten? It's sort of pathetic."

"I assure you, Theodore does not have romantic feelings for the director."

Poppy closed the book. "Did he tell you that? Because if someone has to tell you something, it means the opposite is true. I mean if Etta insisted right now that she's not in love with Carl, we would be wise to assume that she is beside herself with lust for him. Do you see how that works?"

"Poppy!" Etta said as her face flooded with heat.

"Relax, it was a hypothetical. The point is: Teddy is crazy about Hardin. Case closed."

"But he's not. Theodore is in love with somebody else here."

Etta snapped her gaze to Reed. "Please tell me that by here, you don't mean here in this room."

Reed blushed. "Forget I said anything."

Poppy grinned. "Reed, are you and Teddy secret lovers?"

Reed's face flushed an even deeper shade of red. He shook his head.

"Don't tell me he's got a crush on Etta?" Poppy grinned and raised a thin eyebrow at Etta. "I bet he thinks of you when he reads this."

A wave of panic rushed through Etta. She could almost hear Petra's words: *I thought I saw a fox.*

Reed shook his head again. "It's not Etta."

Poppy shifted her eyes from Etta to Reed. Silence settled across the room, and the grin faded from her lips.

Poppy dropped the book in her bag and pulled out a manila envelope. "I found the roster. You said 1985, right?"

Etta had to stop herself from lunging across the bed to grab the envelope from Poppy's fingers.

Etta reached for the envelope, and Poppy jerked her hand back. "First you have to hear how I found it. Teddy's office was a bore, except for that, of course." She nodded toward the Courtesan. "Pens, stationary, budget reports, paper clips. I figured the student records might be kept in that closet next to the administration office. Of course . . ."

"Can I see it?"

"I had to find the key."

"Poppy . . ."

Poppy continued, with an explanation of how she found the key, opened the closet, and found file boxes for each year since 1958. "But get this—there's a blank space between 1984 and 1986. A freakin' hole there."

Etta stiffened. "How did you find it?"

Poppy waved the envelope in the air. "I almost didn't. The 1985 box was totally out of order, sitting right next to the door. And there was so much crap in it—playbills, application packets, this weird handmade hippie yearbook made out of straw and weeds . . . it's a wonder I found this. You shouldn't be too embarrassed for doubting me, Etta. Everyone makes profound misjudgments at some point in their lives."

"I still don't understand why we've burglarized the administration office." Reed's glossy eyes flitted back and forth behind his glasses.

"I would explain if Poppy would let me see that envelope."

Poppy sighed and shoved the envelope in Etta's direction. "I don't think you get it; I was like a Charlie's Angel in there—the one Farrah Fawcett played, except decidedly more stylish."

Etta slid the piece of paper out of its envelope: the school's emblem and the stately typeface of the letterhead were the same as on Etta's acceptance letter last spring.

"Matthew Kenneth Lowther," Etta read aloud from the middle of the list.

"I do not understand." Etta hadn't noticed Reed crossing the room, but he was sitting beside her now, his arm pressed against hers, and Poppy was squeezed on her other side. All of them stared at the sheet of paper in Etta's hands.

"Robert North was here in 1985?" Poppy asked.

Etta's gaze darted down the list. Robert Evan North, two names below Matthew Lowther's.

"I do not understand," Reed said again. "The second name."

"Galen Vincent Buchanan," Poppy read aloud. She met Reed's gaze. "Is this the Galen wandering the school grounds?"

"Is he Vincent Buchanan's son?" Etta asked.

"I don't know." Reed said.

Etta glanced from Reed to Poppy. "Well, I think we need to."

◆

Chapter Seventeen

HUNGER MADE ETTA PULL ON HER RAINCOAT AND SHUFFLE down the path through the rain, hurry around the north side of the Lodge, slip into the theater, and feel her way down the back hallway toward the dining room. She was shaky from low blood sugar, and she couldn't face another stale cracked-wheat cracker, couldn't even look at the last bit of gooey red jam in the bottom of the jar; couldn't choke down another mug of the gray instant hot chocolate with the tiny marshmallows floating on the top.

Poppy had agreed to bring Etta some food tomorrow, but tomorrow was an eternity away. Etta had waited until after nine o'clock, when the kitchen, dining room, and great room were usually deserted. No one would hear Etta sneak into the kitchen. But Etta froze at the corner where the corridor turned toward the dining room. The accented voice was loud and instantly recognizable. Isabella Peña. Etta flattened against the wall, and poked her head around the corner. The lights of the great room were ablaze: a yellow rectangle at the end of the long hallway.

Etta glanced behind her into the shadows. She couldn't turn back now. She was dreaming of cheese—Swiss, Muenster, Brie, asiago, Gouda, it didn't matter. Thick slices on bread, or just a handful of shredded mozzarella, or tortilla chips oozing with melted cheddar. Etta inched down the hallway, running her hand along the wall, feeling for the opening to the dining room. She focused her eyes on the patch of light at the end of the hall and padded along until she felt the door trim. She could hear Isabella Peña's words now, and she stopped. It wasn't what the author was saying. It was the tone of her heavily accented voice. It sounded like she was hurling her sentences at the back of the room.

"So our hero uses his undeniable gift, not to illuminate or enchant, not to make people question or wonder about things. He uses words in the most dangerous way they can be used—as weapons. He uses words to kill and maim, to pillage and plunder, to destroy and conquer. And you wonder who our hero is, you say? You all know him well. You are his protégés."

Isabella Peña paused, and Etta took a step closer to the great room. All she could see was the rectangle of yellow light, and although she wanted to move toward it, to see how her classmates were reacting to Peña's words, she didn't move.

"A more timid woman might have kept her feelings about Vincent Buchanan to herself here, being that he is the founder of your elitist, and forgive me for saying so, but rather paternalistic, institution. However, I've heard you are well-educated and literate young people. The next generation of the American literary intelligentsia. And thus I might expect you to defend your hero, but I would also implore you to leave your minds open. Writers can't afford to close them after all. You are thinking: he is the greatest writer of the twentieth century, three of his books won the Pulitzer prize, and he won a National Book Award. All but three of his novels became celebrated Hollywood films many times over, their budgets exceeding the GNP of most of sub-Saharan Africa combined. How dare a Chicana from the slums of Oaxaca de Juarez ride her burro up north to criticize our hero?" She paused. "But I would challenge you to consider, for a moment, that Vincent Buchanan may not have been a hero at all, but a patriarch, an imperialist, a racist . . ."

Etta gripping the door trim to steady herself.

"Let's examine his short story, 'The Garden of my Summer,' as an example, written in 1967, when your hero was fifty-eight years old. We all know the story, of course. It was a short, rather dull tale about an old man tending his garden, not exactly the most inventive fiction since Buchanan himself had just passed middle age, and the garden was full of the mosses, ferns, and rhododendrons that grow wild just outside these doors, but it was a lyrical, harmless little parable, right? You probably read it in middle school. You undoubtedly learned that the garden was a symbol for America, land of the free and brave—the untamed plants, a vast diversity of them, growing every which way, working symbiotically off each other. America was untamed, but a thing of beauty for all the world to admire. What could be wrong with this little allegory? Well, do you remember how the garden spreads in the story, how the ivy begins to grow everywhere, takes over most of the man's property, encroaches into the forest nearby, even wraps itself around the man's shovel and hoe. The ivy is imperialism. Manifest Destiny. And the rhododendrons, do you remember them? They form a wall, a chamber; they create a secret haven where Payne Morris, the protagonist, goes to feel safe. Yes this is an allegory about America—a place where people are trying to insulate themselves from outsiders, build walls, shut out people from other cultures, of different religions, colors, and creeds, while strangling them with vines. This is your hero's vision for America."

Etta wasn't sure if it was her hunger, or the way it felt like Isabella Peña's voice was slicing the air, but she didn't want to be in the hallway anymore. She slid inside the dining room. Moonlight washed through the windows, bathing the wooden floor and tables. Etta crossed the room and pushed the kitchen door open.

She stepped inside and squeezed her eyes shut against the bright light then brought her hand up and coughed. The smell was unmistakable. It brought back a night at Good Time Charley's in Ann Arbor sitting in the bar upstairs, the outlines of people dancing, the blind date her friend had talked her into meeting, his pack of Lucky Strikes thwacking against his palm, the stream of smoke rising from his lips into the neon lights.

"Just like the blessed baby Jesus, our little Loretta's risen from the dead."

Etta snapped her eyes open, and Good Time Charley's dissolved. Petra Atwell sat on the counter. She brought a squat glass up to her lips and her hand wavered, swaying in front of her. She slammed it onto the counter beside her, and Etta winced. Petra jerked the cigarette up to her mouth. Smoke curled up her face. Her red high heels were splayed on the floor beneath her, garish against the concrete.

"You're drunk," Etta whispered.

Petra laughed. "You're a coward." She tapped the cigarette's filter, and a pile of ashes clumped onto the counter. Petra slithered off the counter. "You want a drink? I found out where the Texan's been hiding the good stuff."

Etta shook her head. Petra laughed and walked to the end of the counter. She poured from a square bottle of amber liquor, swaying slightly. "Suit yourself. Vincent was a snob, a drinker, and too rich for his own good. His liquor collection's been buried in the cellar getting better every year, while he's been decomposing in the ground. The irony."

Petra's cigarette rested on a small plate. A ribbon of smoke tangled its way into the porcelain cups hanging in diagonal rows beneath the shelves. Petra took a sip of her drink and grimaced. "Stop looking at me like I'm a tosspot. Unlike you, I was out there listening to that impudent vamp speak for the last hour." She leaned against the counter. "That woman could have driven the Virgin Mary to the bottle."

Etta walked to the stainless steel table and looked down. When she looked up, Petra was staring at her.

"Why is it that you always look like you're wearing someone else's skin and it's the wrong size?"

Etta glanced behind her at the door. "Excuse me?"

Petra threw her head back and took a drink. "You have a fucking pseudonym. Get over it."

Etta tightened her grip on the table. "I don't know what you mean."

Petra drank the rest of the liquor in her glass and turned her back to Etta. When Petra turned around, the glass was full again. "Jonathan Swift had fifteen. The man probably forgot the name his mother gave him, he had so many make-believe ones. Thackeray had eleven. You've got one rather uninspired pen name and you walk around looking like you've joined the witness protection program."

A strange calmness eased through Etta.

Petra walked to the other side of the counter and picked up her cigarette, leaned back, and closed her eyes. After a second, her eyelashes, thick with black mascara, fluttered up. "I didn't even particularly like Vincent when I met him. He was long-winded, and he followed that pallid poet around with drool collecting at the sides of his mouth, and I swear that waif didn't look any older than fourteen at the time. Vincent never asked how anyone was doing. Didn't give a shit. Just prattled on and on about this damn academy and himself as though he was the center of the universe. The asshole created all of this, because winning every literary award known to mankind wasn't enough for his sense of self importance." Petra took a drink from her glass then pointed her cigarette at Etta. "So, why would I care what that Latina primadonna says about . . ."

"Opal Waters? Did they have an affair?" Etta flinched at the squeakiness of her own voice.

Petra laughed then narrowed her eyes at Etta. "Worse. He was in love with her. The idiotic man was enamored with an icicle." Petra took a sip from her drink. Her hand swayed as she brought the glass down.

"When did you meet Vincent Buchanan?" Etta asked.

"Before you were born I'm sure. This is an unholy place, teeming with vernal innocence to remind you that you're decaying a little more each day." Petra drained the rest of her glass and slid it onto the counter. She pointed a finger in Etta's direction. "You know what's sick? He probably would have wanted to sleep with that priggish diva out there too. She all but called him Goebbels. Referred to him twice as America's 'Propaganda Minister.' You have to admire the woman's bravery, I'll give her that. She should win the medal of courage for impudence. She actually believes *The Western Defense* is responsible for the Iraq War, the plight of migrant farmers, for every impoverished baby born in Tijuana. Yet if that geriatric narcissist were alive, he probably would have wanted to get her out of her cat suit and up to his room. Men are disgusting." Petra lit another cigarette and pointed at Etta. "Almost as disgusting as cowards."

Petra took her time trying to get her high heels on then picked up her glass and sauntered toward the bottle of liquor again, her shoes clicking against the floor.

"I'm not a coward." Etta's voice was a whisper.

Petra spun around and walked toward Etta, the liquor sloshing in her glass with each step. She stopped an inch in front of Etta and took a drag off her cigarette. "We were in the same room for about fifteen minutes several years ago—at one of Marla Epstein's god awful parties. Marla's married to my agent, Peter. It's an incestuous business, Loretta. I feel right at home in it." Petra laughed. "Perhaps you don't remember me? Marla's stuffy soirees can be forgettable affairs. You stood out—can't say why exactly, maybe it was because you were standing in the corner alone playing with that hairless skeleton Marla thinks is a cat, maybe it was because you looked all of thirteen at the time, or maybe you just have a particularly annoying face. Who knows."

Etta took a step away from Petra, her ears swelling with air. She had not forgotten the party. It was her first trip to New York City, the first and only time she'd ever met Marla in person, and sadly the first time she'd ever been to a party where drunk twenty-somethings weren't doing keg stands in the bathroom. She couldn't look away from Petra's face, the swaths of red blush on her cheeks, the way the foundation settled into the furrow between her penciled-in eyebrows.

Petra slid her drink onto the table, the amber liquor sloshing, but somehow staying in the squat glass. "Don't confuse me with your therapist or that priggish bore Dear Abby. I don't even want to begin to guess what could make you such a frightened individual, but I do have some suggestions for you. Drink this. It's more expensive than the piece-of-shit diamond ring my first husband gave me. Stop skipping classes. And, I know, talking to Hardin is about as interesting as reading Proust, but when the man requests that you join him in his office, drag yourself up those stairs even if you're within a minute of your death. Whether you follow any of those recommendations is your own damn business, but I promise you if you ignore this one, you'll spend the rest of your days penning more supermarket bodice-rippers for that half-wit Marla. Do not blow this critique, Loretta."

The door flapped closed behind Petra. The sound of her high heels against the dining room floor gave way to silence.

Etta wrapped her fingers around the squat glass and winced at the burn at the back of her throat as the liquor slid into her empty stomach.

The next morning Etta hurried down the hallway to the classroom. Robert North's voice got louder with each step. She'd woken only minutes ago, pulled her hair into a pony tail, and yanked some clothes on. She'd spent an hour staring at her notebook waiting for something to come to her, writing then crossing it out then writing and crossing it out again. She'd finally reread Matthew Lowther's story again hoping it would put her in the mood to write, but had fallen asleep after the first two pages.

Etta turned the doorknob to the classroom and slipped inside. Robert North stood with his back to the class, his curls outlined against the window. Rain, which had started sometime in the night, streaked across the glass. As Etta eased the door shut, Robert North met Etta's gaze, and stopped talking. A few students turned their heads.

Robert North ran a hand through his hair and strode to the center of the room. "As I was saying, poetry is the most challenging form." Most of the students turned to face the front of the room as Etta let her breath ease out. "Not the form itself, but the length. Novelists, essayists, memoirists, journalists—they're in love with their own voices. They can't edit their nervous chatter. The poet can't get distracted with a character's ex-boyfriend's dislike for rose wine or ramble about an impressionist painting his character saw once in a museum in Rome or concern himself with whatever parental injustices made his character whoever the hell he is today.

"The character is. The moment is. A slice. A sliver. A voice. A flash. A breath. A poem. The poet obliterates all but the essence. The poet writes the truth."

Etta moved toward her seat, slid into her chair, and eased her bag onto the floor, avoiding eye contact with the few students who turned at the sound of her footsteps.

"So why are novelists the celebrities? Why are poets considered eccentrics, flakes, lazy slouches who live in their mothers' basements and can't hold down real jobs? You might think that the poet has been downgraded, that the poet has taken a backseat to accountants and administrators, because of industrialization, or globalization, or capitalization, or some other reason, that the marketplace and the Internet and greed have stripped the significance from the poet?

Robert North paused, his eyes sweeping across the room. "No. The poet has always been scum. Coleridge, Shakespeare, Poe—luminous observers of the human experience—and bottom feeders. The poet suffers; he loses; he hurts; he bleeds; he peers up at society through the sewer grates and tries to tangle existence together with words. That is the poet. Why would anyone suffer like that?"

Robert North turned his gaze on Etta. "Because he has no choice. If you have a choice, take the other route, take the damn exit. Go home."

Etta looked at her lap, but could still feel Robert North's stare. Her hands started to shake.

Robert North cleared his throat. "As you've all probably heard, I'm leaving today, heading up north for another stop on my dreadful tour itinerary. Isabella Peña will take over shaping your young minds this morning. I'm sure she'll be here imminently. Good luck to each of you. If Vincent Buchanan were here, I'm certain he'd be pleased to see a new flock of protégés dwelling in his Shangri-la."

"Thank you, sir," someone said. Etta glanced up. The Poet's Rowers started to clap. Mallory let out a whoop. Someone whistled.

Robert North flung his leather briefcase off the table and clutched his thermos. He strode down the center aisle, his gate long and relaxed, his gaze fixed on the door. Etta felt something on her face, and nearly jumped. It was Maura's breath on her hair. "Are you feeling better?" she whispered. Robert North's hand was on the doorknob now.

Etta nodded and jumped from her seat, wrapped her fingers around the strap of her bag, and flung it over her shoulder. Robert North was nearly at the staircase by the time Etta made it out the door. She broke into a jog. "Wait!"

Chapter Eighteen

◆

Robert North glanced over his shoulder and continued walking. "You were talking to me," Etta called.

Robert North spun around and blinked. He ran a hand through his hair.

"Are you trying to intimidate me?" Etta stepped toward him. Her pulse heaved in her ears. She glanced over the railing. The couch and all of the oversized chairs sat empty, but she lowered her voice anyway. "Did you tell Olivia to leave too?" She felt impulsive, like she did as a kid playing penny poker with her brothers, like there were no stakes. Maybe it was because he was leaving in a few hours. She'd never see him again. Maybe it was the hunger eating at her stomach, coiling around her brain.

Robert North ran his tongue over his bottom lip then laughed.

"Do you get off on killing other people's dreams?" Etta took another step toward him.

"Whose dreams am I killing?"

Etta studied his chiseled features then stared down into the great room. "Olivia's," she whispered, because she didn't want to say, "Mine."

"Jesus. You're the one who seems to be conducting a little investigation into her departure. Surely you've figured out she didn't write those freakish stories. Please tell me you're at least that smart."

Etta glared at him.

He glanced over the railing. "Maybe I would also want to get to the bottom of things if my roommate disappeared, except I didn't, which is the only reason I can still show my face around here."

Etta held her glare.

"Oh Jesus, don't judge me. It's not the same. Matt was a troublemaker, not to say Olivia isn't. But she's more troubled than troublemaker. Matt was intense. He stayed up all night every night pounding on his typewriter, pacing, smoking, muttering under his breath. I requested a different roommate the first week. So, yeah, when he disappeared, I can't say I missed living with the guy. I can't say I put too much thought into where he went off to. Sure, sometimes I feel sorry for that now. But I can't change it. So I'm going to get on with my life. I suggest you head on back to wherever you came from, Ella, and do the same."

"Etta."

Robert North stared at her, his eyes clouding over.

"My name is Etta."

"Well, Etta, I've got a couple hours to kill if you need help packing."

She studied his face. "Matthew Lowther was your roommate." She tried to make it sound as though she'd known. "Where did he go?"

The poet laughed, but it was more of a release of air. "Became a pile of bones in the ground somewhere if you ask that crazy fuck Galen. All I know is I don't want to mess with this anymore and neither should you. Go home. Really, just go home. Stop asking questions." Robert North started down the stairs. Etta watched his figure float down the spiral.

Etta clutched the banister and raced down the stairs behind him. "I'm not leaving." She winced at how loud her voice sounded echoing into the great room. "This is my dream."

Robert North didn't turn around until he was in the foyer. "Well, I'll be gone by afternoon."

"Do you know how hard it is to get into this place?" Etta grazed her hand over the sweat forming on her brow. "The stories, the essay, the interview, the letters of recommendations? I worked on my application for months. I edited it until not one comma was out of place. I cleaned out my savings. I sold everything I owned." She clenched her fists. What she wanted to say but didn't was that she had nowhere to go. No home.

Robert North's laugh was harsh. "Oh Christ, your parents don't own a townhouse on Carnegie Hill or a villa in Tuscany? Then you're right, you completed one hell of an application. Has it ever struck you as curious that nearly all of the aspirant writers the admissions board deems the best and brightest each year are children of the richest and most connected? You've got to give Buchanan credit—convincing upper crust mommies and daddies you can turn their aimless English major or budding adult into the next Salinger or Fitzgerald is profitable deceit."

"You're bitter."

"No, I just know from whence I speak. My grandfather donated the million that built the theater wing. And my father's charitable enough to remind me how I got where I am every time the *New Yorker* buys one of my poems. You really think it was your friend Jordan's writing sample that wowed the admissions board? It didn't occur to you that his old man owns half of New England and publishes the most pompous literary journal in creation? Nepotism is built into the woodwork around here."

"Is that how Galen Vincent Buchanan got in?"

For a moment, she wondered if Robert North had heard her. Then he laughed. "Except Galen has more talent than the rest of us combined. He got your friend Olivia in this place. Talk about a girl who isn't a chip off the old block. Matt may have been an asshole, but he was a hell of a writer."

Etta gasped. It felt as though he'd hurled something at her, and she stepped backward. Matthew Lowther was Olivia's dad. The dad she never knew. The literature professor.

Robert North seemed to realize that he'd revealed something he shouldn't have. He spun around and darted toward the door. "Matthew Lowther was her father," Etta said, mostly because she needed to hear the words aloud. Her voice echoed through the foyer.

Robert North spun around. "You want to be a writer? Stop pretending like you're Nancy Drew and get to work. How's that critique coming?"

Etta's cheeks filled with heat.

"One student messed up his first critique when I was here, and he was back home by Christmas. The most impressive application in the world is not going to help you if you mess this up. Especially if your father can't write the kind of check that sways Hardin. If this is really your dream like you say it is then forget about Matt. Forget about Olivia."

He spun around and wrapped his fingers around the iron door handle. The sound of the rain swelled into the foyer as the door swung shut. Etta stared at the row of rain coats and umbrellas hanging from the hooks. Water had pooled beneath them.

She closed her eyes and tried to remember Olivia's voice.

I'm the product of a one-night-stand. My mom slept with her literature professor.

Does he know about you?

My mom got stoned and forgot to tell him . . .

Etta walked into the great room at the same moment Amanda Watson stepped out of the hallway to the kitchen. Amanda smiled, a tight upturn of her lips. "Are you feeling better?"

"Visiting Carl?" Etta cringed at how high pitched and shaky her own voice sounded.

Mandy blinked. "I stopped in for a quick cup of tea. I slept late today. I'm so embarrassed." She rolled her eyes and pushing her brunette bob behind her ear. "I was up late studying dactylic hexameter. Opal thinks I should write my next work in it instead of anapestic tetrameter. I was originally thinking that I would compose my next work in trochaic octameter, since I love internal rhyme. But I'm starting to think Opal is right. Dactylic hexameter feels grandiose in a way anapestic tetrameter doesn't. It lends itself to enjambment, you know." She let out a nervous giggle. "Oh gosh, listen to me rambling on . . ." Mandy stepped past Etta onto the staircase. Etta watched her for a moment then clutched the banister and followed. Mandy glanced over her shoulder. "It's just so exciting to think about writing something new after working on *After Daisies* for so long. And having Opal as a mentor . . . Anyway, you must be excited for your critique?"

"Thrilled." Etta murmured.

"I'm still recovering from mine."

They stepped into the long hallway at the top of the stairs, and Etta glanced at the portrait of Vincent Buchanan, fixating on his hands clasped in his lap—old and withered, speckled with age spots, resting atop a book.

"It's not so bad. Most people are nice."

Etta flicked her gaze to Mandy. Mandy was already halfway down the hall, her leather backpack bouncing as she walked. She shot a glance at Etta as she thrust the door open, and Etta thought of Chase Quinn and winced. Had she been too harsh on Amanda's critique? She could hardly remember it.

Reed shot out of his seat when Etta stepped inside the classroom. He crossed the room and stepped to her side. The room buzzed with talking and laughter. Isabella Peña was nowhere to be seen.

Reed pushed his glasses up with his middle finger. "I have something to report." Etta stepped toward him to make out the rest of the sentence. "about the mission."

A giggle escaped from Etta's chest. "Listen, maybe we should abort the mission." Another giggle welled through her, like a valve releasing pressure from her chest. Reed pulled the door open and gestured for her to move into the hall. Etta followed him and leaned over, resting her hands on her knees until her laughter subsided. The corners of her mouth ached. "I'm sorry," she whispered, but another bout of laughter surged through her.

The door flung open and Poppy bounded into the hallway. "If something exciting is going on, you guys are in trouble." She flipped her green scarf around her neck and folded her arms across her chest. "I'm in on this too, remember?"

Etta looked from Reed to Poppy and chortled this time.

"What's wrong?" Poppy asked.

"Nothing. Except, my critique's in three days, and I haven't started my story. And get this, Matthew Lowther is Olivia's father." She wiped at her eyes. "He was Robert North's roommate here in 1985. And he disappeared."

A strange sound emerged from Reed's lips. "Like Hans Gretelstien?" he whispered.

Etta met his gaze and then squeezed her eyes shut against the image of Olivia's face in the stage lights after the play, the way her eyes watered and shifted. She was panicked.

Except Galen has more talent than the rest of us combined. He got your friend Olivia in this place.

"Galen wrote her play," Etta whispered.

Reed jabbed a book toward Etta. Etta took it and flipped it over. It had no words on the spine or cover.

Reed's eyes shifted back and forth between Etta and Poppy. "I found it while I was cataloging in the library this morning..."

"Wait a minute, I thought theft was in violation of the academy rules." Poppy giggled.

Etta opened the book. The binding was stiff. The type was typeset crooked on the title page:

Dreams of the Rising Sun: the early imagination of Vincent Buchanan.

Etta dropped her gaze to the middle of the page and gasped.

A Dissertation.

By Matthew Kenneth Lowther.

Presented to the Department of Literature and the Graduate School of Yale University In partial fulfillment of the requirements for the degree of Doctor of Philosophy.
June 1981.
Her hands began to tremble.

Etta read Matthew Lowther's dissertation during the afternoon mandatory writing session. She'd successfully avoided academic writing since she'd graduated from UM. Fortunately Matthew Lowther's dissertation read more like a magazine feature than a dissertation. And within pages, Etta realized she'd known almost nothing about the life of the academy's famous founder.

Vincent Buchanan was born on August 20, 1909 in Buffalo, New York. He was the youngest of five children—three much older brothers: Ambrose, Elias, and William—and a sister, Dorothy, who was born just eleven months before him. He hardly knew Ambrose and Elias. They enlisted in the army the day the United States entered World War I in 1917 when Vincent was just seven. Both perished in Europe's trenches.

For the first eleven years of his life, Vincent and his family lived in Buffalo as the Buchanan family had for generations. Then in June of 1920, as the first Olympics in eight years got underway in Antwerp, Belgium, Vincent's father packed up everything the family owned. They boarded the Nickel Plate Road at the train depot in Buffalo, which took them to Chicago, and then they rode the Union and Pacific Portland Rose to Portland, Oregon.

Vincent's father got a job in the warehouse of the Pacific Coast Biscuit Company. Vincent's mother Edith was a homemaker, but she began exhibiting increasingly troubling symptoms after they moved to Portland. She stayed in the darkened refuge of her bedroom most days, and started mailing letters to her mother, who'd been dead for over a decade. She grew increasingly detached from eleven-year-old Vincent and thirteen-year-old Dottie, as everyone called Vincent's sister. In October of 1921, Edith Ann Buchanan moved out of Vincent's house and never returned. She died on January ninth, 1922, at forty-six years of age, in the Oregon State Mental Hospital in Salem. What she succumbed to, Matthew Lowther did not say. He was more interested in young Vincent Buchanan and his increasing obsession with Japan.

Sometimes an accidental moment, a fleeting event, a mistake, can change the course of an entire life. For Vincent Buchanan that instant was October 4, 1922. His brother William, a delivery driver for Schlesser Brothers' Meats, drove by as Vincent was walking home from school. Vincent begged William to take him on a ride in the Schlesser brothers' 1920 Model H International delivery truck. William finally acquiesced and let his brother climb in. The last stop on William's delivery route that day was Tanaka Grocery in Japantown.

William, 56, a retired machinist living in Portland, Oregon, recounts the day vividly 33 years later. "I couldn't pull the damn kid out of that store. He walked around and touched everything—the silk slippers, the wooden shoes, the kimonos. He even touched one of the dead ducks hanging upside down in the window. It was embarrassing the way he gaped at the Orientals, just trying to do their shopping. I told him to mind his business.

The kid would give me the silent treatment all night if I ran that stop without him, so I started meeting him outside his school at 3:45. It was out of my way, but it made the kid happy, and there wasn't a lot to be happy about those days . . ."

"Can I have a word with you?"

Etta snapped her head up. Director Hardin's head was inches from hers. She heard the slap of something hitting the floor then realized it was her own notebook and Matthew Lowther's dissertation. Her pen slid from her fingers, bounced, and rolled across the wooden planks. Etta leaped to her feet, squatted, and grabbed for the dissertation. A loose page stuck out from the middle of the book. Was it coming apart?

No. It was an envelope.

Etta pushed it back into the pages and shoved the dissertation into her bag. She retrieved her notebook and pen and followed Hardin out of the classroom and down the spiral stairs to the second floor. Teddy didn't stop typing when Hardin led Etta into the administration office, but she could feel his eyes on her as she followed Hardin across the room, past the floor-to-ceiling bookshelves, the upholstery chairs, the table stacked with *Poets & Scribes*, and into his office. The rain drumming against the windows vibrated the panes.

Etta stepped toward the chairs across from Hardin's desk, and jumped backward. A long blonde braid swung across the back of one of the chairs. Etta met Opal Waters' gray gaze.

Hardin closed the door behind Etta, circled his desk, and sat down. "Please sit, Ms. Lawrence."

Etta's gaze went to the window—the swirl of streaky gray, the condensation bubbling the inside of the glass. She sat next to Opal, but stayed on the edge of the seat, her bag still slung across her shoulder.

Hardin rested his hands on the arms of his chair and gazed at a point behind Etta. It was almost as though he was waiting for Etta to talk, and as the silence spread out, Etta considered blurting out an excuse for reading during the mandatory writing session. But something—perhaps Opal Waters' gray eyes on her—told her she was here for something more serious than reading during class.

Chapter Nineteen

◆

"ARE YOU FEELING BETTER?" OPAL SPOKE FIRST. ETTA managed a nod. Director Hardin cleared his throat. He gestured toward a paperback volume on his desk that Etta recognized as the *Buchanan Academy Rules and Regulations,* a tome she'd received in the mail days after she'd received her acceptance letter. "You are familiar with the Regulations, Ms. Lawrence."

Etta nodded.

"So you are aware that students are required to attend all classes, workshops, mandatory writing sessions, meals, and impromptu events, readings, and speeches, except on Sundays, which have been set aside as free days." Hardin rapped his fingers against his desk. "We have been fortunate, in that we've never had a serious illness strike one of our students. We attribute our residents' health to their engagement in the creative process, the environment of learning, the salubrious nature of literature, and to the fresh air and beauty of the grounds."

Etta dropped her gaze to the floor.

"I will remind you of our policy on illness." She heard the thin pages of the book slap against each other. "Page sixty-one: To protect all residents, any illness must be reported to the director

144

or his assistant within twenty-four hours, either in person or by proxy."

The room grew silent, and Etta lifted her gaze to meet Hardin's. He stared at her over his spectacles. "You can understand how this is particularly urgent if the illness is of a contagious manner. We have an agreement with Dr. Herbert Mansheim, a general practitioner in Jackson. He can be here in less than forty minutes. Shall I phone him?"

Etta tried to shake her head. "I'm fine . . ."

Hardin brushed his hand through his wispy hair. "I will not belabor the point, except to say that we take the codes seriously here. With Vincent no longer with us, they are all we have to ensure his legacy remains unspoiled. I am willing to overlook one transgression, especially under the circumstances." He closed the book and rested his hand on it; his gaze drifted toward the window. "We also have arrangements with a psychiatrist—Dr. Evelyn Ryder of Portland, who has counseled many of our students over the years. Perhaps you would like to talk to her?"

Etta glanced down and saw Opal's slender fingers reaching for hers. She instinctively drew her hand away. Then she tried to smile, but Opal looked away, her hand fluttering to her lap.

After a moment, Opal spoke: "I've consulted with Dr. Ryder myself. She's a good listener, and she can prescribe medication for depression, whether it's seasonal or . . ." Her words trailed off.

Etta stared at the blue veins laced beneath the poet's pale flesh. She thought about extending her hand toward Opal's, but hesitated. "You were depressed?"

"When I heard of my father's passing, the isolation of the lodge . . . I've lived here on and off for thirty years, you understand, and it's always been a sanctuary, a muse—but it became, well . . . It was nothing really. Listen, you may have heard that sadness is part of the artist's soul, that it breeds imagination or makes you see the world more clearly, but it's simply not so. Dr. Ryder can help you, maybe as soon as tomorrow."

The vein that threaded up Opal's brow to her hairline was just barely visible. Etta thought of Petra's words. *Vincent followed that pallid poet around with drool collecting at the sides of his mouth, and I swear that waif didn't look any older than fourteen at the time.* A tendril of hair had come loose from Opal's braid and fallen across her cheek. Etta glanced at the director, and followed his gaze toward the window. She became aware again of the sound of the rain, softly drumming against the panes.

"Did Olivia talk to her?" Etta asked.

Hardin took off his spectacles and set them on the desk. He closed his eyes and massaged his temple. Without his glasses, he looked tired, the flesh below his eyes sagging into his cheek bones. "I'm sorry, but I cannot discuss Ms. Saxon's medical condition."

Hardin looked as though he might say something more, but Opal spoke next: "Did Olivia seem depressed to you?"

"She cried sometimes," Etta said, thinking of Olivia's muffled sobs in the night. Why hadn't she asked Olivia about it? Of course, they were strangers at first, but later, she could have asked. She should have.

"Did Olivia confide in you?" Opal asked.

Etta opened her mouth to say no, and then thought better of it.

After a moment, Opal continued, "Being the confidant of someone who is unstable is not easy. Perhaps that is what brought on your own troubles."

Etta stared at the books on the shelves behind Hardin. Did Etta have troubles? She hadn't eaten in days, she'd hardly slept, she couldn't write, and she'd gotten Reed and Poppy involved in something she could hardly put into words, something that didn't make sense even to her.

"It may help to get it off your chest, I mean, whatever it is Olivia confided in you," Opal said.

Etta met Opal's gaze. "Olivia thought Jordan was in love with someone else." Etta only said it to watch Opal's reaction, but Opal's eyes revealed nothing. The poet brushed the strand of hair off her face and tucked it behind her ear.

"Did Ms. Saxon and Mr. Waterhouse have a . . ." Hardin cleared his throat. "Were they violating the regulations?"

"Where is Olivia?" Etta sensed the meeting wouldn't last much longer, and she'd regretted not asking Hardin last time she'd been sitting across from him.

"I understand it is difficult, but you must try to move past this. I will have Theodore telephone Dr. Ryder. You can meet with her in my office. I'm confident she can help you work through any lingering" —he rolled his eyes toward the ceiling— "emotions."

Etta nodded, because she wasn't sure what else she could do. But her heart hammered against her chest. Did she need help? Or medication? She clutched the strap of her bag against her shoulder.

"One more thing." Opal smiled at her—a tight, close-mouthed smile. "We're looking forward to your critique. What's the title of your story?"

Etta bit the inside of her lip. "Cherry Blossom," she whispered, because it was the only thing she could think of.

Etta's pulse raced as she stepped into the hallway outside the administrative office. At the bottom of the stairs, the commotion of lunchtime drifted from the dining room. Etta slipped to the back side of the staircase and stepped into the shadows. The stairs matched the architecture so well with its unfinished log banisters, wide plank steps, and general rustic splendor that Etta assumed it had been built with the rest of the lodge during the Depression, but according to Carl, Vincent Buchanan had added the staircase when he acquired the lodge in the late fifties. He'd been enamored with the lighthouses on the Oregon Coast when he was a child and had wanted to emulate the feeling of spiraling toward light.

Etta crouched. The air was stale and dusty. Some words were etched into the baseboard. Etta leaned closer and ran her finger over them: WPA 1936. Then she pulled Matthew Lowther's dissertation from her bag and fingered the envelope that protruded from its pages.

As Etta stepped into the dining room, everyone seemed to be discussing Isabella Peña. The visiting author had never shown up to take over Robert North's class that morning. Winston Goss had appeared at ten to oversee the mandatory writing session and apologized for the "lack of communication" concerning the morning class.

"If she thinks Buchanan was so awful, why is she here?" someone asked.

"She's practically a fugitive."

"I wish she'd go home."

Chase Quinn's voice rose above the rest for a moment. He was talking to Jordan, who sat across from him. "America's Propaganda Minister. What kind of crack is she smoking? We'd be speaking Japanese right now if it wasn't for Buchanan."

Etta dropped into her chair, so intent on overhearing Jordan's response to Chase's analysis that she hardly noticed Reed and Poppy.

"Is everything okay?" Reed asked. Etta jumped and then plunked her bag onto the floor and slid it under her chair.

"We saw you leave with Director Hardin." Reed whispered. His blue eyes darted back and forth behind his thick lenses.

Etta could only think of the rice paper envelope, thin and fragile. She'd decided it would be best not to open it crouched behind the stairwell and had returned it to the pages of the dissertation. But she'd stared at it long enough to memorize everything on it—the three cent stamp with Thomas Jefferson's profile on it. The postmark: Seattle, Wash, August first, 1940. And the address, written in careful cursive letters: Vincent Buchanan, Box 7502, Portland, Oregon.

"See, I told you." Poppy pursed her lips and blew on her jambalaya.

"Told you what? Told him what?" Etta jerked her gaze to Poppy. Poppy brought her spoon up and took a bite of her jambalaya. The sight of it made Etta's stomach growl.

Poppy set her fork down. Etta grabbed it and stole a bite of sausage.

Poppy cleared her throat. "We think . . ."

"It's unimportant," Reed jumped to his feet. "I will get you some lunch. Would you like a beverage? Milk, iced tea, juice, coffee, herbal tea, water?"

"Water. Thanks."

Reed disappeared. Instead of jambalaya, his plate had pear slices and what looked like a plain cheese sandwich.

Etta scanned the room. At the director's table, Teddy and the major sat with their backs to Etta; Opal and Hardin hadn't arrived yet. Were they still upstairs discussing Etta? Poppy tapped her fork against the edge of her bowl, a quick, steady beat that grew louder and more rapid.

"Can you please stop that," Etta said, a little louder than she'd intended.

Poppy raised one of her wire-thin eyebrows and continued tapping.

"Why are you doing that?"

Poppy shrugged and rolled her eyes to the ceiling, letting her fork sink into her bowl. She drummed her nails across the table.

"Poppy. Please. Stop. It."

Poppy rolled her eyes. "That's exactly what I was saying. You think you're in charge of us."

Etta glanced over her shoulder, hoping to see Reed with her meal. Instead she glimpsed Carl's cowboy hat floating above the crowd. She snapped her gaze back to Poppy. "I don't know what you're talking about." She tried to keep her voice measured, even though her hunger, combined with the sight of Carl, made breathing feel impossible.

"You're keeping stuff from us."

Etta shook her head.

"Reed and I are your underlings. You treat us like children. Even worse, like step-children."

She did tend to think of herself as much older than Poppy, who was all of twenty-three. The smell of Poppy's jambalaya swirled all around her.

"You want the glory."

"Glory?" Etta snorted. "What glory?"

Poppy stared at her.

"There's no glory here. I don't even know what we're doing. I don't understand any of this—Olivia, Matthew Lowther, Robert North. Galen. Jordan. Opal. Any of it. I haven't eaten a meal in a week, and I'm so ravenous that it's all I can do not to grab that sandwich off Reed's plate, and I've been waking up about ten times a night if I can even get to sleep, because when I close my eyes, I see Olivia standing on the stage next to Robert North, and I hear her crying. I actually hear her. And if I don't write a story in two days . . . I have nowhere to go when they expel me—no house, no family, no money."

Etta felt someone next to her and jerked her head up. Reed's gaze flitted away. He set the bowl of jambalaya on the table, his hands trembling. The water sloshed over the sides of its glass as he set it down.

They ate in silence. Etta shoveled spoonfuls of jambalaya into her mouth, hardly chewing, only momentarily savoring the way the green chilies complimented the Creole spices and the smoked Andouille sausage. "Where did he go?"

Poppy glanced up for only a second then stared back at her bowl. It was the first time Etta had ever known Poppy to hesitate to speak. Etta shifted her gaze to Reed, whose face was still pale, his glasses sitting slightly crooked on his long nose.

"Robert North. He left two hours ago. I saw him go outside, out into the rain. Carl's the only one who could drive him to Jackson, right? And Carl's over there. So where did Robert go?"

Poppy dropped her fork into her bowl and pushed it away. Their heads drifted toward the middle of the table.

"He said Galen got Olivia into this place, which means Galen wrote her story and Galen wrote the play." Etta brought her hand down, and Poppy and Reed both flinched at the clatter the dishes made. "Hans is Matthew Lowther, right. He was at the academy looking for the truth. The truth about Vincent Buchanan?"

"I do not understand. Do you think they led Matthew Lowther into the forest, because he knew something?" Reed whispered.

"Olivia was acting so strange that night . . . terrified." Etta glanced toward the director's table. Hardin and Opal were there now, seated in their usual spots. "No. Not scared. She was furious." Etta dropped her voice. "At Hardin."

Chapter Twenty

◆

AFTER LUNCH ETTA, REED, AND POPPY WALKED TO THE THEATER. While Reed fiddled with the switches on the light board, Etta drifted onto the stage, moving toward the place where Olivia had been standing the last time she'd seen her. Etta stood in the spot for several minutes and stared into the shadows beyond the curtain. "Here?" she mumbled to herself.

"You found it in the theater?"

Etta had almost forgotten she wasn't alone, and the sight of Poppy on the floor in the middle of the stage with her legs folded beneath her sent a startle through Etta. "I was just wondering if this was where Olivia . . ." The name caught in Etta's throat.

Poppy stared at her, lines forming at her brow. "Did you even hear my question?" She pulled her fine hair into a ponytail then let it fall across her shoulders.

Etta shook her head.

"You've got to be kidding me. I asked you three times."

One of the velvet curtains wavered, and Reed stepped from behind it. The reverberation of his footsteps rippled across the stage. "We should not stay long if we wish not to be interrupted." He spoke just above a whisper. "Winston will arrive in fifteen minutes."

"Why is Winston always in here anyway? It's creepy." Poppy's voice echoed into the narrow room.

"This is where he writes," Reed whispered then glanced over his shoulder. "I saw him one day when we were preparing the production, and . . ." Reed looked from Poppy to Etta. "He was standing in the middle of the stage speaking into a voice recorder. It was as though he was watching a production unfold in front of him. He recited every stage queue, described the sets, the music, random sounds, the lights. Later I saw him transcribing his recordings onto a legal pad, the sound of his own voice filling the theater. He seemed to be in some sort of trance. I read an interview years ago, where he said, away from the stage, he cannot write a word."

Etta folded her arms across her chest and rubbed at her shoulders, even though she knew the chill that had rippled through her had nothing to do with the temperature. It was the idea of words springing forth when someone stepped into a theater, of words springing forth at all. Would that ever happen to her again?

"For the fourth time, where did you find this letter?" Etta jumped at the sound of Poppy's voice. But Poppy didn't seem to notice. "I bet it's worth a fortune. I saw this guy on *Antiques Road Show* who had a signed edition of *The Triumph of Folly*. It was worth, like, three thousand dollars. Can you believe it? Just for Buchanan's stupid signature."

Reed shoved his hands into the pockets of his khaki pants and began to pace, his shadow mimicking his curved spine. "Poppy is correct. Buchanan ephemera is valuable. That's why Buchanan's personal correspondence, interviews, notebooks, and other such documents are stored in the archives. Unless the letter is of no relevance, perhaps?" Reed stopped pacing and stepped toward Etta, peering at her through his glasses. His feathery hair was coiled into tight curls. It apparently reacted to rain in the same way Etta's did.

Etta slipped the dissertation from her bag, sat down on the edge of one of the folding chairs and opened the book to where the envelope lay between its stiff pages. The name on the envelope made her heart pound, just as it had the first time she'd seen it: Vincent Buchanan.

Etta slipped the stationary from the envelope and unfolded it. Careful cursive letters filled every inch of the page. Etta read, her voice tumbling across the stage:

July 20, 1940
Dearest koibito,

In a few weeks time, I will be on the other side of this ocean we share, but I assure you that nothing can ever wash you from my heart.

It gives me great shame to recount this even now. You probably believe that a mother always loves her child, but for a long time, it was only my sisters my mother loved. She would say her Issei child would ruin the family long before I knew what Issei meant, before Issei Child became my name. In Portland I was an extra mouth to feed. My sisters were my family's future. The Nisei era will blossom, my father said. My parents saved every coin to send Natsuki to the university. They planned for Natsuki and Miki to buy land for us and to run our store when they came of age. They hired you to teach English lessons only to Natsuki and Miki, because I would need to learn to read and write no more than my mother had. I was able to join them only because I begged and refused to eat for many days. I only tell you this now, so you will understand that your friendship was like the sun on my face at the end of a long, cold winter.

When we returned to that foreign place my parents called home, I was sure I couldn't survive the ache I felt for you. I could not say your name aloud, because mother would turn her silence on me for weeks, and Natsuki and Miki would run about the house taunting me with "rabu rabu." That's when Mother began to call Natsuki and Miki gaijin, outsiders, because they were not born in Japan. I became the favorite, but I could never forgive that she could treat love like rice, giving it and taking it away so easily. I was afraid to leave Natsuki and Miki alone with her. Her anger was like those black tornadoes of dust that swept across America a few years later.

One time Mother threw all of Grandmother's tea bowls, the only valuables in our small house, across the room, shattering them one by one, yelling about that day my father was forced to put the sign in the window of our store proclaiming we were Japanese. Do you remember that day? There were so many tears in Nihonmachi that day, but it is yours that I remember still. How could a stranger feel such sorrow for my family?

Each time my parents said we had come home to that strange city of Kyoto, I knew it was not home, because there could never be a home without you. I read the books that you gave me and practiced my English every day, and I repeated your promise over and over inside my heart until I could bear it no more. The seasons turned from spring to summer to fall to winter. When the snow blanketed the trees, I stopped believing you would come.

Then you were there in the garden, as full of life as the first time I met you, and I thought I would never let you leave my sight. I never told you this, but now that I will never see you again, secrets seem as futile as dreams. As a child I wished I was one of the picture brides on the boat with us, girls who seemed so old then, but were younger than I am now, dressed in their nicest kimonos. I watched their wedding ceremonies on the boat. White men climbed aboard dressed in strange clothes and filed past us, taking their hats off, holding black-and-white photos in their scrubbed fingers.

I knew even as a girl that I did not want a marriage like my mother's, a sea of loneliness, with a man who only knew obligation. I wanted poetry, someone who would lie awake at night listening to my heart. I found you, my koibito, and I would never leave you, except I am terrified for your safety as these two great lands I've called home dissolve around us.

Etta glimpsed the last sentence before she read it. Her hands started to quake, and the rice paper slipped from her fingers and wafted to the stage. It folded over itself and landed face-down next to Poppy's boot. Reed crouched to retrieve it, squinted, and read the last sentence, his baritone voice resonating across the stage:

I hope you will find comfort in the words my grandmother spoke to me before I crossed the ocean for the first time. It is impermanence that gives the monotony of breathing its radiance.

Yours forever,

Sakura

Reed stared at the letter then he folded it and passed it to Etta, pushing his glasses up with his index finger. Poppy's round cheeks glistened. Reed noticed Poppy's tears at the same moment as Etta did, and he dropped to his knees and knelt beside her, clearing his throat several times.

Poppy waved her hand in the air then wiped at her eyes with the back of her hand. "You should have seen me the last time I watched *Pretty in Pink*. I went through an entire box of Kleenex."

"*Pretty in Pink* wasn't even a sad movie."

Poppy snapped her gaze to Etta. "Are you kidding? It was the greatest movie of all time. Remember when Andie and Duckie—"

"Excuse me," Reed interrupted. He looked as surprised as Etta that his deep voice had sliced through Poppy's. "Forgive me, but we need to put the letter away now. Winston will be here soon. We should not stray off topic."

"Sorry," Etta and Poppy both mumbled at the same time.

Etta slipped the letter in its envelope, staring again at the neatly-written address. "Sakura is Yumi."

Reed stared at her, unblinking.

"Are you speaking English?" Poppy asked.

"'Impermanence gives the monotony of breathing its radiance.' It's the last line of 'Cherry Blossom.' Lowther must have stolen it from this letter. In the story Peter Morrison meets a beautiful woman in a garden, a shop keep's daughter named Yumi. Peter Morrison is Vincent Buchanan, and Yumi is Sakura."

Etta grabbed the dissertation off the chair and started flipping through the first chapter.

"It sounds like a line from a fortune cookie." Poppy wiped at her cheeks with the back of her hand.

"Maybe Matthew Lowther brought his dissertation here with him. Vincent Buchanan was obsessed with Japantown as a child. He went with his brother for the first time when he was eleven or twelve, always to the same store." Etta flipped through the pages, her fingers turning back to lobster claw, fumbling with the thick paper. "Tanaka Grocery. That must have been Sakura's family's store."

Poppy stretched her legs out in front of her. "So Vincent Buchanan wrote to a woman named Sakura? So he went to Japan? I'm sure he did a lot of things. What does any of this have to do with Olivia?"

Reed cleared his throat then stood and started to pace again. "It would be of great interest if Buchanan had a relationship with a Japanese woman. I prepared my honors thesis on Buchanan's use of symbolism in *Rebellious Tides*. *Rebellious Tides* made Buchanan into a household name, a celebrity even. It won the Pulitzer Prize in 1938. It's still considered by many to be Buchanan's best work, although it was all but forgotten after *The Western Defense* became such a sensation. *Rebellious Tides* became a Bette Davis movie in 1940, and some think the movie's success incited William J. Donovan, the man who oversaw Franklin Roosevelt's Office of Strategic Services to tap Buchanan to help with the anti-Japanese propaganda effort."

Poppy laughed. "You sound like Isabella Peña."

"Well, her rhetoric may be hyperbolic, but her contention that Buchanan worked for the OSS is not implausible. Steinbeck is the person who encouraged the president to create the propaganda office in the first place. He wrote *The Moon is Down* about Hitler. Hersey wrote *The Bell of Adano* about Italy. The Office would have been looking for a celebrated author to write a piece about Japan. And a fictional attack on the West Coast would have been just the sort of novel they would have commissioned—a story that would build American anxiety about Hirohito and bolster the public's resolve to sacrifice for the war effort in the Pacific. It would explain why Buchanan, by all accounts, had unprecedented access to military and naval information while writing *The Western Defense*. He purportedly even toured the map room with Roosevelt and Churchill."

Reed stopped pacing, and silence engulfed the stage. Etta was startled to see that she was squeezing the dissertation so tight her knuckles were white. She relaxed her hands.

"Is it true that Truman was reading *The Western Defense* when he decided to drop the bombs?" Poppy asked.

Reed pushed his glasses up. "That story was originally reported by Milton Warren, a reporter for the *New York Post*, who was known to fabricate a canard or two."

"You know a lot about Buchanan," Etta said.

"I studied literature because of Vincent Buchanan. He's the reason I wanted to be a writer."

"Yeah, you and every other male English major," Poppy mumbled, rolling her eyes. "Buchanan or Hemingway."

Reed stared at Etta. "Honestly, I'm bewildered by this letter. I've examined every secondary resource available about Buchanan, at least everything held in the libraries at Boston University and Harvard, and I don't recall a single mention of Buchanan ever going to Japan or stepping foot in Japantown as a boy. These revelations would be of incredible interest to Buchanan scholars."

"It seems like Buchanan didn't want them to be." Etta stuffed the dissertation into her bag, and silence eased across the stage.

"Don't ask me." Poppy pushed herself to her feet. "I studied botany." Poppy swung the striped tote bag over her shoulder. "I only switched to Creative Writing because my parents were too thrilled about the botany thing, boasting to all of their Connecticut Rose Society friends that I was following in their footsteps, babbling about how I would surely be the next Almira Phelps."

"You're not the only one here going against your parents' wishes."

Etta leapt to her feet and spun toward the voice. Winston Goss stood behind her, dressed in gray slacks and a beige button-down shirt. Etta's hands shook. She hadn't heard a sound, not the wing door creaking open, not Winston's footsteps behind her, and she had the same tongue-tied feeling she'd had the few times in the past when she'd been gossiping about someone just as the person happened through the door. Except no one had said anything about Winston, and he was smiling at them, looking from one to the other expectantly.

"My father made it known to me before my fifth birthday that I would become the next director of Goss Family Memorial Services—no matter that I became hysterical when I accidentally killed a spider by washing him down the wash basin and had full-blown panic attacks at the thought of siphoning blood from human corpses."

Poppy giggled. "Sarah Orne Jewett's also to blame," Poppy said.

Etta tried to make the words make sense.

"My junior year I went on a weekend trip to Maine and picked up a copy of *A Country Doctor*. I changed my major to Creative Writing the day I got back."

"Ah, yes, Ms. Jewett. For me it was Vincent Buchanan."

Etta would have usually smiled at Winston, nodded, politely laughed, or chimed in that it was Virginia Woolf's essay "On Being Ill" that had first inspired her to write, a line she'd repeated so many times she almost believed it. But the chill was back, spreading through her at the mention of Vincent Buchanan's name, and she wanted away from the stage, with its bright lights and cavernous echo.

Chapter Twenty-One

◈

WINSTON EXPLAINED THAT HE'D LEFT HIS NOTES IN THE STAGE wings, and needed them because he'd be teaching the afternoon class. He walked to the classroom with Etta, Reed, and Poppy. As always, Winston wrote the theme of his lecture in small print on the chalkboard behind him: *Creating believable characters.* Then he stepped behind the podium, cleared his throat twice, adjusted his glasses, and read from the text in front of him in his nasally voice: "Hamlet, Willie Loman, and Abigail Proctor walked off the page and onto the stage . . ."

Etta heard a distant rumble outside. The rain had become even heavier in the last few hours, muddling the landscape into hazy gray mush. Was it thunder? No. Etta leaned forward and blinked, making out the glow of the truck's tail lights floating down the narrow road on the south side of the lodge past the garden and disappearing into the haze. Was Carl taking Robert North to Jackson?

Puddles of water pooled on the window sill. The realization overwhelmed her. She wanted to leap from her chair and shout it aloud. But Winston was still reading from the papers on his podium, his voice hardly registering any inflection. Reed was scribbling notes. Poppy chewed on her bottom lip and coiled a piece of blonde hair around her finger.

Galen, Etta wanted to shout. We must go find Galen.

Etta and Reed trekked up the steep hill to the south of the women's cabins. Etta closed her eyes against the ice-cold drops pelting her forehead. Reed had voted to wait until the weather cleared up to go looking for Galen, and of course, he'd been correct, but Etta wasn't ready to admit it quite yet.

As she propelled one foot in front of the other, Etta thought of Poppy's excuse for not coming. "The trim of my rain coat is faux fur," Poppy had explained, "I'm afraid it's functional and stylish in drizzle to moderate rain conditions, but wholly inappropriate in downpours." Poppy had brought more clothes with her than anyone. Yet, she'd arrived at a location boasting an annual rainfall of eighty inches with only one raincoat inappropriate for downpour conditions? Now, Etta wanted to shout at the idea of Poppy snuggled under Etta's comforter with Matthew Lowther's dissertation open on her lap and a cup of hot chocolate on the nightstand beside her.

Reed and Etta crested the hill and followed the trail to the west. The rain seemed to let up somewhat, if only because they weren't walking into the wind anymore. They walked for a long time and then came to a fork in the trail. Etta took off her gloves and rubbed her hands together to try to warm up her fingers. Reed took off his glasses and cleaned them with a small piece of material he'd evidently brought along for that purpose.

Etta surveyed both trails. On her runs, she had only taken the one that went east and circled the lodge. It was a good path, wide and maintained, whereas the trail to the west looked more like a deer path—a narrow strip only wide enough for one. But Carl had said Galen had been seen at an old cemetery that was west of the swimming hole.

Reed was busy situating his glasses on his nose, using both hands to straighten them. Etta gestured toward the deer path.

Reed nodded, although Etta was sure she saw his blue eyes flicker with worry, or fear?

The canopy of the forest closed in around them, blocking out much of the rain, wind, and light. Etta's eyes eventually adjusted, and she got into the rhythm of meandering with the trail through the trees. They climbed over several downed trees and forded two streams. The brush cut into the path at times, scratching against her rain pants,. It felt like they were weaving aimlessly through the forest. And they'd been walking for so long. Too long? Maybe they'd already left the academy grounds and entered federal wilderness land, which bordered the academy on each side? Except wouldn't there at least be a wire fence indicating the boundary? They would need to turn around at some point, but every time she glanced behind her, Reed forced his lips into a brave smile, and Etta couldn't bear to tell him.

Etta stopped. She heard something. A car? She snapped her gaze to Reed. Her instinct was to raise her finger to shush him, but he wasn't speaking. She spun around and stared into the forest, surprised at how hard the rain was falling around them. Everywhere she looked she saw tree trunks, undergrowth, moss hanging from branches, water pooling on leaves.

But it was definitely a car or a truck. The chugging began to fade. It had been close before. She thought she'd even felt the rumble in the ground.

She started to run, and then sprint. The trail twisted again to the west, and she picked up her pace.

Then she was standing in the middle of a road. An iron gate towered in front of her. She turned in a circle. For a moment she was sure she saw exhaust diminishing in the rain. Or was it just fog? She tried to quiet her breathing to listen, but the forest was still except for the patter of the rain.

Etta moved toward the iron gate and blinked as the cemetery seemed to sprout from the ground before her—grave stones, miniature iron fences, chipped and broken sculptures, a knee-high stone wall. Everything was sunken and decayed, grown over with moss. Ivy crawled up part of the iron gate.

Reed stepped up beside her and slid his hood off. "This was in the play." His glasses were foggy and streaked with rain. "Winston changed the scene, because we didn't have time to make a set. In the original, Hans buried the truth in a cemetery."

Did that mean Olivia knew about the cemetery? Had she been here?

The rain picked up as they stared through the iron rungs, and they decided to come back on a drier day. They took the road this time and walked for a long while in silence.

"We should find Buchanan's grave."

Reed pulled off his hood. "Vincent Buchanan's buried in Riverview Cemetery in Portland. Haven't you been to his grave?"

Etta shook her head.

"It's a tourist attraction, a stop on the Rose City Walking tour. I've visited twice. He's buried next to Winona, his second wife. Their marriage was quite unhappy by all accounts, but his will stipulated that he was to be buried beside the mother of his children. His second marriage was the only of his legal unions to produce offspring, and although his children were mostly estranged from him by all accounts, they followed his wishes. Several years later a private donor had a bronze statue of him placed behind the graves."

Etta was sure someone had told her Vincent Buchanan was buried near the academy grounds. It seemed absurd now. Why would an author of Buchanan's fame be buried in a dilapidated pioneer cemetery?

"You said legal union. Did he have illegitimate children?"

"Honestly, no one knows. There's a lot of speculation. I've read that he and Winona had a daughter and son who supposedly want little do with the estate or academy. But his personal life is not well chronicled. Buchanan was intensely private. He threatened a journalist with a WWII bayonet once when he'd drunk a few too many before an interview. And he made sure another reporter was fired for reporting about his marital problems. I suppose it worked. Even after he died, journalists and biographers, have by and large, stayed away from his private life. That's why Matthew Lowther's revelations are so compelling."

"But delving into private lives is America's favorite pastime, isn't it?"

Reed smiled. "Buchanan's estate is supposedly quite litigious. Besides no one cares about novelists, do they? Even today. How many children does Tom Wolfe have? Joyce Carol Oates? Philip Roth?"

Etta thought about it. "Good point."

"I've heard Winona never resided in Roosevelt Lodge. She kept up a household in Portland, and Buchanan visited her there. For a long time Buchanan seemed to think it was the perfect union; he could write and she could have her independence."

"Except she had to raise the children by herself."

"Yes, well, perfect for him."

"So Winona was Galen's mom?"

Reed gave her a thoughtful look, although his crooked glasses and wet curls made him look more clownish than serious. "I suppose so."

The front gate of the academy grounds emerged through the trees. A chill rose through Etta at thought of standing at the gate of the cemetery. Galen could have been lurking in the shadows just beside her.

Etta stayed up late that night reading the rest of Matthew Lowther's dissertation. By the time she finished, it was past midnight and rain was still drumming against the rooftop. She crossed the room to her desk, retrieved her notebook, and jotted down notes.

Katashi Tanaka owned Tanaka Grocery, the store in Japantown Vincent Buchanan began visiting each afternoon. Tanaka was a prominent businessman in Portland for a time during and after World War I. He owned three stores—one in

Portland, one forty miles down the Columbia River in Hood River, and one in Seattle.

Vincent Buchanan began tutoring all three of Katashi Tanaka's daughters—the eldest was Sakura—in the spring of 1922, just months after thirteen-year-old Vincent's mother passed away in the Oregon State Hospital in Salem.

Vincent and Sakura sat at a card table in the back of the grocery store—a dusty store room filled with boxes. Sakura struggled to conjugate a verb, her eyes drifting to the exposed rafters. "I am, you are, she is, we are, they are," she said. The air was fishy. Sakura's two younger sisters sat on each side of their sister, both staring at the gangly boy who came each day after they finished Japanese school. The boy hardly noticed the little girls though, because he couldn't draw his eyes away from Sakura, her long neck and delicate chin, the drape of her black hair across her shoulders. When Sakura leaned forward, a beam of sunlight fell across her face. "It is impermanence that gives the monotony of breathing its radiance," she whispered.

With a jerk, Etta sat up. She'd fallen asleep, her pen falling from her fingers and hitting the floor. Matthew Lowther had written only a single sentence about Buchanan tutoring Katashi Tanaka's three daughters, mentioning it with a litany of other chores young Vincent performed for the Japanese businessman: bookkeeping, unpacking boxes, stocking shelves.

Matthew Lowther painstakingly documented the state and federal laws passed during the second decade of the twentieth century, which made the West Coast an increasingly unfriendly environment for the Japanese.

The Supreme Court ruled in 1922 that Japanese-born immigrants, or Issei, were ineligible for citizenship. The Oregon Alien Land Law of 1923 prohibited Issei from owning land, and the Oregon Alien Business Restriction Law of 1923 forced all Japanese merchants to post a sign indicating their nationality in their store windows. And the 1924 Immigration Act prohibited any further entry of Japanese into the United States.

In 1925 a mob of whites violently drove Japanese sawmill laborers out of Toledo, Oregon. The Toledo Incident pushed many Japanese immigrants to return to their homeland, because they feared for the safety of their children. The Tanaka family was among them.

Katashi Tanaka might have been especially concerned about Sakura, since she was one of the four people in the household who'd been born in Japan, as had he, his wife, and his wife's sister.

The biographical portion of the dissertation ended with the Tanaka family leaving for Japan in 1929 when Vincent was twenty years old. It didn't mention anything about Buchanan visiting the Tanaka family in Japan.

Matthew Lowther instead turned to an analysis of *The Western Defense*, theorizing that Buchanan wrote about Japan's aggression during World War II as a genesis of his boyhood interest in Japan. Etta's mind began to wander, and she had to reread several lines. His thesis just felt anemic. Isn't that why people studied things? Because they were interested in them? Etta's eyes fluttered closed again.

Somewhere on the borders of slumber, she realized that Matthew Lowther's research felt incomplete because it was. He'd come to the academy to finish it. Then he'd disappeared.

Chapter Twenty-Two

◆

Bang, bang, bang. Etta pushed herself up. The digital clock on her nightstand read 7:44. Fifteen minutes until class. The cabin door shook with another series of bangs. Several seconds passed. Etta slid from her bed, padded across the room, and rested her ear on the door. Rain pattered against the tin porch roof. Marla, who thought Central Park was wilderness, had mailed Etta bear spray as a congratulatory present for getting into the academy. Etta had decided not to bring it. Now she wished she had.

It was Friday. By one o'clock Etta was supposed to make copies of her story for each student and the resident authors. The class would have two days to read it and write their first critique for Walker's Monday workshop on plot. Etta laughed out loud, but the sound died in the air—high-pitched and shrill.

Etta glimpsed her cellular phone on the corner of her desk, where it had been charging for months. She unplugged it, turned it on, and fought a wave of dizziness. Olivia beamed back at her. Etta had taken the photo not long after she'd met her new roommate. They'd been on a picture-taking frenzy, snapping photos of everything: their new room, the lodge, each other sitting at their writing desks. Olivia's face was flushed, her teeth gleaming white. When Etta had taken it, she'd pegged her

167

new roommate as sweet, flirtatious, friendly, giggly, easy to talk to—fun.

"Who are you, Liv?" Etta whispered.

Etta clicked on her list of contacts and scrolled down to Olivia's name. They'd exchanged phone numbers in their first weeks at the academy, when they were used to everyone being a phone call or instant message away. They'd wandered up the hills surrounding the lodge several times looking for a spot with cellular coverage. A few students had reported getting a few bars on a hill near the swimming pool. But Etta and Olivia hadn't had any luck, which had disappointed Olivia more than Etta. Olivia had left a boyfriend named Kody behind in New York, whom she talked about in her first few weeks at the academy then seemed to forget entirely once she met Jordan. Etta, on the other hand, hadn't been sure whom she'd call even if they'd found a patch of coverage. Maybe her brother Cook—just to hear his voice. Then she'd hang up.

Etta closed her phone and slumped into her desk chair, staring at the pile of books that sat there. She ran her finger along the one on top of the pile, leaving a line in the layer of dust there. Reed had brought them, handed them to her. She'd slid them onto her desk. But, why? She closed her eyes. A memory drifted somewhere just on the edges of where she could retrieve it. And then she remembered.

She yanked her bottom desk drawer open, pulled out "Cherry Blossom," and turned the pages over. The call number: BL UB271.J3S4 P.98.

The books didn't have library labels on the spines. They'd been rebound in hard covers, with no titles, authors, or words of any kind on them. Etta opened the book on top of the pile. Her hands trembled when she saw the call number scrawled in tight cursive on the first page. BL UB271.J3H297. She compared it to the call number on "Cherry Blossom." Close. She flipped to the title page and her pulse thundered into her ears. It was in Chinese . . . or Japanese. Etta flipped through two more books with similar, but unmatching, call numbers, both in Japanese.

Etta opened the fourth book and drew in a breath: BL UB271.J3S4. She thumbed to the title page. *Japanese Espionage in the West* by David Nash. Copyright: 1943. Etta studied the call number on Matthew Lowther's story. P.98? Page ninety-eight? She flipped through the book until she found it. A grainy black and white photo filled the page. In it, about twenty Japanese men posed for the camera. Most of them were dressed in suits; a few donned black robes. Three of them stood out, because they wore round glasses with black frames.

Etta read the caption: *It is believed that a few Americans and Britons have ties to Japan's notorious ultranationalist secret societies, including the Dark Ocean Society, the Black Dragon Society, and the League of Blood. According to one source, the man sitting in the top row, second from the left in this rare photograph of a Black Dragon Society meeting in Kyoto in 1932 is an American ex-patriot named Peter Morrison.*

Peter Morrison? That was the main character in "Cherry Blossom." Etta flipped the story over and stared at the typewritten pages. But the Peter Morrison in Lowther's story was a fictionalized Vincent Buchanan. Or was he?

She squinted at the photo in the book. The man sitting in the top row second from the left wore a suit and tie and had dark hair like the rest of the men. But the photo was washed out, and Etta couldn't make out his facial features.

She thumbed to the index and found the Black Dragon Society. Chapter four was all about the Black Dragon Society, a secret society originally founded in 1901 to support Japan's military efforts to take over Manchuria up to the Amur River. Its membership included cabinet members, military officials, and professional spies. *In the nineteen thirties the Black Dragon Society expanded its activities around the globe and stationed agents in Europe and the United States.*

Etta flipped back to the photo and studied it again. Then she crossed to her bookshelf, pulled down *The Western Defense*, and stared at the grainy, black-and-white photo of Vincent Buchanan on the back. She studied the photos, and then dropped both books into her bag along with her notebook, the dissertation, "Cherry Blossom," and the 1985 class roster.

She closed her eyes, trying to conjure up images of Vincent Buchanan and Sakura, but her mother's lined face emerged instead, pinched in the tight expression Etta had last seen in her rearview mirror the last time she'd seen her family—more than a year ago.

Etta didn't even know her own mother. How was she going to understand someone she'd lived with just a few months, let alone a long-dead writer she'd never met? Coldness eased through her limbs. She couldn't shake the feeling that her safety—her life even—relied on her understanding.

Etta crouched in the shadows next to Buchanan's portrait and watched her classmates file down the staircase. Mallory Chambers' voice boomed above the rest: "Now is the winter of our discontent. Made glorious summer by this sun of York; And all the clouds that lour'd upon our house. In the deep bosom of the ocean buried . . ."

Etta recognized Gloucester's soliloquy from *Richard III*. Reciting Shakespeare was one of Mallory's favorite ways to show off, and these were some of his favorite lines to recite. Etta had heard Mallory pronounce the same sentences with the same flourish at least a half dozen times as she'd filed out of class.

Mallory also liked *Macbeth* and *Hamlet* soliloquies, the prologue to *The Canterbury Tales*, and he seemed to have an endless arsenal of poems memorized—Robert Frost, Alfred Tennyson, William Butler Yeats, W.H. Auden.

As Opal Waters bristled by, her hair long and loose down her back, Etta tried to will herself deeper into the shadows, letting her breath out as Opal descended the stairs without noticing her.

Poppy and Reed did not emerge. After several minutes, Etta crept down the hallway and peered around the doorway into the classroom. Everyone was gone. Etta slipped back into the shadows and waited for the students to amble up the stairs and trudge back to the classroom. Then Walker Ryan strode by and closed the door behind him.

Where were Poppy and Reed? Etta's heart drummed against her temples. She raced to the stairs, taking them as quickly as she could, and then crossed the great room and emerged into the rain. She raced around the lodge to the back entrance, pulled the theater door open, and blinked into the darkness. Silence hung in the air with the dust. "Reed . . ." Etta's voice echoed through the hollow room.

"Poppy?"

Silence.

Etta spun around. Were they in one of their cabins?

She hardly felt the rain as she ran, keeping her eyes glued to the trail, ignoring the way her bag flapped against her back.

"Whoa. Watch it!"

Etta jerked to a stop and brought her head up. Jordan and Chase were standing in front of her, staring at her. After an awkward moment, they stepped around her and continued down the trail toward the lodge, disappearing into the trees. Etta spun around and broke into a run again. She didn't stop until she was in the clearing in front of the men's cabins. She turned in a circle. Which one was Reed's? She picked a cabin, climbed the steps, and rapped on the door. No answer. She raced to the next cabin, pounding as hard as she could. By the time she'd knocked on all of them, her knuckles were raw.

Etta jogged down the shortcut to the women's cabins, heaving from the exertion. When had she grown out of shape? She made a beeline to Poppy's cabin, took the steps two at a time, and pounded on the door. She only heard her own breath in response—short, frantic intakes of air. Etta whipped around and squinted through the rain, which fell in drifting sheets through the clearing.

She took a step forward and then the blood drained from her face. The door of her own cabin was open. She went numb. She heard a low sound—a voice?

She ran down the steps and into the rain, fighting to keep her footing on the trail to the men's cabins and back to the theater entrance. She slipped inside and hunched forward into the darkness, bringing her hands to her knees, flinching against the sharp pangs in her sides. The door creaked open behind her.

She spun around and stared into the darkness. Her body started to tremble. "Reed?" she whispered.

"Good morning, Loretta."

Etta cringed at the sound of her given name. She inched backward into the blackness. "Hi Teddy," she whispered. If she ran down the aisle and onto the stage, could she find the stage exit in the dark?

"I am under orders to bring you to the director's office. Will you comply, or shall I use force?"

Was Teddy laughing?

"Force?" Etta asked as calmly as she could muster.

"Force is the last resort of any good officer. However, I'm under orders, and disobeying the lawful orders of a superior has consequences. My grandfather and uncles are peace officers. Hauling in outlaws, man slayers, perps, and women of the street is in my genes. I won't hesitate to use my taser if I have to. Have you ever felt fifty thousand volts coursing through you?"

Teddy was talking a little like Dirty Harry, and Etta had a sense that he neither had a taser gun on him, nor was he prepared to use any other kind of physical force against her. "Teddy, you're a secretary at a literary academy."

"I am the administrative assistant to Director Edwin J. Hardin, and he, as my superior, ordered me to escort you to his office. I advise you to stop resisting and follow me. Insubordination is what gets cadets court-marshaled."

Court-marshaled? Etta didn't bother to ask. Perhaps Teddy had an actual psychosis that made him believe he worked at a military school. She stared behind her into the emptiness and tried to make out the shape of the velvet seats, the stage, anything. If she ran, and by some miracle managed to make it through the darkness, onto the stage, and out the stage-wing door, where would she go then?

"Okay," she finally said. "Let's go."

Chapter Twenty-Three

◆

Etta pretended to scan a *Poets & Scribes* article about the best five MFA programs in the Northeast, while Teddy reclined in his chair staring at her, his navy tie thrown back over one shoulder. After several minutes passed, she dropped the magazine onto the table next to her and forced a smile. "If the director is busy, I can come back later."

Teddy narrowed his eyes at her. The stiff hair product he usually slicked his curls back with must have washed out in the rain, and his hair was a mess of loose curls.

When Hardin's door finally swung open, Etta jumped to her feet.

Reed stepped out and froze when he saw Etta. His eyes flashed to the floor and then back to her face.

"Reed," Etta whispered. She reached for the bookshelf beside her. Reed made a beeline toward the door. The door didn't make a sound as it slammed shut behind him. Or maybe it did, because Etta realized someone was saying her name.

She snapped her gaze to Hardin. His lips were moving, but it was Reed's voice echoing through her head. It felt as though he'd shouted the words at her, even though she was sure he'd only mouthed them. Two of them: "I'm sorry."

Opal stood near the windows behind Hardin, her gray gaze set on Etta. The vein down her forehead was more prominent than usual. Hardin was in his chair. His sagging face revealed nothing. He gestured for Etta to be seated.

Hardin and Opal glanced at each other, and then Opal stepped away from the window. "You were not in class today."

It wasn't a question, but they both waited for Etta to speak. "I've had some stuff, um, issues of a personal nature." Etta hoped the subject might dissuade any further questions.

Opal glanced out the window, and then fixed her gaze on Etta. "We expect a certain caliber of performance from our student writers, and frankly, you are not meeting that standard. You've missed sixteen classes and eight mandatory writing sessions in the last month, and you've consistently been absent for meals. During writing sessions, you've been observed reading, doodling in your notebook, and staring out the window. You were sighted yesterday outside of the property boundaries—a direct violation of the codes.

"We have reason to believe you may be conducting some kind of personal inquiry that is distracting you and others from writing. Is this true, Etta?"

Etta tried to swallow. She couldn't find words. She couldn't get past the words "personal inquiry."

"Writing is the only reason any of us is here." Opal said. "Is that why you're here?"

Etta looked from Opal to Hardin, trying to get words to come out of her mouth. Finally she nodded.

Hardin cleared his throat. "Good. We'd like to review your first semester story now. It is due today, as I understand it."

Etta clutched her bag closer against her chest, trying to imagine what Reed might have meant when he'd mouthed, "I'm sorry."

"It's in my cabin. I'll go get . . ." She scooted to the edge of her seat.

"No," the director interrupted. Etta winced. "That will not be necessary. May I have your handbag, Ms. Lawrence?"

Etta stood up. "Why?" She stepped backward and glanced at the door behind her, and then spun around, took the four steps to it, and reached for the doorknob. As she twisted it, panic gripped her. The door was locked. She reeled around, her gaze going to the windows.

Opal stepped to Hardin's side. "Please calm down. The pressure of the creative life can exacerbate personality disorders. Dr. Ryder, the psychiatrist we told you about, is on her way. She has been delayed by the storm, but we expect she will arrive in a matter of hours."

Etta tried to speak, but couldn't get any words to come out.

"You will wait for her right here. Now I'll need your belongings." Hardin stepped toward Etta.

Etta gripped the strap of her bag. "No," she snapped, and the director stepped backward. "Why do you want my bag?"

"We need to make sure you're not a danger to yourself," Opal said.

"Dr. Ryder believes you are exhibiting signs of Paranoid Personality Disorder. Have you ever been diagnosed with a psychiatric condition?" Hardin asked.

Etta shook her head.

Opal spoke more slowly: "People with PPD believe others are out to get them. They tend to create conspiracies and become fixated on them. They stop leaving their homes; they stop seeing other people; they stop eating and sleeping; they worry incessantly about problems or situations that do not exist. Do these symptoms sound familiar?"

Tears welled near the corners of Etta's eyes. She felt like she might be shaking.

"Living in a small community like the one we have here can be difficult for some, not to mention the pressures of the writing life." It was Opal again, but her voice sounded far away, like she was at the end of a long tunnel.

Etta felt faint. She reached for the bookshelf next to her, her other hand clutching her bag so tightly her hand shook. All she could think to say was: "Am I going to disappear?" But the words sounded so paranoid that she couldn't bring herself to speak them.

When Opal and Hardin left the room, and the lock clicked behind them, Etta made a beeline to the windows and pushed on both. She'd spent her childhood living in the only old farm house on the outskirts of Temple austere enough to suit her father, so she was all too aware that wood expands in moisture, making windows in old dwellings useless for months of the year. That didn't stop tears from welling at the corners of her eyes when neither budged. Condensation clung to the inside of the panes. Etta rubbed at the glass with her sleeve. Even if she got one open, what would she do? Jump? Maybe she was a danger to herself.

She moved toward the photograph of Vincent Buchanan hanging between the two windows. It was different than the portraits that hung all over the lodge. It wasn't posed. Buchanan was standing in front of a lighthouse. He looked to be around Etta's age. Or a little older?

Etta crouched, pulled the dissertation out of her bag, and flipped it open to the first page. *Vincent Buchanan was born in Buffalo, New York on August 20, 1909.* So the photo might have been taken around 1939? By then Buchanan had already won the Pulitzer Prize for *Rebellious Tides*. Etta flipped to the page of the dissertation where the envelope lay. The rice paper looked wilted, like an autumn leaf clinging to a branch. She tried to still her trembling hands and removed the letter. *July 20, 1940 . . . In a few weeks time, I will be on the other side of this ocean we share.* Could Sakura have taken the photo?

Etta returned the letter to its envelope, tucked it back inside the dissertation, and shoved the dissertation in her bag. She pushed herself up and walked to Hardin's desk.

The executive chair squeaked under her weight. A cigar rested half-smoked in an oversized ashtray, which looked as though it had been scrubbed clean since the cigar had been smoked.

How long would Hardin be gone? It was lunchtime. An hour? Maybe a little more. Etta tried to push through the tightness pulsing at the back of her throat.

She opened Hardin's lower left drawer. A bottle of Macallan rolled toward Etta. She thought about taking a drink. She could almost feel the burn at the back of her throat, the calmness sinking into her stomach. But she slammed the drawer shut. She needed to stay sharp.

Etta found little of interest in Hardin's desk, except for a handful of letters from authors requesting permission to visit the academy. Marilyn Bernard, one of Etta's favorite authors, was among the applicants. Etta had pre-ordered her most recent book, *Water on the Moon*, months in advance. What would the author's workshops be like? Then a chill washed through Etta. She would not be meeting Marilyn Bernard. She was locked in an office awaiting a psychiatrist's pronouncement that she was insane.

Etta moved to the wooden filing cabinet across the room. The top drawer contained information related to donors and bequests: legal forms for archival and monetary donations, a donor's bill of rights, a transfer of stock form. There were annual reports to donors for the previous five years and individual files for past donors. Another file was labeled "prospective donors" and stuffed with a thick fading list of names, which had been printed on a dot matrix paper. The second drawer consisted only of budget spreadsheets, as well as contracts for repairs to the lodge, work on the grounds.

Etta wondered if directing a writer's academy was the most boring job on the planet, worse than temping at Morgan, Kane, and Associates, until she pulled open the third drawer. It was slightly more interesting. It contained files for authors, and Etta recognized many of the names instantly. Had they all visited the academy at some point? Was Robert North in there? Isabella Peña? Etta tried to push some files back to see the names in the middle, but they wouldn't budge. Something must have fallen and jammed everything. Etta opened the drawer all the way and reached for the back, her fingers wrapping around a thick file lodged there. She pulled it out, and her eyes registered the name on the typewritten label at the same instant that she heard Opal's voice in the reception area.

Etta snapped her gaze to the door then slammed the drawer shut and stepped away from the door. She expected to hear the click of the lock, to see the doorknob twist. But several minutes passed. She couldn't make out words, but she could hear the cadence. They were arguing. Etta clutched the file folder and padded closer to the door until her ear was pushed up against it.

"Does anyone with a Y chromosome turn your mind to putty? We should have reunited that last one with her fucking father like she wanted."

Silence. Etta forced air into her lungs and pressed her ear closer to the door.

Opal spoke again, but Etta couldn't make out her words.
More silence.

Opal again: "Consider what's at stake here. The major needs to be involved in this one."

Hardin now: "We already decided. Nothing is at stake. We'll expel her for misconduct. We'll have Evelyn sign the report. We'll release that to every news station in the country if we ever hear from her again."

"That was before we talked to her. She's . . . Maybe you were right about the last one. All the Waterhouse boy had to do was say hello to her. But this one, watch her eyes. She knows more than you think."

"She doesn't know anything."

Opal's voice faded. Did she step further away? Etta slid her ear down. "I'm going to get Mills."

"Opal..."

A door slammed shut. Then it creaked open and slammed shut again.

Etta gazed at the folder in her hand, at the way the typewritten name had yellowed and faded over the years. *Lowther, Matthew Kenneth.*

It's amazing what a woman will do when she's desperate.

Those were the words on the cover of *Dissatisfaction,* Etta's first Courtesan romance, just under the title. They coursed through her mind now as she strode to Hardin's desk and picked up the ashtray. The half-smoked cigar rolled to the floor. Etta weighed the glass in her hand. Ten pounds maybe.

In Loretta Ann Fox's first Courtesan romance, the heroine, Miss Kristine Richards, found herself trapped in a house fire. Kristine, a woman who could never decide what to order for dinner in a restaurant let alone how to handle an emergency, locked herself in her second floor bedroom and waited for her beau Morgan Kane to arrive. As the flames ate their way through her house, Kristine was convinced fate was on her side. Her fiancé was Morgan Kane, a strong, handsome fire fighter, who she'd chosen over Henry Ross, a nice, but too-talkative reference librarian at the Detroit Public Library. Morgan was late, as usual, for their date, but he would arrive soon to save her. Except as the black smoke slid under Kristine's bedroom door, and she breathed in the acrid air, Kristine began to wonder if Morgan wasn't on his way after all. That's when she got desperate.

"It's amazing what a woman will do when she's desperate," Etta said out loud.

In Kristine's case, it was a library book—an oversized coffee table tome about sea turtles that Henry Ross had recommended when Kristine had stopped into the downtown branch of the Detroit Public Library a week before. Henry had remembered from their coffee date several weeks before that Kristine liked sea turtles.

In Etta's case it was Director Hardin's ashtray. Etta hurled it toward the window, aiming for the spot toward the lower left corner that she'd researched was the best spot for Kristine to hurl her book—the spot near the sill where a window was most likely to shatter if struck. Sure enough, the glass burst. Etta gasped at the sound of the glass shards tumbling over each other on their way to the floor. Then the roar of the rain thundered into the room.

Chapter Twenty-Four

◈

Etta had done more research for *Dissatisfaction* than she did for all of her other romances combined. She'd volunteered at the Ann Arbor Library a few evenings a week so she could understand the day-to-day minutia of her hero, Henry Ross' career. And she'd learned how to do taekwondo and make a martini, two of Henry Ross' other specialties.

She also interviewed Bart Townsend, her friend's brother, a fire fighter-in-training at the Ann Arbor Fire Department to better understand the handsome, but two-timing Morgan Kane, whom Etta named after the law firm where she temped during the day while she worked through the nights writing her first romance novel. Bart had explained what a woman stuck in a raging house fire should do, and Bart's words came to mind as Etta stood at the sill of the director's shattered window, glass crunching beneath her feet, and blinked to try to make out the ground one story below. "Your lady'd be crazy to jump straight out of a high-up window," Bart had said in the macho way Bart said everything.

Etta hadn't entirely believed Bart since he seemed to exaggerate the dangers of everything a woman might want to do, but now the ground did look far away. She squeezed her eyes shut, trying to remember Bart's words. "She should cover any sharp edges sticking out of the sill by draping a towel or blanket across it then throw as much clothing or bedding out the window as she can to soften her landing. Then she's gonna want to lower herself down as far as possible, even just arms length, before letting herself fall to the ground. Then that lady needs to get her ass up off the ground pronto and run away from the building.

Etta set her bag on the floor, unzipped her coat and draped it across the windowsill, folding it over itself until she couldn't feel anything sharp as she padded her hands along it. Then she pulled her wool sweater off, shivering against the icy rain that pelted her arms. She balled it up, leaned over the sill, and dropped it straight down. Etta searched the room for anything else that looked soft. A jacket? A sweater? She tried to pull the cushions from the chairs. They wouldn't budge.

Etta walked back to the window, flung her bag across her shoulder, and stepped onto the window sill. She crouched, squinting against the rain, searching for a ledge or a tree branch to help her to the ground. There was nothing.

Then Etta did exactly what Kristine Richards had done. She inched herself around, clutched onto the window sill, and lowered herself to arms' length. She hung there until her arms ached, praying that a wool sweater would somehow miraculously break a one-hundred-and-ten-pound woman's fall. Then she let go.

Unlike her heroine Kristine Richards, Etta didn't believe in fate. She'd only put it in the plot of *Dissatisfaction*, because she liked the idea that checking out a library book could be the piece of fate that saved a woman from a house fire instead of getting engaged to a handsome fire fighter. While Kristine Richards was saving herself from the fire, fate had it that Morgan Kane was spending his dinner break in bed with Kristine's best friend

Melinda, climaxing at the moment that Kristine let go of the window sill. Fate was a romance writer's best friend.

Etta picked up her head and blinked. She tried not to breathe through her nose. She pushed herself up and flinched as an earthworm crawled out of the decomposing kitchen waste next to her foot. The compost pile stank, but she couldn't have asked for a softer place to land. Fate? Carl had started the compost bin during the summer, collecting the kitchen scraps and garden debris daily and piling them in this bin. Had he done it for her, to give her a safe place to fall? Or to make her realize what it was that she had to do next?

Etta heaved herself over the wall of the bin and lowered herself to the ground. Her sweater was nowhere to be seen, and the idea that she'd been counting on it to break her fall made her nauseous. She clutched the strap of her bag, and started toward the back door to the kitchen. Goose bumps rippled across her arms beneath her long-sleeve T-shirt, and her teeth began to chatter. Either the scent of the compost was lodged in her nose, or she was covered in it.

Etta rapped on the outside door to the kitchen, waited, and then pounded again. Her gaze flitted from the door to the trees behind her. Tears burned at her cheeks, but she kept pounding. What else could she do?

The door cracked then flew open. Etta inhaled. She'd never been so happy to see Candy's fluff of blonde hair under her hair net or the bubbly words on the intern's apron: *Some things are better rich: coffee, chocolate, and men.* Etta opened her mouth to speak then the back of her throat started to close. The flute, the gongs, the synthesizer. New Age music. Carl wasn't there.

The chef's quarters sat between the theater and the kitchen. He had an exterior door, which Etta hadn't known was there until Candy pointed it out. But she'd heard his wind chimes before—a low, haunting sound she'd never placed. She stared at the door, and then wiped at the beads of water rolling down her face, and lifted her hand to knock.

The door swung open before Etta's knuckles touched the wood.

Carl was looking down, zipping up his corduroy jacket. He glanced up and stepped backward. The corners of his mouth turned up then a coldness crossed over his eyes, and he looked past her

"Carl," she whispered, but the clatter of the wind chimes swallowed her voice.

Carl stared past her for what felt like several minutes then stepped back and waved Etta inside. He closed the door behind her, and she melted into the warmth of the room. The walls were painted a rich terra-cotta color and covered with oversize paintings of desert landscapes: saguaros, red canyons, cracked soil, rock formations—all of them lit by track lights. Etta opened her mouth to ask who'd painted them, and then saw the easel set up next to his window, a half-finished desert scene propped against it.

Carl's double bed was covered with a Native American blanket decorated with red and black diamonds. Across from it was a fireplace with a couple of acoustic guitars and a small stringed instrument Etta didn't recognize propped in stands on the hearth

"Need some food?"

Etta snapped her gaze to Carl, stung by the flatness in his voice. "Your room . . ." she whispered. "It's . . ." She'd always pictured Carl as the type to have few possessions—a bed and a desk, a couple of chairs. But his room looked like something out of a magazine. "Beautiful."

"Been out here for awhile. Had a little time to decorate." Carl put his hand on the doorknob. "I hate to end this little show and tell, but I've got to run."

Etta tried to steady her voice. "I need a ride to Jackson."

Carl stared at the door. "You get permission?"

Etta stared at him.

"You know the rules. You need permission from Hardin if you want to leave the grounds. And, here's the thing, in the last five years, Hardin's never given a student permission to leave the grounds."

The tears broke loose, like a cap bursting off of an overheated radiator. Sobs sputtered from somewhere inside her, shuddering through her. "Fine, I'll walk." She stepped toward the door.

Carl blocked the door. "Jackson's thirty-five miles away."

"Excuse me," Etta whispered.

He didn't move. The pressure started to build again.

"If you won't help me, let me go."

Carl put his hand on her shoulder. "What in the devil's gotten into you?"

"Let me go," Etta's words dissolved into tears.

"I can't just leave. I gotta tell Hardin if I'm heading to Jackson. I gotta let Candy know she'll need to make dinner."

"No. No. No." Etta backed up. "Don't tell Hardin I was here," Etta heard how hysterical she sounded, but she couldn't control her voice. Her gaze flitted around the room. There was a door on the far side of the room. She'd seen it from the other side. In the back hallway to the theater, across from the stage-wing door. Etta swirled around and raced toward it, her shoes squeaking against the wood floor.

Carl's hand descended on her shoulder when she was halfway across the room. "Jesus, Etta." He pulled her around and draped his coat over her shoulders. His hands were shaking. "I'll take you."

Etta and Carl didn't speak as Carl pulled the truck out of the garage, eased it along the narrow road, and wound through the trees to the front gate. Carl stopped there, pulled the emergency break, and reached behind the seat. He pulled out a crumpled blue rain parka, opened his door, and swung his long legs out of the truck, holding the parka over his head as he slid off the seat. The windshield wipers slid back and forth, with a swish.

Etta grabbed her bag off the floor, yanked the flap open, and pulled out the file folder: Lowther, Matthew Kenneth. She set it on the seat next to her and tried to stop her hands from trembling. The pages inside the folder were loose and Etta had to rest her hand on them to keep them from catching the blast of air from the heater vent.

The light was low, but Etta registered instantly what was on top: a medical report. *Paranoid Personality Disorder. Extremely aggravated. Obsessed with conspiracy . . .* She started to shake.

"It's stuck."

Etta snapped her gaze to the door. She hadn't even noticed Carl opening it, even though he had to shout over the roar of the rain. "The combination won't work. Happens sometimes when it rains a lot."

Carl stared at her then slammed the door shut again, and pulled the parka over his head. He was a blue blur sprinting back toward the gate.

Etta glanced into her rear view mirror, but couldn't make out anything except streaks of rain. Then she heard something she hadn't said in more than a decade tumbling from her lips. "Our father who art in heaven, hallowed be thy name, thy kingdom come, thy will be done on Earth as it is in Heaven . . ." The words kept coming again and again, even as Carl climbed back into the truck.

He pulled on the emergency break, and the truck eased forward. They turned onto a wider gravel road.

"I've never seen anyone look as scared as you looked back there."

"Is there another vehicle?" Etta asked even though she knew the answer.

Carl glanced at her. "There's the van, of course, and Buchanan owned a 1959 Roadster and a 1963 Edsel truck. Both of them are still parked in a storage barn a ways from the lodge. I don't reckon they're going anywhere though."

The van was a Chevy cargo van parked in the garage next to the truck, kept there only to drive the students to the academy and in the case of an emergency evacuation, since no one left the academy under normal circumstances. Etta could still hear Hardin's voice echoing through the great room during orientation: "This is your year of solitude. Your Walden Pond. Most writers only dream about this kind of isolation."

Now Etta was fleeing the most prestigious writing academy in the United States, not with a certificate or a half-dozen short stories to publish or the beginning of a serious novel as she'd envisioned, but as a fugitive.

"Please drive fast," she whispered.

"I'm going just about as fast as I can go."

The windshield wipers whirred as the truck drifted down the gravel road. Finally they turned onto the highway, gaining speed.

Etta nearly jumped when Carl spoke: "So, you going to tell me what's going on?"

Chapter Twenty-Five

◆

CARL SPOKE AGAIN AFTER A FEW MINUTES. "MY OLD MAN worshipped Townes Van Zandt. Saw him for the first time in 1973 at The Old Quarter in Houston. I didn't see much of him 'til after Townes drank himself to death. I thought Dad was such an asshole back then, but I get it more now, you know, following your dreams, even if your dreams are a wreck of an old musician."

Etta realized that the radio was playing and maybe had been playing for awhile. The sad, crooning voice must be Townes Van Zandt, whoever that was. "Are you following your dreams?" Etta asked, more to fill the silence than anything else.

Carl didn't speak for so long that Etta forgot she'd asked the question. The song ended and another began. "I might've dreamed about sitting this close to you once or twice."

Etta felt the corners of her mouth turning up. She stared out her window.

"Course, you're probably asking if my plan was to live in the middle of nowhere cooking meals for a bunch of pretentious snobs. I've been out here too long to think anyone comes here following anything. We're all just running from things."

Headlights blurred by, lighting the cavity of the truck. The windshield wipers glided back and forth. "Except for Olivia,"

Etta murmured, glancing at the papers from Matthew Lowther's file, surprised to see them scattered across the seat between them. She reached for one of the sheets, but her hand was shaking, and it slipped from her fingers. She inhaled, startled by the sensation of Carl's warm hand covering hers.

"What're you running from now?"

Etta couldn't bring herself to look up.

"Fair enough, I'll go first. My girlfriend died."

Etta jerked her gaze up, meeting his for a minute until he stared out the windshield again. "Don't go feeling sorry for me. We'd been broken up for a good six or seven years. She was even married to someone else—a middle-school teacher from Tulsa. They lived in Austin, and I'd moved up to Portland by then. Just opened my dream restaurant serving up Southwestern French fusion in the Alphabet District, if you can imagine anything more awful. I was working sixteen hour days, obsessing over the amount of time between courses, tearing into servers if they were three minutes behind schedule delivering a salad." He laughed. "Had an actual breakdown once when a server crumbled a cork into a one-hundred-and-fifty-dollar bottle of Pinot.

"I hadn't talked to Brooke in years. Then I woke up one morning, got the worst call of my life, and she's all I could think of. I went over every word that woman ever said to me. To this day, I wonder if that's what seeing a ghost is. Not some apparition in the doorway, just not being able to forget someone, living with them every second of every day. It's the worst kind of agony."

Carl shifted the hand that was resting on top of Etta's. "So how did you end up here?" Etta whispered.

"You know that short story Isabella Peña's so hell-fire incensed about: 'The Garden of my Summer.' That was Brooke's story. She wrote her master's thesis on it. She was the type who couldn't read a damn thing to herself. I swear, she read that story aloud so many times, I wanted to burn her *Norton's Anthology*. By the time we broke up, I could've recited that story in my sleep.

"And this day comes when I know I'm never going to give enough of a shit about my restaurant to make it go, never goin' to get all worked up about whether some rich guy has to wait a minute too long between a round of escargot chilé and a salad, never going to shed tears if a sea bass is too underdone or a filet comes out looking like charcoal. I see this job in the paper and come out here for an interview, thinking it might be nice to get out of the city for awhile. I walk the grounds to get a sense of the place and end up in that old cemetery. Damned if I don't recognize it from that story. It was May. Everything was overgrown. The rhododendrons were blooming.

"I know it sounds crazy, but I just knew Brooke was trying to tell me something. She was good at that. Giving advice."

Silence filled the truck, except for the voice of the radio deejay, so soft that Etta couldn't make out his words. Etta shut her eyes and thought of the cemetery, the sunken graves and mossy headstones, and the overgrown path. "We need to go back."

Carl fixed his gaze on her. "We're just a couple miles out of Jackson."

Etta glanced out her side mirror. A blur of yellow lights trailed behind them. "I need to go to that cemetery. I need to find Galen. " Silence settled between them, and Etta wondered if Carl had heard her. "You know, Galen . . . "

"Yeah, I know. Why on Earth would you want to talk to him?"

Etta stared at the seat between them. "If I told you something terrible is going on, that Hardin and Opal Waters and Major Mills and possibly Jordan Waterhouse are in on it. That people have disappeared. Would you think I was crazy?"

Carl started to laugh, and then the sound died in the air. "You're serious?"

"Olivia . . ."

"Christ. Please tell me this isn't about Olivia."

Etta clutched the door handle to stop her hand from trembling.

"Listen, I was the one who drove her to the hospital in Salem that night, and that girl wasn't right. She was shrieking, kicking, yelling, crying. I've never seen anything like it. She scratched Hardin's arm so bad it was bleeding. They had to sedate her just to get her in the truck."

"Who? Who sedated her?"

"Mills. He's trained as a medic."

Etta gasped. "Is she still there? In Salem?"

Carl lifted his hand from hers and it started to shake. "I reckon her family would've moved her somewhere closer to home. Where's she from?"

Etta rifled through her bag and pulled out her cell phone. Its bluish light lit up the truck, making it seem darker outside. Her pulse raced when she saw the two bars indicating service. She found Olivia's number in her list of contacts and dialed. It rang five times and died. Etta dialed again then stared at her phone. What was Olivia's aunt's name? Didn't she live in Syracuse? Or Rochester? Etta turned to Carl. "Where did you send her stuff?"

Carl reached for the gear shift. The truck was decelerating. "Hardin had me take it in a storage unit in Jackson. Said her family was planning to have it shipped."

"I have to talk to Galen. Please turn around."

"Jesus, you want to go hunting for a certified insane man in a cemetery in a storm. You really think I'm going to let you do that?"

The truck decelerated more. They passed a wooden sign lit from beneath by a spot light. *Welcome to Jackson, Population 4300.* Then they passed a gas station and a store and a couple of empty lots, deserted under the dim street lights.

"Fine," Carl whispered.

Etta snapped her gaze to him.

"I'll take you to talk to Galen, but only because he's a hell of a lot closer than you think. Robert North convinced me to give him a ride to a cheap motel on the other side of town two nights ago. I don't see as how talking to someone as twisted as Galen is going to do you any good, but I'll take you. On one condition."

Etta wiped at her tears, anticipation and panic jumping to the back of her throat.

"Don't even think about leaving my sight when we're with that crazy asshole."

"Word of advice?" Carl pulled to a stop in the parking lot for the Jackson Motor Motel, a two-story L-shaped building. A few dim bulbs lit up some doors on the second floor, and a vacancy light glowed red above the washed out wooden sign. His face was submerged in shadows, but Etta could just make out his motions. He took off his cowboy hat, set it on the seat between them, and ran his hand through his hair. "Don't mention his father." Carl opened his door, the sound of the rain thundering inside. The dome light illuminated his tall frame as he slid off the seat.

Carl's door slammed shut and darkness washed over the truck again. Carl was the last one who'd seen Olivia, Etta realized. Olivia had sat exactly where Etta was on the last night anyone had seen her. A shiver swept up Etta's spine.

Her door creaked opened. The sound of the rain and Carl's face next to hers filled her senses. He reached for her arm. She let him take it, her feet finding the ground. The rain was icy on her face. They climbed a rickety iron staircase. Carl stopped in front of room two-o-eight, one of the doors lit by a bare light bulb. The flickering blue light of a television eased from the sliver between the drawn curtains.

Etta winced as her knuckles struck the cold metal door.

She knocked again, harder.

The door flew open, and Etta reeled backward. She recognized him. She'd been peering at his face for months. It hung in every corridor of the lodge, in the library, in Hardin's office. "You look just like him," Etta whispered, even though he looked less like his father every second, because the images were still, and Galen's face never stopped moving. His lips moved even when he wasn't speaking—pursing, smacking together. His pale face was grooved with creases, his black hair streaked with white.

"What are you selling? Girl Scout cookies, sex? I got no use for either one." Etta's gaze went to the hole where Galen's two bottom teeth should be.

Galen's gaze shot to Carl, and recognition washed over his face. When he looked at Etta again, the intensity of his gaze made her hands shake. "Bobby told me I had about as much chance of seeing you as a man has of dying of a shark bite in Kansas. Fancy metaphors for such a waste of a man. Doesn't give a damn if a friend gets murdered, but cries like a little girl if one of his piece-of-shit poems gets a bad review. What layer of hell do you suppose the devil reserves for fucks like him?"

"Mind watching your tongue?" Carl's voice was low.

"It's okay," Etta said. Was Galen talking about Robert North?

Carl stepped closer to Galen and glared at him

"How do you know who I am?" Etta asked.

"If you don't mind, I was locked inside a building for three decades. I can't stand being outside anymore." Galen jerked away from the door and shuffled into the room.

Etta took a step forward to follow him, but Carl grabbed her arm. "I don't think this is a good idea," he growled.

Etta gave him her most pleading look, and he dropped his hand. The smell of the cigarette smoke hit her first then the heat. Sweat beaded on her forehead. There were piles of paper stacked everywhere—on the floor and table, the TV, which was on, but without sound. Its flickering light was the only light in the room, except for one of the bedside lamps, which illuminated the floral-print wallpaper and the stacks of paper splayed across the bed. "I thought you lived in the forest."

Galen set his black eyes on her for a moment then laughed—a hacking raspy sound. "Do you think I'm Rumpelstiltskin?"

"No. I . . . How do you know who I am?"

Galen paced. He was thin and wiry, and his body seemed to jump when he moved. "Bobby told me some girl was asking questions. Figured it was the same girl Matt's girl talked about. I looked for you." Galen stopped pacing, his skin shining blue in the TV light. His face became still for a single second then his lips started to move again. "I was afraid you'd end up where she is. Where I was." He brought his hand up and ran his finger along a scar from his chin halfway up the side of his cheek. "They diagnose you, so no one ever listens to you again. Who's going to believe someone in an asylum? It's as good as killing you. Better. Nobody's gonna turn up a body."

He moved to the bed, leaned over, and sorted through a stack of papers, his hands jerking. A soft grunting seemed to come from somewhere deep in his throat. Then he stepped toward Etta.

Carl stepped in front of her. "Don't lay a hand on her."

Galen extended a crumpled piece of paper toward Etta. She reached past Carl's outstretched arm to take it.

A nine line stanza and a six line stanza. A sonnet. Etta's gaze dropped to the bottom of the page where the initials M.L. were neatly scrawled. She jerked her head up to meet Galen's blinking gaze. "Was going to leave it with that." She followed his gaze to her thumb, to Olivia's tourmaline ring. She'd slipped it on after she'd found it on her porch and had all but forgotten it. "Thought about trying to roll it up and stick it in there, hoping you'd find it, but the rain never stops pissing down around here, does it? Don't know what the Jap-lover thought was so holy about that place. Being out there was worse than being strapped down with white coats cramming pills down my throat. Course the Jap-lover had his whore geishas to entertain him."

Etta looked from the poem to Galen. "Is the Jap-lover your father? Vincent Buchanan?"

Immediately, she regretted the question.

Chapter Twenty-Six

◆

WHEN GALEN GOT ANGRY, HE MOVED MORE THAN USUAL, NOT just the twitching and blinking and shaking, but jerking and pacing, his hands flailing out to his sides. His speech dissolved into mumbling. One of his eyes watered, a steady trickle down his cheek that glimmered when he turned toward the TV. And for several minutes "white coats" and "Jap-lover" were the only words Etta could decipher.

Carl stood with his arms crossed over his chest glaring at Galen. Occasionally he shot Etta a look, which she supposed was meant to convey a message—either *I told you not to bring up his father* or *Let's get the hell out of here*. It didn't matter. Etta wasn't planning on taking either suggestion.

As Galen's nonsensical mumbling gave way to teeth gnashing, Etta stepped toward the brass lamp on the wall next to the bed. She squinted at the paper, blinking to make out the typewritten words in the sporadic television flickers and read aloud:

> *Winter comes to the garden of dead dreams*
> *Rain puddles on yesterday's lives decayed*
> *Wilts azaleas once lovingly displayed*

Turns decay to life with relentless streams
Washes away September's pale sunbeams
Winter clouds above and memories fade
Moss coats barren bark in the season's shade
Here, truth is more enshrouded than it seems.

I have searched the deserted forest floor
Have hunted secrets sleeping with the souls
Have sought out stories about peace and war
and pondered the men who once dug these holes

The garden of his summer you must score
The truth is there behind her marking stone

M.L. November 2, 1985

The room was silent except for a low wheezing whir that seemed to come from somewhere deep in Galen's throat, like he was struggling to push air in and out of his lungs.

"Matthew Lowther was a poet?" Etta said the words aloud mostly to distract herself from the sound of Galen's breath.

"He was a genius. Renaissance man. Martyr." Galen rubbed at his face, his pale fingers trembling so badly that Etta looked away. "The Jap-lover . . ." he mumbled.

"You sick pervert," Carl cut him off. Etta spun around.

Carl had moved from her side to a particle-board writing desk, which looked as though it was about to collapse under the piles of paper stacked atop it, some of them bundled in rubber bands, their yellowed pages curling up. Etta moved toward him. He held a faded photograph. Even in the shadows, Etta knew the face instantly: the dark eyes and olive skin, the flushed cheeks. The little girl staring back at her was perhaps three or four, but Olivia's features had hardly changed at all. "Was this his?" Etta spun around. "Was it Matthew Lowther's?"

Galen paced. "I found Matt's little girl. He talked about her all the time. They thought I was doped up and semi-consciousness in their asylum, but I found her, all grown up. Got her into their snooty little academy. Found Bobby too. The only thing that kept me going all those years was dreaming of the frigid geisha's face when Bobby swaggered through those doors.

"I should've known Bobby wouldn't do Matt justice. All that hair dye seeping into his brain." Galen laughed. He stopped pacing next to the bed, his face lit in the lamp light. "Tell me, your dad ever cheat on your mother?" His face was still for a minute then one eye pinched shut as though a gnat had flown into it, and his lips started to move again.

Wallace Fox left the house at seven thirty each morning after a bowl of rolled oats with a teaspoon of brown sugar and eight ounces of orange juice. At noon he ate a turkey sandwich with a slice of tomato and one sprig of iceberg lettuce, and then prayed for the remainder of his lunch hour. His leisure reading material consisted of exactly one book: *The New Order Translation of the New Testament*, which he read every evening between nine thirty and ten, at which point he turned off his light and inserted his ear plugs. Etta couldn't imagine Wallace Fox breaking from his routine to have sex with anyone, even her mother. But her mind went to Lewellyn, the organ player at church, who always waddled to her father's side after service. And the students who waited in the straight-backed chairs in his secretary's office, waiting to consult with her father about biblical passages or position papers or vexing moral quandaries. Nausea churned through Etta's stomach at the thought of her father sleeping with any of them, which, she realized, had been exactly Galen's intention.

She dropped her gaze to the piece of paper, and read the poem again, trying to make sense of it. The garden of his summer. Truth. Truth? The play. Hans staggering through the forest. "Something's buried in the cemetery?"

Galen's hands trembled and his pace quickened as he walked toward the TV and back again. "Matt wasn't a poet. Only reason he'd write a sonnet was for Bobby. The prima donna was obsessed with them. Thought he was going to be the next Petrarch. Matt left it in Bobby's desk. Probably hoped if something happened to him, the worthless sack of bones would read it and go find the manuscript he'd been working on. Too bad Bobby doesn't give a shit about anyone but himself. Didn't even show anyone the poem till I tracked him down last summer."

Etta gasped. "Maybe I have it." She lunged to her bag and tugged on the straps. "His manuscript. Maybe he didn't bury it in the cemetery." She thrust the dissertation toward Galen. "It's about your father."

Galen seized the book and heaved it into the wall. It plunked to the shag carpet.

"Don't call that useless Jap-lover my father. He kept his Jap geisha and her half-wit son down the road dressed in silk and pearls. My mother died of desolation, of abandonment, and he sent me to rot in a head case house while his geisha's little boy ran that store."

Galen stepped in front of Etta, his eyes flashing blue in the television's reflection. She inhaled the scent of him—acrid, stale, and sour—but forced herself not to break his gaze.

Galen jerked his chin toward the dissertation. "You think a man gets killed because of a pedantic piece of academic shit like that? So what. The famous writer had a Jap geisha whore on the side. He took up with a frigid poet half his age. He had affairs with a half-dozen other slut Lolitas. One of them thought people gave a shit and did a series of interviews with the *New Yorker* just before the Jap-lover died, tried to expose America's beloved patriot as a letch. Guess what? People worshiped him more. He liked his liquor in large quantities and snorted lines of blow so he could stay awake through the night pounding away at his Remington, storming at anyone who knocked on his door—even his six-year-old son. No one gives a shit. Americans want their luminaries blemished and raw, deranged and narcotized. Makes 'em more intriguing."

Galen stepped closer to Etta. His breath grazed her hair. "Whatever's buried in that cemetery will bring down the Jap-lover and his precious academy, and the henchmen and frigid geisha bitch who hijacked his royalties by convincing him to send me to putrefy in an asylum. It's not some soap opera sob-story about a half-orphaned kid making friends with a Jap girl who ruined my mother's life. It's something they're dead serious about keeping in the ground."

Carl lunged between Etta and Galen, his dark gaze lancing Etta's. All of the hairs on Etta's body stood up at once. Panic surged through her. Carl had worked for Hardin for years. He'd always been willing to fill in as needed, to do whatever Hardin asked. He's the one who walked the grounds searching for Galen. He's the one who got rid of Olivia. What had made Etta think she could trust him? She took a step backward. Her calves struck the edge of the mattress.

Then the world went black, and she was on the ground, her elbow grinding into the carpet, Carl's weight crushed against her. Then he edged off her, and she felt a cold dampness swirling with the heat and heard the sound of rain roaring into the room. Had the door blown open?

A voice sliced through Etta's ears like a knife blade. It was unmistakable.

The major.

Uriah Winston Mills' thin, wiry shadow darted in front of the TV. Then the world went black again. Etta forced her eyes open and saw a flash of metal. Major Mills' outstretched arm moved in a slow arc from side to side in front of the TV, the outline of the handgun juxtaposed against the talk show. Behind it a smiling host leaned forward in her chair gesturing at her panel of guests. Tonight's topic was uplifting if their smiles were any indication. The camera panned the audience—a hundred smiling faces.

Major Mills aimed the gun at Galen. "Hello old friend. So this is where you've been." His voice was friendly, like he'd run into an acquaintance in the grocery store. He took several strides and held the gun only an inch from Galen's chest. "Should I finally do you the favor?" His tone sounded warm for a man shoving the end of a pistol into another man's flesh.

Carl moved again, squatting in front of Etta, blocking her view of anything except his broad shoulders and her own knees. Galen wheezed. A pounding seemed to come from the floorboards, except it was coming from Etta's own chest.

"That would be too kind. Honestly, I thought you'd do the job for us by now. All those attempts at the hospital." Major Mills snorted. "'Leave it to my fuck-up kid,' your father said. 'Can't even get it done after five tries.'"

Galen's breath grew more labored.

"Course, even your old man was wrong a few times. He thought Dos Passos was better than Hemingway." The major laughed. "Worse, he liked Shakespeare's comedies better than his tragedies. Didn't appreciate *Hamlet* like you and me, Galen." His voice became louder, as though he was facing Etta and Carl now. "The bard understood the ecstasy of watching life surge from a woman's flesh—Ophelia, Juliet, Desdemona, Portia, Cordelia. He loved to send innocent young women to violent deaths, to watch them suffer. Staged his plays with sheep entrails, lungs, hearts, and livers. Even strapped human corpses from the arbors. Now there was a man after my own heart."

Carl's weight pressed into Etta's shins and then he shot up and lunged forward. "Don't lay a hand on her," Etta thought he said, but his voice sounded garbled and far away. For what felt like hours, Etta hunched, paralyzed, watching the hulking figures above her. Then she realized that Carl was giving her an opportunity—to move, to get away. She crumpled the poem, shoved it into her coat pocket, and twisted around, inching toward the end of the bed. Her bag was lying on the floor several feet in front of her. If she could make it there, she could . . .

"Would you like a shower in your boyfriend's gray matter?"

Etta froze. The major's voice still had the same breezy quality, but his tone was patronizing, like he was talking to a naughty child. Etta's body began to pulse, to vibrate.

"Stand up."

She didn't move.

"Stand," the major barked again. "Or I'll treat you to a show of carnage the mobs at the Globe Theater would have salivated over. It's a shame they didn't have firearms back then. Imagine the dramatic effect. Scarlet explosions raining across the London stage."

Etta pushed herself up, surprised she was able to stand on her trembling legs. She turned slowly. Then a high-pitched sound burst from her throat, which seemed to surprise the major as much as it did Etta. Carl and the major were inches from her. Etta could smell the onions on the major's breath. The gun was jammed into Carl's jaw.

"Just like they teach you in SERE training: threatening to execute a prisoner's loved one gets better results than threatening to kill the prisoner himself. And they say humans aren't altruistic."

Chapter Twenty-Seven

◆

Etta and Carl followed the major's orders. They left Galen in the shadows of his sweltering room, and moved down the walkway single file. The staircase rattled beneath their weight. The rain had given way to mist, and at the bottom of the stairs, Etta raised her face into the spray of moisture. Swirls of clouds blotted out the stars. She trudged through the puddles toward the black Ford Taurus parked sideways next to the truck. She opened the back door on the driver side, as the major instructed, ducked her head, and eased herself inside.

"We've got lakes smaller 'an this in Texas," she heard Carl say as she pulled the door shut. Darkness descended over her and a calmness washed through her. It was like leaning back in the dentist's chair. There was nothing she could do about anything now. Everything was out of her hands. She almost felt like she was floating. Did Matthew Lowther feel so at peace near the end?

The driver-side door buzzed, bathing Etta in the dome light. Then Carl climbed into the driver seat in front of her. "Etta, listen, the story, that story."

The passenger door swung open and Carl's voice died in the whirring buzz. Carl's panic was palpable, but sound itself seemed to dance away from Etta. Listen. The word was weird. Hissing. She wanted to feel it on her tongue. The major climbed into the passenger seat, again jamming the gun into Carl's temple. Then the major slammed his door. Blackness enveloped the interior of the car again.

"Take forty-eight west," the major barked.

Carl slid his seat back, slamming it into Etta's knees. She winced.

The car hummed to life. It rocked through the parking lot, over pot holes, through puddles. The glowing red vacancy sign was blurry through the condensation on the windows. The blinker clicked and they turned right onto the two-lane highway. Back toward the lodge?

The major laughed. Etta blinked, trying to make his shadow out of the darkness. He'd lowered the gun from Carl's temple. Had he spun around in his seat? Was he staring at her? A shiver crept through her. "I wrote your final scene that day you came with all of your curious questions. Tell me what you think. There's a clearing past the swimming hole, a grove of cedars, where the light slants through the branches in the morning like spotlights on a stage. That's where the secret lovers die, naked, twisted in each other's arms. The audience stumbles upon them, a student first, perhaps Morinsky. Then the others. They shudder. They stare, in that way you must when something is both gruesome and beautiful. Didn't the careless lovers know that there are wild carnivores in the woods? Lions who strike without warning, tearing into that bundle of nerves at the base of the neck, stripping the flesh from human bones?

"One second, the lovers themselves are animals. Moans and growls escape their lips. Then they are prey, and their screams slice the autumn air. Blood pools across their pale flesh into the crisp red leaves beneath them. Ecstasy and death entwined. Art. The French call the orgasm 'La petite mort,' the little death. The Bard, too, equated the act of orgasm to the moment of death.

"It will be my most impressive scene yet." The major laughed again, a thin, wiry sound. "The last one was just as masterfully plotted. But disappearances are anticlimactic. The county sheriff ambled up to the lodge seven months later and asked a couple of bored questions. Then nothing. Two decades of silence. His classmates were comatose. Never underestimate the apathy of the young."

Etta's legs, jammed against Carl's seat, were going numb.

"Then you walk into my office and I hear his name again for the first time in twenty years. And as you sniffle and quiver in the doorway, your last scene forms in my mind. So I set it into action. I plant the dissertation for your pathetic friend Morinsky to find, thinking then that it might be him who breathed his last breaths tangled in your arms. It's better this way. Perishing in the arms of the hired help."

The car jerked, and Etta brought her hand up to clutch the seat in front of her. The major must have sensed her movement. He swung the gun around and aimed it at her. Etta's torso began to pulse. Finally the major slipped the gun into his lap again. His voice was taunting: "Do you think Shakespeare's characters ever surprised him? Mine never do. Morinsky brought that dissertation right to you, didn't he? You two led me right to Galen's door." The major cackled.

"If you were so hell-bent on finding Galen, why'd you leave him there?" Carl drawled.

The major's gaze left Etta, and a knot of tension released from her spine. "I keep my eye on that boy for my own entertainment more than anything else. Talk about a living catastrophe. He's tried every felo-de-se except a pistol—razor blades, poison, pills, carbon monoxide. The boy roped a noose up in his closet, but all he did was bruise his elbow when the pole crashed to the floorboards. If he's too big a coward to use a gun, I'm sure as hell not going to stand in as his courage." The major laughed again. "Next time I want to bask in his self-destructive decline, he'll be right there in that putrid room failing at everything he tries. I don't waste my time with characters like him or that crybaby daughter of Lowther's. I don't need to turn their lives into tragedies. They've done it all on their own."

A sound escaped from Etta's throat, something between a gasp and a scream. The car seemed to be accelerating. Rapidly.

Etta's pulse thudded in her wrists. She grasped for the seat in front of her, her gaze flying to the front windshield. The yellow line blurred in the headlights.

Matthew Lowther's name brought her attention back to the major. "Shakespeare would have appreciated my dramatic choices. Sending an egomaniac to a nameless grave. A loud mouthed know-it-all buried alive, with no one in fifty miles to hear his complaints. I'd do some revisions if I were to undertake the project today, of course . . ."

"Carl," Etta choked. She leaned forward, trying to get a glimpse of the speedometer. The major spun around, jerking the gun up again.

"Get down." Carl's voice echoed through the car. "Now. Etta. On the floor. Now."

Etta hurled herself to the floor, tucking herself between the seats. Her knees smashed to her chest, her cheek ground against the carpet. A sharp chemically smell filled all of her senses. Then the world began to spin. Around and around.

She thought she heard the major yelling although she couldn't focus on his words. All she could hear was the words that were slipping from her lips: "Our Father, Who art in heaven, Hallowed be Thy Name. Thy Kingdom come. Thy Will be done, on earth as it is in Heaven . . ."

Etta's eardrums burned. Pain shot through her temples. Then her phone rang, a shrill high-pitched ring tone that Etta didn't remember picking. It went on and on, whiney and whirring. Whoever was calling must be in terrible trouble, Etta thought.

Then she realized that it wasn't her phone at all, but her eardrums that were ringing, aching and pulsing. The ringing was accompanied by a low hiss, like a slow leak from a tire. Then the smell of sulfur hit her, and she remembered. The major. Carl. The car. Spinning and spinning and spinning.

The car was no longer moving, Etta realized. Everything was still.

Etta's body was coiled up, tingling from head to toe, pains shooting through her shins. She wrenched her chest up, squeezing her shoulders between the leather covering the two seats. The strap of her bag sliced into her shoulder.

She blinked, staring up. The car was awash in the dome light, and someone had strewn silver glitter through the air. It shimmered and danced in the light. Etta blinked again, though, and it wasn't glitter at all, but a fine white dust.

Oversized trash bags billowed from the dash. Not trash bags. Airbags. That's when it struck Etta that the front car doors were wide open. Carl and the major were gone.

A hand clutched Etta's shoulder and the warmth of someone's breath raced across her neck. She yanked her body around, pain tearing through her back and neck as she tried to kick away from the person, propelling herself across the backseat. Her feet struck something hard.

Carl's face was framed in the door frame. Relief washed through Etta, but only for a moment. Then it occurred to her that his mouth was opening and closing. He was speaking. And Etta couldn't hear a word. Crimson gushed across his cheek. Blood, Etta realized. A lot of it. She squeezed her eyes shut. "You're hurt." Either the words didn't come out or she just couldn't hear them.

Carl reached for her arm and pulled her from the car. She stumbled along beside him. Then he tightened his grip on her hand and broke into a run. Her bag slammed into her hip. She glanced over her shoulder at the car. But all she glimpsed was the giant tree trunks rising up in circles of white light. She snapped her gaze back to the front, blinking at the wall of blackness in front of them.

Carl's grip tightened again, and Etta's fingers felt as though they might crumble. Her body hurt everywhere—her knees, her back, her head.

Then Etta remembered standing with Carl in the library, his shadow long against the window. He wore running shoes. It felt like a lifetime ago.

Are you a runner?

Only if something's chasing me, Carl had replied

Etta glanced behind them. Everywhere she looked, there was darkness. And then her body remembered how to run, her lungs filling with the chill of air, her brain rushing with familiar waves of endorphins.

They ran for what felt like hours, but might have been fifteen minutes. Etta realized two things: Carl was in good shape, and he knew where they were going. They were on a road; Etta recognized the sensation of gravel crunching beneath the soles of her running shoes. Occasionally she stepped in a puddle, water seeping into her shoe.

The ringing hiss buzzed on and on, and the exhaustion that had eased around the corners of her mind over the past few weeks threatened to overtake her.

Then a glimmer appeared in the darkness, a light. Carl seemed to be steering them toward it, leaving the road they were on and turning onto another one. A tiny cottage rose out of the darkness, its porch light a luminous window into the night. The house was blue and yellow. A row of garden lights lined a narrow stone walkway.

Carl slowed his pace from a sprint to a jog, pushed the gate open, and climbed onto the porch, still clutching Etta's hand.

The door swung open. A tall brunette with flushed skin stood framed in the doorway. An overweight tuxedo-colored cat spilled out of her arms. The woman's lips spread into a wide smile as she reached up and unlatched the screen door. Then her face fell, and she dropped the cat to the floor, clutching Carl's arm, peering at his face. Etta followed the woman's gaze to Carl's face. Dizziness seized her. The world flashed red. Carl's hair and collar were soaked with blood.

The woman pulled Carl inside, leaving Etta on the porch. The screen door flipped back and forth. The cat stared at her with round eyes. The woman led Carl into the blue bathroom. She helped him sit on the edge of the bathtub and then rushed around the house grabbing things. Then she went in the bathroom and closed the door behind her.

The house burst with color. Etta could see into every room, all of them painted a different soft shade—lemon, peach, sage, sky blue, and lavender. Her eyes were drawn to the lit fireplace in the living room. A painting hung above it. Reds and oranges. A desertscape. One of Carl's.

Something made Etta turn her gaze back to the cat. He was still staring at her, cocking his head, his mouth open. Was he meowing? "I can't hear you," Etta whispered.

Then terror gripped her. Like breath rippling across her flesh, Etta was sure she'd heard the major's cackling laugh weaving through the darkness behind her. She grabbed for the screen door, pushed her way inside, and slammed the door shut behind her, fumbling to engage the old brass lock. Her chest heaved as she leaned on the door, alone except for the fat black-and-white cat, who didn't seem pleased to see her.

Chapter Twenty-Eight

◆

IT TOOK AWHILE FOR THE ROOM TO COME INTO FOCUS—THE hand stitched quilt and floor-to-ceiling bookcase, the easel in the corner lurking like a leggy insect in the shadows. Light crept in under the curtains, the flush of early dawn. Slowly it all came back to Etta: the woman named Violet, with the dewy face and brunette hair streaked with gray. She'd scrawled her name for Etta in swirling cursive, made her chamomile tea, and drawn a hot bath for her. She'd peered inside Etta's ears with a flashlight and dripped some herbal oil in them, and then rubbed circles on Etta's temples with her finger tips. Etta was dressed in Violet's clothes, cotton that smelled as though it had been dried in the sun, even though the sun hadn't shone for weeks.

She rubbed her eyes, pulled her damp hair into a ponytail then released it, letting her damp curls tumble across her shoulders. She switched the lamp on next to her bed, blinking into the circle of light. She moved her arm and an ache shot through her chest and biceps. Images of the night before flooded to her: Galen's face seizing up on one side, the major jerking the gun from his lap.

Etta cleared her throat and started at the guttural sound of her vocal cords constricting.

"I can hear," she said aloud. Tears burned at the corners of her eyes when she heard her voice.

"You're awake." A creak echoed through the house. Etta slid down, wiping the tears from her cheeks.

Heat swelled into her chest.

"I saw your light." Carl stepped into the doorway and then crossed the room, a lumbering shadow in the low light, and sat on the edge of the bed. Etta pushed herself up and winced at the soreness in her muscles. Carl pushed a piece of her hair behind one of her ears. "Are you okay?" His voice was a whisper.

Etta looked down.

"Damn it, I should have told you to cover your ears. Airbags are damn loud." Carl dropped his hand, but Etta could feel him staring at her. Finally she looked up. His shirt was freshly-laundered. *Portland Culinary Academy Open Chef's Night.* The bandage taped to his cheek was stained with old blood.

"It's just a cut. Mills looks worse, trust me." Carl touched the bandage and flinched. "They used to think airbags could replace seat belts, you know, but if you're in the front seat without a belt on, you'll just fly right over the damn bag, right through the windshield. When I realized we'd be heading toward Violet's . . ."

Etta squeezed her eyes shut. "Is he alive?"

"He was bleeding pretty bad."

Carl adjusted his weight and his hand brushed Etta's. A prickle raced through Etta's body. She crossed her arms in front of her, and stared at the light easing its way through the cotton curtains. "What about the gun?"

"It was dark. The undergrowth was thick."

"What if he followed us . . ."

Carl shook his head. "He didn't."

Etta could tell there was something more Carl wanted to say, but they sat there for a long time, both of them staring at the bed. "You still have that poem Galen gave you?"

Etta stiffened.

"All I could think of on that ride last night was that poem." Carl looked at the door "Member how I told you my girlfriend Brooke wrote her thesis on 'The Garden of My Summer?'"

Etta nodded.

"She was right, wasn't she? It's about grief."

Etta wasn't sure what to say. She vaguely remembered reading "The Garden of My Summer" in high school, but remembered nothing about it.

"Guess I didn't think much of her thesis. Brooke thought everything was about grief. Her aunt and uncle owned a morgue up in the Hill Country. So she spent her summers watching funerals while the rest of us watched *Dukes of Hazards*. Let's just say, she was more occupied with the dark things in life than most. We'd go out for dinner with friends, and she'd start talking about all the dismal, macabre things people spend their whole lives trying to avoid thinking about. I'd shift in my seat while the other couple's faces went white. Brooke didn't even notice. I think she was amused that other people carried around too much baggage about death.

"Her theory was compelling enough. She thought the main character, Payne Morris, wasn't planting a garden at all, but was building a sepulcher for his lover, that everything in the story, including the name Payne, was a symbol for loss. She thought it was autobiographical, that Buchanan must have lost someone close to him around the time he wrote it. She originally thought it must be about his wife, except the story was published before Winona passed. Brooke wanted to do some biographical research to find out.

"Our advisor Phillip Bullock, or as Brooke called him Full of Bull Shit, was a devotee of New Criticism, studied under John Crowe Ransom himself at Kenyon College. So, of course, he insisted that consideration of a text had to be independent of biographical or historical context. He demanded Brooke revise her theory."

"You studied literature?" Etta's voice was sharper than she expected it to be. "You said our advisor. You have a Master's degree in literature?" Etta cringed at how accusing her voice sounded. It was a graduate degree, not a prison record. But why had Carl never mentioned his knowledge of different literary schools of criticism, not to mention Brooke herself, or Violet, who apparently had piles of Carl's clean T-shirts in her drawers next to her herbal oils?

Carl lowered his voice. "Not exactly. Brooke could go from polar to red hot in under a minute. She thought Bullock was a world-class idiot, and she refused to stay in his department. Of course, I couldn't stay either, which was just fine with me. It turns out not too many people pursue a graduate degree in literature because they like to read. Most of 'em just like to scrutinize the written word to ashes."

Etta stared at him and tried to make sense of his words. Not about him, not about Brooke. But about what he was really saying, about the story. Grief. Death. Blood started to course through Etta's neck and face. "He wrote it for Sakura," she whispered.

Carl didn't hear her. He kept talking, but all Etta could hear was Galen's words. *He kept his Jap geisha and her half-wit son down the road dressed in silk and pearls.* She blinked. Sakura Tanaka must have come back to the United States, like in 'Cherry Blossom.' But she stayed. Did she and Buchanan have a child together? Etta tried to swing her legs over the side of the bed. They smacked against Carl. He jumped up to move out of her way.

Etta stood up and recoiled at the iciness of the air on her arms. She swirled around, searching for her bag and clothes, for the jacket of Carl's that she'd been wearing. She shuffled into the living room.

Sunlight slanted through the muslin curtains. Carl's jacket hung on the coat tree next to the door. Etta staggered to it and groped at the pocket. She seized the crumpled paper and stared at the last two lines: *It's winter in the garden of his summer. And I left truth behind her marking stone.*

Carl stood in the middle of the room. His jeans were creased down the middle of each leg, as freshly laundered as his tee-shirt. "You told me Vincent Buchanan was buried in that cemetery."

Carl stared at her.

"Why'd you say that? He was buried in Portland."

Carl shrugged. "I don't honestly remember saying that."

"Tell me about "The Garden of My Summer." Etta crouched down, grabbing her shoes from next to the coat tree. "Everything. Everything you remember."

"What are you doing?"

Her shoes were a little damp, but someone had washed them. Etta pushed them on over the rag wool socks that Violet had lent her the night before and yanked the laces tight, rolling up the cuff of the wide-legged pants. She glanced up at Carl. "This sepulcher Payne Moore was building for his lover, what did it look like?"

Carl cocked his head. "Rhododendrons," he finally said. "Payne obsessed over the smell of them, had dreams about them. Cinnamon and nutmeg—that was the smell."

"What else?" Etta stood.

"Where are you going?"

"What do rhododendrons look like?" She'd never paid much attention to plants.

Carl gazed at her. "They're all over out here, like plumbago in Texas. Listen, what I was going to say is that I've got to call the sheriff. Report the accident. You need to explain why Mills might have come after you with a gun."

Etta grabbed Carl's coat off the hook and pulled it on, zipping it to her chin. It was still damp. She reached for the brass lock, jerking back when the fat tuxedo cat came out of nowhere, jumped up on the door and stretched its tufty paws up to the doorknob. "Go away, kitty," Etta said, surprised by how sharp her voice sounded. She reached down and tried to push the cat away.

The floorboards creaked behind her, and she sensed that Carl was standing only inches from her. She pushed herself between the cat and the door, wincing at the yowl the cat let out. She twisted the lock and pulled the door open. A blast of cold air cascaded across her cheeks.

"Jesus Christ, you can't just leave. I'm coming with you."

Etta pushed through the screen door and spun around when she was on the other side. The first thing she saw was Carl's bare feet then the silhouette of Violet standing in the doorway of her bedroom, her long bare legs, the pile of thick hair atop her head. "Carl?" The tall woman strode to Carl and wrapped her arm around him, her hand settling on his hip.

Etta blinked back tears and jogged down the two porch steps. She made her way across the stone pathway to the fence, which was made of stripped willow branches. She focused on the gravel road in front of her. Douglas Firs loomed up on each side of it. A few branches were strewn across the road.

Etta halted where Violet's road met a wider dirt road and looked both ways. Which way was the lodge? One thing was sure and her certainty of it stole her breath for a minute—it was near enough that Carl could slip away late in the night to knock on Violet's door.

The sun was low in the sky when Etta approached the clearing. Sunlight filtered through the cedar grove, slender beams plunging into the thick rug of moss, ferns, and ivy carpeting the forest floor. Etta dropped to a crouch, rolled up Violet's wide-legged pants, and tried to catch her breath. Something rustled near her. Her gaze went to a patch of mushrooms sprouting from the bark of a downed cedar. A grey squirrel stared back at her then darted into the brush.

Etta winced against the pangs in her hamstrings and quadriceps. She dragged herself across the clearing, climbed the three steps, and rapped on the door. Her heart thumped against her rib cage.

She knocked again.

Was it Sunday? Etta wasn't sure of anything. She glanced across the clearing. Then she sensed something behind her—a noise, a motion?—and spun around.

"Poppy," she called out, unsure how loud the name came out or whether it came out at all. A woodpecker hammered its beak into a tree trunk. The sound echoed across the clearing. Etta's gaze shot to the doorknob, as the door creaked open a slit. Poppy appeared, blinking, the corners of her eyes heavy with sleep.

"Please get dressed. You've got to come with me. I'll explain on the way."

Poppy stared at her. Her head fell to one side, and her ponytail flipped from one side of her face to the other. It was all Etta could do not to grab her friend's shoulders and shake her. She slid past Poppy into the dim cabin, and blinked, trying to adjust her eyes to the light, pulling the door shut behind her. "We've got to go to the cemetery. Can you identify a rhododendron? Please hurry. Please get dressed."

"I'm a charlatan."

Etta jumped. The voice was deep and familiar. "Reed?"

Reed rose from behind Poppy's bed, clutching Poppy's pink comforter around his chest and torso. His glasses sat crooked on his face.

"Reed?" Etta whispered again. She stepped backward. "Oh god, were you . . ."

"I'm so sorry."

Etta gazed at him then raised an eyebrow at Poppy. Poppy stared at the floor.

Reed pushed his glasses up and sat down on the edge of the bed, clutching the comforter at his collar bone. Lines creased his forehead. Etta glimpsed his khaki pants crumpled next to his foot and what might have been boxer shorts. She looked away. "Please tell me you're not hurt," Reed whispered.

Etta blinked. "Hurt? No, of course not. Just surprised."

Poppy's laugh interrupted Etta. "Did you sleep in the free box at a thrift store?"

Etta glanced down at Carl's corduroy coat, which came almost to her knees, Violet's purple pants were rolled up to her shins, and the wool socks were mostly saturated with mud.

"You look . . ." Poppy didn't finish the sentence, but Etta could tell by her pursed lips that it wasn't going to be a compliment. Then Poppy's face changed. "There were two men at your cabin last night."

"We watched them with Reed's infrared binoculars." She nodded toward a pair of camouflage binoculars propped on the windowsill.

Reed's face grew long. "They were plain-clothed FBI."

Etta gasped. "How do you know that?"

"They weren't wearing FBI jackets."

"But how do you know they were FBI?"

"They had forty-caliber Glock semiautomatics. Standard FBI issue firearms."

Etta's mouth fell open and then panic convulsed through her. She reached for the wall. "I've got to go."

"Wait. I'll get dressed."

Etta snapped her gaze to Poppy. "No. You might be in danger." An ache radiated through Etta's arms, surged into her chest, and for a moment, she wondered if something terrible was happening, except then a surge of energy followed, pulsing through her. She stepped toward the door then whipped around. "What does a rhododendron look like?"

Poppy narrowed her eyes. "Don't they have rhodies in Michigan?"

Etta shrugged.

"Well, there are over a thousand species in the genus."

"Do any of them smell like nutmeg and cinnamon?"

Poppy stared at her for a long time then shrugged. "Only rhodies with white or pale flowers are fragrant."

"Okay. So I should look for pale flowers?"

Poppy's thin eyebrows came together. "Sure. In April or May—when they're blooming."

Etta's heart raced.

Poppy moved toward her bookshelf, which was crammed with horticulture tomes. "It could be fragrantissimum. It's the most common fragrant variety. I've never thought it smelled like nutmeg and cinnamon, but I suppose. The flowers are large." Poppy held up her hands to indicate the size of the flowers. "Mother planted them. She loves smelly things. The bush itself is rather uninspiring, kind of straggly." Poppy's gaze lifted to the ceiling. "This time of year, they'll still be green, with dark, sort of hairy leaves. Fragrantissimum is sparse. A lot of gardeners use it for trellises and walls."

"Yes," Etta whispered. "For walls. That's it." She spun around, grasped for the doorknob, and hurled herself outside, bringing her hand to her eyes to block the sunlight. She propelled her aching legs forward one step at a time.

Chapter Twenty-Nine

◆

Etta Would have assumed that nobody else had visited the cemetery for decades—even a century—if she hadn't known that Galen and Carl had both been there in the past month. Within a couple of steps, ivy, ferns, and shrubs tangled around her feet. The paths had long given way to foliage, which was now gnawing away at the graves themselves. She halted, blinking at the beams of sunlight that eased through the gaps in the canopy.

A fallen Douglas fir lay decomposing over a family plot in front of her. A wooden grave jutting from the remains said *Baby Mary* in rudimentary carved letters. Etta knelt and cleared the vines from a granite face in front of her. Moss had filled the hand-carved letters, making most of them unreadable. She traced her fingers along them, making out only *Sarah, wife of* and the year 1843.

Etta sat down on Sarah's headstone. Her chest ached with each inhale. Everywhere she looked were dark green leaves—coiling, climbing, and tangling. She might have sat for a long while mesmerized by them, watching the way the breeze made them dance, as though they were teasing her.

The voices brought her attention back to the forest's chatter—the low groan of the trees, the birds and squirrels scuttling through the branches, and Reed and Poppy arguing.

"She's okay," Poppy said.

"Betrayed persons often experience post-traumatic-like stress symptoms."

"What are you talking about?" Poppy let out a high-pitched laugh. "You seriously think she's in love with you?"

Etta stiffened. Reed either didn't respond or his response was smothered by the sound of the bird warbling far above.

"She's not in love with you . . ." Poppy struggled to speak through her laughter. "She's in love with Carl," Her voice echoed through the cemetery.

Etta cringed and pushed herself to her feet, spinning around to face the gate. Poppy straightened her lime green jacket and glanced up then caught sight of Etta and jumped backward. Poppy's buggy eyes swept back and forth across the cemetery. "This place is spooky."

Etta followed Poppy's gaze. A beam of sunlight fell on a crude statuette of an angel. Its wings were eroded, half of its face eaten away by lichen. Reed stepped to Poppy's side. "Is Galen here?" he whispered.

Etta's pulse swelled into her temples at the thought of Galen—his nervous tick, his stammer, the crack of the dissertation striking the wall, the gun against Carl's jaw, the explosion of the airbags, the car spinning around and around. She tried to focus her eyes on something, anything. The jungle of plants seemed to have multiplied in just the last minute. "We'll never find it."

"Where's the garden?" Poppy asked.

Etta stared at her.

"Fragrantissimum doesn't grow wild." She wrinkled her forehead and glanced around.

"No. Vincent Buchanan would have planted it. The year he wrote "The Garden of My Summer," which was . . ." Etta looked at Reed.

"1967," he said.

Poppy's eyes grew wide. "Well, I guess some rhodies do have a long life expectancy. The species that grow wild here are Pacific Rhododendron, or macrophyllum." She pointed to a thick shrub on the other side of the gate. "That's one. With the spotted leaves. They bloom bright pink in the spring. Fragrantissimum looks different . . ." Poppy moved forward, weaving around brambles and headstones, picking her way through the undergrowth, pausing occasionally to touch a leaf, to lean over and examine a plant, her ponytail swinging behind her. Etta and Reed followed. They walked for awhile, stepping around graves and trees, meandering through the undergrowth. It quickly started to feel like a labyrinth with no end.

Had Matthew Lowther walked this path thirty years before, looked for the same plant? They halted in front of an iron fence. It was smaller than the fence they'd entered through, but everything else looked the same. Poppy bit her lip and turned in a circle.

"They look like monsters." Reed pointed to some deciduous trees a few feet away from them. They'd already lost their leaves, but thick moss clung to their claw-like limbs, dangling like fringe. Ferns sprouted from their mossy bark.

"They're Big Leaf Maples." Poppy stepped toward the trees, "Oh my gosh. Look." She weaved through the cluster of maples, ducking under the moss hanging from the low branches. Etta and Reed followed.

Poppy moved toward another tree. It stood alone in a clearing—skeletal, a tangle of barren branches twisting from a gnarled trunk.

"Sakura," Poppy whispered. Etta snapped her eyes to Poppy's, but Poppy just stood gazing at the tree. "It's a sakura."

Etta pushed down a wave of dizziness. "I don't understand."

"Sakura means cherry blossom in Japan. They're kind of like Japan's official tree. They grow over three hundred species of them. I'd guess this one's a weeping variety." Poppy stepped back and looked around. "Cherry trees require a lot of sun. Someone probably cleared the area to plant it, which might be why that cluster of Big Leaf Maples grew. They like land that's been cleared, like clear-cut areas."

"Someone planted it?" Etta whispered.

"The cherry tree, I mean. No one would have intentionally planted Big Leaf Maples in a cemetery. The roots destroy whatever they come into contact with—patios, foundations, sidewalks. Gravestones, coffins."

Etta tried to push away the image of coffins being ripped apart by twisting roots. "When was it planted?"

Poppy squinted at the cherry tree then brought her hand up and touched the bark. "It's lost some limbs and the bark's cracking. It's near the end of its life. Some cherry trees don't live long at all – fifteen to twenty years. Others live nearly a century."

"They symbolize death." Etta jumped at the sound of Reed's voice. He stepped toward her. His glasses were sliding down his nose. "That's why the Japanese celebrate them. They represent the transience of life. The blossoms burst into brilliance and die only days later at the pinnacle of their splendor. Just like soldiers. During World War II, they painted them on the side of their kamikaze planes."

Poppy stepped toward the maples. "If they started growing shortly after the cherry tree was planted . . . They don't look full grown. But they can live for three hundred years or so, so I guess that doesn't say much."

Etta thrust her fingers into her pocket and grabbed at the crumpled paper, trying to steady her hands enough to smooth it out. The paper was worn and disintegrating at the corners, but the typewritten words were still legible. She tried to find words to explain where it had come from, and then gave up and read it aloud:

Winter comes to the garden of dead dreams
Rain puddles on yesterday's lives decayed
Wilts azaleas once lovingly displayed
Turns decay to life with relentless streams

Washes away September's pale sunbeams
    Winter clouds above and memories fade
Moss coats barren bark in the season's shade
    Here, truth is more enshrouded than it seems.

I have searched the deserted forest floor
    Have hunted secrets sleeping with the souls
Have sought out stories about peace and war
    and pondered the men who once dug these holes

The garden of his summer you must score
    The truth lurks there behind her marking stone

M.L. November 2, 1985

Poppy gasped. "We're not looking for the fragrantissum. We're looking for the snow azalea."

"No. It's got to be a rhododendron," Etta snapped.

"Azaleas are rhododendrons. And this one is popular in Japanese gardens. Plus, it has a strong scent—like cloves." Poppy spun in a circle then she was on the move, picking her way through the brush. "Rhodies like shade," she called. Etta hurried to follow, but her shin collided with a granite gravestone buried beneath the undergrowth. She hunched over to grab her leg. She limped to catch up to Poppy, moving to her side, clenching her teeth.

Poppy grinned as she stared at a woody bush that towered over her and Etta. She plucked off one of the oval leaves and rolled it around in her fingers. "It's a snow azalea." Then her grin faded. "Now why are we looking for it?"

Before Etta could comprehend the next sound, Reed's voice echoed into her head. "Get down." He was pushing Poppy to the ground, his hands flying over his head.

Etta spun around and blinked. It took a moment for the figure to come into focus—the silken braid across the shoulder, the fitted leather jacket, the skin-tight leggings, the gun pointed at Etta. "I told you to go home." Opal's voice was taunting.

Edwin Hardin stepped up beside Opal Waters, his flesh more waxen than usual, his eyes sunken.

"Of course, I didn't realize you weren't welcome there. It turns out heretics who defile the Holy Testament by churning out soft core porn aren't welcomed back into the folds of fundamentalism with ice cream socials. How much self-loathing does it require to create an entirely fictitious identity for yourself, Loretta? And I thought you weren't creative."

Etta's mouth fell open.

"Yes, your mother does like to chat, doesn't she? Especially about you."

Etta tried to force in a breath. She brought her hand up and grasped at her neck.

"You thought you were the only one who could play sleuth?" Opal's gray eyes moved back and forth. "What exactly do you think you're going to find here? It's all ashes and dust. Nothing more."

Etta felt something crawling up her shin. She stiffened and jerked her head down, ready to shake whatever it was from her leg. Poppy was yanking on her pant leg, her buggy eyes bulging.

Opal laughed. "I suppose we should give you credit. You've surpassed at least a dozen worthless idiots who call themselves Buchanan scholars. Of course, academic research is laughable. The morons are so taken by a shift in narrative style in an author's fourth work, so intent on establishing whether he fits into Modernism or Post-Modernism that they somehow miss that he wasn't who everyone thought he was." Opal cackled, and this time it sounded so loud and out of control that Etta's body seized. "Not bad, Loretta. But the proof is all that matters. Without that nobody is going to believe a washed up romance writer with nothing but a pile of badly-written trash to her name, depending on what name she decides to use that day, of course. The thing about lying—once you make it into a habit, no one believes anything you say."

"Loretta's books are rather titillating, but badly written?" Petra Atwell's raspy voice echoed into the clearing. "No offense,

Opal, but I imagine most people would choose them over your maudlin verse. Besides, one might think that a vamp who trades sex for a job and uses it to steal an old man's estate might be less priggish about such matters."

Etta blinked. The rifle the memoirist gripped in both hands dwarfed her small frame, and her hair glowed in the beam of sunlight glinting through the trees.

"I didn't realize we were having an Annie Oakley look-alike contest." Opal's voice was ice-cold.

"Annie Oakley shot a twenty-two." Reed, who was standing now, scrutinized Petra's gun through his crooked glasses. "Ms. Atwell's is a thirty ought six."

"Very good," Petra rasped. "What's Opal's carrying? A cap gun?"

Reed squinted at Opal. "It looks like a forty-five."

Etta jerked her gaze to Poppy, who was tugging at her pant leg again. Violet's pants were so loose Etta feared they might slip off her hips if Poppy kept it up. Poppy was mouthing something.

"Now, let's think," Petra said. "Why would Opal be pointing a forty-five at Loretta? And why would Edwin be standing there like the wench's hapless sidekick? Go ahead, Edwin, tell me. Don't worry about surprising me. Naïveté has never been my virtue."

Hardin's gaze shifted from Petra to Opal.

"Don't tempt me by being coy." Petra took a step closer to Opal and Hardin.

"Ignore her," Opal snapped. "Firing that gun would throw her halfway across this cemetery."

Etta didn't register what was happening until Petra's upper body jolted backward. At the same moment, the blast roared, and Etta hands reflexively flailed up to her ears. She snapped her gaze to Hardin. Both he and Opal stood blinking, staring at the undergrowth between them. Petra clicked the rifle's bolt action into place.

"Tell me, Edwin, what brings us here?" Petra asked. "Did Loretta inquire about how a huckster book salesman who's never published as much as a short story became director of a prestigious writing academy? Or maybe I should ask Opal." Petra turned her glare and the gun on Opal. "Did she suggest that a woman who cons an old man out of his estate, or has an affair with a student half her age, might be morally bankrupt? We all might be wanting for a bit of drama out here, but can't we solve our differences like adults? Forgive each other over some nips of Vince's Balvenie 191?"

"She's right. No one needs to get hurt." Hardin took a step forward, his eyes flitting from Reed and Etta to Opal. "Why don't both of you put the weapons down." His voice cracked.

"Edwin," Opal barked. Her handgun was still aimed at Etta's chest.

Petra twisted her head, her gaze meeting Etta's for a minute before darting back to Opal. Etta's legs began to tremble. In that second, Petra had looked nearly as terrified as she was. "Your own reputation is the only thing you would murder for, and everyone knows you seduced Vincent and swindled him into naming you his beneficiary, so you wouldn't be flinging that dainty little pistol around over that. Please say this isn't about that preppy Waterhouse boy. Sleeping with him may get you on the editorial board of his dad's magazine. Who am I kidding, you'll probably own *The Drinking Gourd* before you're finished. But tell me you wouldn't kill someone over that half wit. What? What is it, Edwin?"

Etta tried to swallow. Lines were growing blurry, the ground becoming less firm. Opal Waters was the only other person in the world—her gray eyes, the pistol clutched in her slender white fingers. Etta struggled to inhale.

Poppy's voice brought everything back into focus, the words vaulting into the silence. They were familiar, although it took Etta a few moments to place them.

Then for the first time, she heard the wind in the trees, a low whooshing, and the leaves clinking together like wind chimes. The putrid smell of the autumn forest wafted to her—damp fir and cedar needles, fallen leaves, and decay.

And she heard her own voice repeating Poppy: "It is impermanence that gives the monotony of breathing its radiance."

Chapter Thirty

◈

Etta dropped to her knees beside Poppy and thrust her hand into the undergrowth. Her hand struck something solid and slimy. She yanked at the ground, uprooted a sapling, and tore at a fern. Her heart stopped then came hammering back into her chest. When she glanced up, she was surprised to see Poppy still beside her, sitting back on her heels. She helped Etta hold the brush away from the polished granite. It said only the words Poppy had just spoken aloud: *It is impermanence that gives the monotony of breathing its radiance.*

A plaque? An unmarked grave? Etta ran her fingers over the words, and other words flooded to her. *Your friendship was like the sun on my face at the end of a long, cold winter.* Etta stared into Poppy's blue eyes. "Is Sakura buried here?"

Etta winced. The feel of the icy metal against her skull was unmistakable. Then Opal's voice was just behind her, above her. "Where's the manuscript?"

Manuscript? The word sent electricity zinging up Etta's spine.

"I don't know," Etta whispered.

"Don't entice me, Opal. Remove the gun from Loretta's neck, or I'll blow your sidekick's groin into mincemeat then I'll shoot you. I'd be doing the literary world a favor, extinguishing one of its minxes while she's just sashaying past her prime." Petra cackled. "Not the jeune fille of a Lucretia Davidson or Sylvia Plath, I suppose, but still with a few years of potential left."

A whimper pierced the air. Hardin choked out a plea for Opal to drop the gun.

Then silence. A gust of wind set off a tumble of leaves, and a bird let out a chick-a-dee-dee-dee in the trees. Etta's pulse writhed through her chest. Then as quickly as it appeared, the steel barrel was no longer pressed into the base of her skull, and she fell forward, gasping for breath.

"Reed. Take the gun." Petra barked.

"Don't even think about it," Opal retorted.

Etta glanced over her shoulder, and pain shot through her neck and back. She froze. Poppy was crawling headfirst into the rhododendron bush.

"What are you doing?" Etta hissed.

Poppy jerked, and her ponytail snagged on a branch. She wrenched her arm around to untangle it. "I see something," she mouthed.

"Opal." Hardin's voice was tight as though through gritted teeth.

"Stop whining," Opal said. "She won't shoot you. She's not even that crazy."

"Funny, that's exactly what my father told his campaign manager. Those exact words," Petra laughed again. "Except in his case, he didn't think I was 'even that crazy' enough to ruin my own father's career. He doesn't make assumptions about my sanity anymore."

"Please . . ." Hardin's voice trailed off. Etta realized Petra probably wasn't merely aiming the gun at Hardin; the barrel was almost certainly jammed into his flesh.

"When they give me what they came here for, this will all be settled," Opal said.

Hardin let out another groan, so guttural that Etta squeezed her eyes shut. What was Petra doing to him?

"I'll shoot him. I'll revel in it. Give Reed the gun."

"Please." Hardin moaned.

"No." Opal's voice was staccato. "They'll close us down. They'll take everything."

The gun roared. Etta's hands shot up to her ears. She squeezed her eyes shut. Flashes of white light sparked against her eye lids. When she dropped her hands from her ears, it was so silent that she was sure she'd descended back into the tinny muffled world of deafness again. Then Hardin's voice rang out: "Please . . ." It dissolved. "We don't know . . ."

"Yes we do." Opal cut him off. "You think they let the Rosenbergs go back to their freelance work? Did they slap Alger Hiss on the wrist and tell him to hurry back to his peace work with the Carnegie endowment?"

Etta tried to follow Opal's strange, high-pitched verbiage and make sense of what she was saying.

Then coldness descended over Etta. The Rosenbergs. Alger Hiss. The were spies. Traitors. She remembered Galen's snarl: *It's something they're dead serious about keeping in the ground.*

What had Opal just said? *They somehow miss that he wasn't who everyone thought he was.*

The realization felt like a tornado churning through her. She thought of the photo in the library book of the Black Dragon Society meeting, the American ex-patriot named Peter Morrison. There was no Peter Morrison. It was Vincent Buchanan.

Vincent Buchanan had ties to Japan's notorious ultranationalist secret societies. Vincent Buchanan spied for the Japanese.

Matthew Lowther was at the Buchanan Academy to out America's greatest patriot as a traitor. Etta braced herself against the wave of dizziness that surged through her.

The snow azalea shook. Etta craned her head and let all of the air out of her lungs when she saw Poppy, her cheeks flushed, her eyes glistening, slithering beneath the branches with only one hand on the ground. She clenched something to her chest with the other. Etta stretched forward. Poppy dropped the object on the ground and pushed it forward with her free hand, prodding it until it was within Etta's reach.

Was it a tool box? Etta dragged the object from beneath the bush. The rusted tin box certainly looked like a tool box, except it was smaller than most toolboxes. A tackle box perhaps? Too fancy. A floral pattern had once decorated the sides, although now the red, green, and white design was barely visible beneath the dirt and rust. The hinged lid was ornately molded with a small oval handle on the top, entirely corroded by rust. Etta lifted the box. It felt weightless.

"It's like a little room in there." Poppy whispered. "This was by itself in the clearing, half-buried"

Etta gasped and nearly lost her grip on the box. Were Sakura's ashes inside? No. It was too light. Then again, how heavy were ashes?

"Give it to me," Opal said. "And I won't tell anyone you spent a half-decade penning housewife smut."

Petra let out a gravelly laugh. "Reed. Take the gun."

Behind her, Opal let out an angry sigh. Etta twisted her head to shoot a glance at her. But she could only see Reed. He was trembling so much that for a moment Etta didn't see the pistol clutched in his pale hands. She followed the barrel of the gun to Opal. The poet's face was frozen, her arms folded across her chest. A few feet behind her, the director was pale and shaking, Petra's rifle still jammed into his crotch.

"It won't open," Poppy said, tugging at the latch on the box.

"Don't just stand there, Edwin. Take the box from them. Get the fucking manuscript," Opal shrieked.

"Manuscript?" Petra readjusted the rifle. Hardin responded with a groan. "What in hell kind of manuscript is Opal risking your testicles for?"

The latch was corroded with rust, and it wasn't budging. Poppy found a stick, and jammed it between the latch and the box, jimmying the fastening up.

Poppy pried the lid open with a crackling pop. "It's empty. There's nothing here." Poppy tipped the box so everyone could see the empty rusted tin box.

"Then where is it?" Opal's voice was shrill. "Where's the fucking manuscript?"

"What manuscript? I don't know what you're talking about." Etta made her way around a crumbling headstone and pushed the box toward Opal. The poet didn't reach for it. She just stared at Etta with her icy gray gaze.

Petra let the rifle drop from the director's groin and moved toward Etta.

"How'd you know to come?" Etta asked.

"I hadn't seen Vincent's fucked up kid for almost thirty years," Petra said. "Then he comes knocking on my door at midnight." Galen must have driven Carl's truck to the lodge after Etta and Carl left with the major.

"I need the truck." Etta stared into Petra's dark eyes. "I'll call the police in Jackson."

Petra glanced at Hardin and Opal before she released a manicured hand from the rifle and thrust it into the pocket of her fitted wool pantsuit. She produced the Texas-shaped key ring Etta had seen clutched in Carl's hand so many times. Carl must have slipped the key to Galen the night before when the major wasn't looking. Etta reached for it and folded it into her palm. "You sent two men to my cabin. They're not FBI agents, are they?"

Petra laughed. "They work at the Highlander, a dive in Jackson. They make a decent Tangueray and tonic for a backwater. Let's just say, the boys owed me a favor."

Etta didn't even want to ask Petra whose Glocks "the boys" were armed with. She smiled at the memoirist and began picking through the undergrowth.

Etta halted when she finally spotted the gate and glimpsed the sunlight glinting across the windshield of the truck just beyond it. The effect of the light as it rippled across the glass made it look as though someone was sitting in the driver's seat. But

Etta blinked, and no one was there. The faint scent of gasoline hung in the air with the damp fir needles.

Etta glanced over her shoulder. Everywhere she looked, plants ate away at the past. She dropped her gaze to the rusted box gripped in her left hand. Galen was wrong: Matthew Lowther hadn't left a manuscript buried in the cemetery for Robert North to find. He'd left his roommate something else—a box, an empty tin box.

Etta pulled over outside of Jackson at the first spot where her phone indicated cellular reception, dialed 911, and gave the operator directions to the cemetery. Her next stop was a Shell Station off Interstate Five in Salem, where she bought a bag of pretzels, a chicken-salad sandwich, a frosted snack cake, and a map of Portland. She sat in the truck and devoured most of the convenience-store sustenance, and then watched cars pull up to the gas pumps as she dialed the phone.

She first talked to a reference assistant at the main branch of the Multnomah County Library, who put her on hold for several minutes then transferred her to a brusque reference librarian. He explained that while someone might ordinarily be able to glance at some old city directories for Etta, the reference desk was understaffed on Sunday afternoons. He suggested that Etta try the research library at the Oregon Historical Society. The Oregon Historical Society library was closed on Sunday afternoon, but the baritone voice on the answering system announced that the Society's museum was open. Etta dialed the number.

The volunteer who answered the phone at the Oregon Historical Society museum sounded close to ninety. She asked Etta to repeat her question three times. Each time, she responded with a long murmur. Etta was about to thank her and hang up, and then the woman exclaimed that she had a dear friend named Peggy, who was a volunteer docent at the Oregon Nikkei Legacy

Center. Peggy led tours through the Japanese American Historical Plaza, and the volunteer was sure Peggy would be thrilled to talk to Etta about "the Japanese."

Etta wasn't so sure, but she dialed Peggy's number. Peggy had a chirpy British accent. She called Etta "lovey" and she did seem excited at the opportunity to talk about Portland's Japantown.

Peggy suggested Etta park at Union Station. "It's a short walk," she chirped. "And be sure to visit the Chinese Gardens while you're in the neighborhood. It's splendid, just splendid, especially in the rain."

The next morning Etta pulled into a parking spot in front of Union Station and glanced up at the clock tower. It was nearly ten. It was only six blocks from Union Station to the corner of Northwest Fourth and Davis, but Etta would have been soaked by the time she reached the edge of the parking lot if it wasn't for her new black umbrella. She'd found the Gap Outlet store at the Woodburn Outlet Mall between Salem and Portland. The sales clerks glared at Etta as she trudged around the store in Carl's coat, Violet's muddy socks, and her filthy running shoes, but it had been worth it.

She'd stood in the motel shower for more than an hour the night before, and this morning she'd pulled on a brand new pair of black slacks, a button-down shirt, and a black rain coat. Then she cleaned out her courier bag and transferred everything to the black shoulder bag she'd grabbed from beside the Gap counter. Etta had hardly recognized herself in the bathroom mirror. She'd lost at least fifteen pounds and her hair was longer than it had been in years, curling below her shoulders.

As the light changed on Irving, Etta clutched the strap of her bag and the plastic bag she'd carefully wrapped the tin box in, and continued on, stopping only once under an awning to pull the rusted box out, open the lid, and glance inside at the label. It was faded and hard to read. Etta wasn't sure if it was an old label or a stamp, but the type was still clearly legible: Tanaka Grocery. Selling Asian goods since 1917.

Portland's Chinatown was surprisingly deserted for a Monday morning. According to Peggy, Portland's Japantown, Nihonmachi, once stood here. But it all but disappeared in the spring of 1942 when the Japanese on the West Coast were rounded up and moved to ten different internment camps in the interior of the country. "Gila, Granada, Heart Mountain, Jerome, Manzanar, Minidoka, Poston, Rohwer, Topaz, and Tule Lake," Peggy had listed off the camps from memory.

"Tanaka Grocery?" Peggy put the phone down while she went to find a tourist map the Nissei Center had reconstructed of Nihonmachi in the twenties. When she was back on the line, her voice even more chirpy than it had been before. "Oh yes. Four hundred NW Third. It's called Eastern Imports now. It's near the garden. The tourists love their cheap imports, you know?"

"Is there any possibility that the same family still owns it?"

"It's unlikely. After the exclusion order, the Nikkei were forced to sell their homes and businesses in only a week. Some sold to white friends, sympathizers, people they trusted, hoping they could get their property back someday. I suppose it's possible the Tanaka family did something like this and resumed ownership when they returned home." Peggy was silent for a few moments. "The owner of Eastern Imports is active at the Nikkei Center. I'm sure of it. I just don't recall his name. The brain doesn't work as well at my age. I could look it up for you. I have a list of donors somewhere. It might take me awhile to find it though."

Etta told Peggy that wouldn't be necessary, mostly because she needed to get on the road if she were going to make it to Portland before dark and find a hotel. Peggy told Etta about the reparations given to the internees in 1988 and about the Japanese American Historical Plaza built on the banks of the Columbia River in 1990. But Etta's mind wandered.

Katashi Tanaka had left Portland long before the Exclusion Order of 1942. He'd taken his family back to Kyoto in 1929 and had never returned as far as Etta knew. But one Tanaka definitely had returned to the United States at some point. Etta closed her eyes and tried to remember exactly what Galen had said: *That*

Jap-Lover sent me to rot in a head case house while his geisha's boy ran that store. Vincent Buchanan and Sakura must have had a son.

Chapter Thirty-One

◈

THE FADED EMBOSSMENT ON THE GLASS DOOR WAS THE SAME logo as on the inside on the tin box. *Tanaka Grocery. Selling Asian goods since 1917.* She collapsed the umbrella and reached for the brass door handle.

Bells jangled overhead. A sea of paper lanterns swayed from the ceiling. A wooden table in front of the door overflowed with ceramic tea sets, dishes, and brightly-painted enamel jars with red sale tags attached to them. The bells clanged again, and Etta realized she'd let the door handle slip between her fingers.

She moved toward the long counter that ran along one wall of the store. A sign behind it read Chinese Green Tea by the ounce in block letters. Bronze canisters filled the two glass shelves beneath the sign, each of them labeled with Chinese characters. The counter was bare except for an old cash register.

A girl's face rose from behind the counter, and Etta stepped backward. The girl was young—eighteen at the most. She had dark eyes, high cheekbones, and streaky blond hair. Her cheeks sparkled with pink glitter. She stared at Etta then plucked the white headphones from her ears, unleashing the faint bass of hip hop music.

"Hi." Etta's cheeks filled with heat. "Do you work here?"

The girl rolled her eye, her blue mascara-coated lashes flicking up and down. "No. I just like it back here."

Etta forced a smile. "Is the owner here?" She held her breath.

The girl studied Etta for a moment then reached down and switched her music player off. Black polish chipped off the tips of her fingernails. "Shit. Are you the new accountant? Please don't tell Dad what I said. If he finds out I was listening to my music, he'll take it away, and it's deadly here without it." She pushed a piece of hair off her face. "Are you starting today?"

Etta stared at her for a minute then nodded, hoping the girl would continue.

"Please don't tell him. Will you?"

Etta watched the girl's eyes.

"I mean, he complains about Ojiisan making him work here, and he does the same thing to me. It's, like, a human rights violation. "

Ojiisan. It sounded Japanese. A rush of heat raced up Etta's spine. "Ojiisan?" she said aloud.

The girl rolled her eyes again. "Are they making you come to the party? I don't know why Mom insists on throwing another one for him. She's incapable of listening to anyone. He wants us to celebrate on New Year's, that's the Japanese way, but Mom ignores him every year. Sorry they're making you come. It's a family business, they're always saying. That's probably what drove Rachel out in the first place. The whole forced family thing's a little creepy, kind of like the mafia, don't you think?"

"Rachel?"

"The last victim. I mean accountant."

Etta laughed. "Ojiisan. That's your grandfather's name?"

The girl looked at Etta as though it was the stupidest thing she'd ever heard. Etta tried to smile. "I mean, can you remind me again, what's his name?"

Every movement the girl made exuded boredom, from the downward turn of her lips to the way she mindlessly chewed on the tips of her fingernails to her blue lashes clumping lazily up and down. "It's the same as dad's. Joseph Thompson."

Etta's fingers went numb. She'd been so sure the girl would say Buchanan that she couldn't speak. She glanced behind her, not knowing what to do next. "Do you think it would be possible for me to talk to him? Or to your father. It's really important that I speak with one of them. Right now."

The girl blinked at Etta. Etta wrapped her fingers around the tin box. Tears welled near the surface of her eyes, pulsing with a knot of tension at the base of her spine. She tried to push both down. The girl shrugged and nodded toward a curtain at the back of the store next to a display of Chinese silk pajamas. She inserted one headphone back in an ear. "Oji's back there, as usual."

Etta forced a smile and pulled the tin box toward her chest. She tried to propel herself toward the curtain despite a wave of dizziness.

"Hey," the girl called. Etta stopped. "Shout. He's like totally deaf."

The old man sat craned over a table reading a newspaper. Steam rose from a teacup next to him, glistening into the beams of the track lighting. Boxes were stacked all around him, teetering next to dusty rice paper floor lamps, teak chairs and tables, stacks of prayer cushions and tatami mats, and a table scattered with porcelain dolls. The newspaper crackled and Etta snapped her gaze to the old man. She gasped and stepped backward. He was peering at her, his shriveled hands folded atop the newspaper.

Etta took a step toward him and introduced herself.

The old man stared back at her vacantly. She repeated herself, louder this time. Her voice shook. He just gazed back at her and panic knotted through her chest. She was sure he'd heard her this time, but still he said nothing.

Etta pulled the tin box from the plastic bag, walked to the table, and dropped it in front of the old man. She leaned her umbrella against the chair adjacent to him and jammed her trembling hands into her pockets.

He stared at the tin box then reached for it. He turned it over in his hands and opened the lid. Rust flakes scattered across his newspaper. He looked up at Etta. His face was jowly, his white hair thinning and slicked back, his mouth and flat nose strangely puckered. Grooves laced out from his black eyes. "Where are the letters?" he whispered, meeting Etta's gaze.

"You knew Matthew Lowther." Etta's voice echoed into the room.

The old man dropped the box. He leaned forward, pressed his hands onto the table, and pushed himself up. His chair fell backward and thwacked the floor.

The hair on Etta's arms prickled. She'd seen something in his eyes. She was sure of it.

"Who are you?" The old man's voice was deep and nasal.

"You knew him? Matthew Lowther?" Etta couldn't stop the tears now. They burned down her face. At first the sound of the words tumbling from her lips startled her. She hadn't realized she was going to tell him everything, but she couldn't stop herself. She told him about the Buchanan Academy, the play, Olivia's disappearance, reading "Cherry Blossom," Galen's insistence that Matthew Lowther had left some kind of manuscript. Her voice got louder as she talked and took on a frenetic quality that she hardly recognized. "This is it. This is all he left." She picked up the tin box and thrust it toward the old man. "Maybe it's a clue. Maybe he was trying to tell his roommate where he left the manuscript. That's all I can think of. Maybe it's here?" She let the words trail off. The old man's dark gaze did not move from her face. He was just a stranger again, an old man with a crooked back and frightened eyes. But there was that moment. She was sure he'd recognized Matthew Lowther's name.

"Go away. Leave me alone." Joseph Thompson shuffled away from her, weaving around the tangle of tables and boxes.

Etta followed. Before she could reach him, the old man exited through a door, which clapped shut behind him. A lock engaged. Etta halted in the middle of the room next to a tall wooden mask with a crack down the middle, which leaned against a stack of boxes.

A heater clicked on. Rain pattered against the windows. A buzzing coursed through Etta. She wiped at her tears with the back of her hand then wove around the boxes and pounded on the door. "Mr. Thompson, please." She didn't even know where it went. Maybe he was outside, in another building. She couldn't control the sobs. Her voice sounded high-pitched, hysterical. "Matthew Lowther was murdered. My best friend disappeared. They're trying to kill me. They'll find you. They'll find your family." She collapsed into the door and thought she heard movement behind it, but it didn't open. "You have to talk to me."

Energy surged through Etta. She clenched her fists and pounded on the door again. "I know who your father was. I know Vincent Buchanan spied for the Japanese. I know he was a traitor."

The door swung open. He was in a closet. A bare light bulb swung over his head, and inches behind him a wall safe stood open. He was clutching a box in both hands. "You don't know anything."

Etta's entire body pulsed, the blood surging through it in waves. She could wrest it from his hands. He was an old man. How hard would it be? He looked frailer standing than he had when he was sitting, gravity dragging his spine down. But something about his face, the way it had sunken in on itself, the way his body curled toward the floor, made Etta step backward. "That's it?" Her voice was a whisper.

"My uncle Katashi always said, 'Let what is past flow downstream.' You do not follow this advice either, I see." The old man walked past her and shuffled toward the table. Etta followed. He sat and set the box on the table. He poured water in his teacup, his hand trembling then took a drink and licked at his thin lips. Etta sat across from him. "Tell me, why would a brave family live in shame?" he asked. He hardly opened his mouth when he talked, and his words came out with a slight lisp.

He gazed at her as though he was waiting for her to answer his question. Silence settled between them. When Etta couldn't stand the sound of the heater and the rain anymore, she spoke. "Were Vincent Buchanan and Sakura Tanaka your parents?" She slid her fingers into her bag and pulled out the stack of books and papers inside. "Cherry Blossom" was on top. She wanted to tell him how beautiful his parents' love story was. She wanted to show him Sakura's letter, but she only sat staring, her hands shaking.

"Matthew Lowther." He gazed at the short story. "He's why you've come? I did not know him. He came to visit me once."

Etta felt as though she would collapse, as she waited for him to speak again.

"He asked me to read what is in here." He rested his withered hands on the box. "He said he would be publishing it and wanted me to read it first. He would return in two weeks. He told me it might be hard for me to read, that it would change the way I think of my family. I could not sleep for many days. Maybe I knew what was inside. Maybe I did not. I did not want to know. Then in a dream, my cousin Sakura came to me and told me a man would bring our family from the shadows.

"Sakura had been dead for a long time, and my father had just passed on after a long illness. That morning I awoke weeping. Then Mr. Lowther came, and I felt weightless. You might not understand this feeling, but I carried my ancestors with me every day. Then these two weeks, I could breathe again. We would stop living in shame.

"When Mr. Lowther returned, I would tell him to publish whatever he wished. But I would not read it. I worked in the store all day and stayed until long after the sun went down, pacing back and forth, watching the headlights pass by through the windows. He never arrived, and then I was relieved. I almost set this aflame that night. I had a match lit beneath it." The old man dropped his eyes to the box.

Etta coughed against the spicy scent of incense easing its way in from the front room. "I don't understand. Sakura wasn't your mother?"

The man glanced at the curtain separating them from the front room. "That was the beginning of our lies. My mother was Sakura's aunt, Yoshizaki Sinobu. I never knew her. She died in 1929, just after my family returned to Kyoto when I was only months old. From then on I lived with my aunt, my uncle Katashi, and my cousins Sakura, Miki, and Natsuki. It was not easy for my aunt and uncle to have a haafu in their home during that time. I brought them many years of shame."

Etta rubbed her hands on her black slacks. "A haafu?"

"Mixed blood. Half and half."

Etta gasped. "So Vincent Buchanan was your father?"

The old man smiled. It was the first time Etta had seen his expression change. "Vincent Buchanan was a deity. I met him once when I was a baby, when I was too young to remember such things. I only knew his loyalty was as wide as the Pacific Ocean. To my uncle Katashi, this man was not mortal. It was only many years later I discovered he was flesh-and-blood. He was my uncle."

Etta sat back, staring at "Cherry Blossom" until her eyes blurred. She met the old man's eyes. "I don't understand."

"My father was William Thomas Buchanan."

Etta brought her open palm down. The table shook, and the old man reached for his teacup. "Vincent Buchanan's brother."

"It was not such a lie. My aunt wanted nothing to do with me. Sakura was as close to a mother as I would know. Sakura was the one who taught me English and told me about the place were I was born. Sakura told me who my father was. She spoke of this place so differently than everyone else, and I dreamt of coming here every day, this place where my father was."

"When did you come?" Etta asked after many moments of silence.

"I was nearly a man, almost sixteen years old. We forged papers saying Sakura was my mother. She hoped it would allow her to stay if she was the mother of a Nissei, married to her son's white father. She thought marrying an American would protect her, and it did. It was only many years later that I realized it is never an answer to live in the dark."

Etta sat for a moment trying to make sense of what he was saying. "So Sakura married Vincent Buchanan's brother?"

"Oh no, deceit grows like moss on trees." He drank from his teacup. "My father paid an older man who worked as a butcher in the store to become my father and marry Sakura. He bought the man a house near here and set up a vanity for Sakura, lined the closets with her clothing, hung pictures of us on the walls. I hardly knew this man. But his name is mine, Joseph Thompson, and on my citizenship papers, he is my father and Sakura is my mother. You must understand, I knew who my father was. He was a loving man. I knew it was his famous brother, whose loyalty made everything possible."

For a second, Etta thought she saw the resemblance between Joseph Thompson and Vincent Buchanan, something about his eyes or his chin, but then it was gone. He poured more water in his cup and gazed down. "You might judge me—building a life on lies." He met Etta's gaze. "But sacrifice and fortune had always been my companions. Kyoto was spared the bombings. Only miles from us, Osaka, Nagoya, and Kobe were destroyed. Do you know, Kyoto was on the list of cities for the atomic bomb? Hiroshima, Nagasaki, and Kyoto. Fate left Kyoto in splendor. Can you imagine such fortune?

"I never knew a mother's love, never felt her breath on my cheek as I slept, never smelled her perfume. I never heard her sing. But I found my father. I finally found my father."

He stared somewhere past Etta and grew silent again. She leaned forward, holding her breath, waiting for him to continue.

"In Kyoto after the war, school children were given black markers and told to mark out the part of the national history that may offend our new occupiers—anything about the military, about our proud Kamikaze spirit, about the brutality of the

Allies. We were to ink it out of existence. Why couldn't I also choose a new history for myself?"

He picked up the box, and for a second, Etta was sure he was going to pass it across the table to her. Her hands started to tremble. Then he set it down and folded his hands over it again.

"You can't go back. Your children, your grandchildren, they become your lies. They do not know themselves. I have asked myself so many times, is this what I will leave for my grandchildren—a trail of false stories?"

He stared at the box, and silence settled between them again.

"We have more in common than you might think." Etta's voice trembled. "I just need to know. I need to know what Matthew Lowther left for you."

Joseph Thompson's gaze settled on the stack of papers and books in front of Etta. His eyes were glossy. "Oh yes. Mr. Lowther. He came to the store in the afternoon and walked around for a long time before he spoke to me, looking at things, holding them up and setting them down. Then he approached me and asked me if we could talk alone. It will sound funny now, but I thought he wanted to buy the store. I dreamt of selling it so many times. I could not, of course. It did not belong to me, even if my name was on the deed. It was my uncle Katashi's. It was Sakura's. As my father said, Nihonmachi was gone, but the Tanaka family was still here. But I was forcing my own son to work here instead of going to a university, instead of becoming his own man. If Mr. Lowther had offered to buy the store that day, I wonder . . ." His voice trailed off. He poured more water in his teacup, but he didn't drink.

"I offered Mr. Lowther our finest tea, but then he began asking questions. Not about the store. About my family. He said he knew Sakura was not my mother. And he mentioned Vincent Buchanan's name many times, which made me tremble. My father never wanted anyone to connect me to his famous brother. If he'd been alive, he would have been outraged someone was asking questions." He lowered his head and picked up the tin box. "I gave him Sakura's letters in this box." His voice cracked. "I still don't know why. He intimidated me. The way he talked, his eyes . . ." The old man set the tin box down and picked up the manuscript box, turning it over. The pieces of tape sealing the box were old, discolored—untouched.

Etta lifted her gaze to the old man's. "You never opened it?"

"I knew my uncle Katashi was a member of Kempaitai and the Black Dragon Society. I knew my father and uncle had secrets. But who was I? I wasn't sitting on the Tokyo Tribunal. These men were my family, my ancestors. They had given me everything I'd ever had. How could I pass judgment on any man's choices during a time of war when I was a boy at home with the women? How could Mr. Lowther judge? He did not watch the refugees with burned faces and crying babies trudge in from Kobe and Osaka. He did not wait every day for a bomb to fall. He did not see the hunger in his cousins' eyes when the rations ran low. You think Vincent Buchanan was a traitor? A monster? Never forget, he loved my uncle Katashi. He loved Sakura. He loved me. To us, his loyalty was as wide as the Pacific.

Etta nodded, watching as the old man ran his hands over the box, flipping it over again and again.

"Not long ago, I asked my young katakana to type Mr. Lowther's name into that computer of hers. She insisted she could find anything. She read me a story about him, and I understood for the first time why he did not return. Someone didn't want him to publish this. I still wonder if my wishes were answered that day, or if I was cursed."

A chill rose up Etta's spine. The old man pushed the box toward her and stood. "A brave family should not live in shame." Etta rose to her feet too. The old man looked so sad that she wanted to grasp his arm, but she reached for the box instead. The cardboard was brittle.

The old man shuffled through the maze of boxes then turned and looked at Etta, the light from the windows catching his white hair. "Soon, I will see Sakura again. Perhaps she sent you from the heavens to bring my family from the darkness."

Epilogue

◆

TEN MONTHS LATER.

Olivia's dark gaze sweeps the crowd, and no one seems to breathe. She leans forward, wrapping her willowy fingers around both sides of the podium advertising the Strand's eighteen miles of books. She's framed by the narrow window behind her, a black sliver between the floor-to-ceiling bookshelves. Her hair is short and layered around her face, and her cheekbones are more pronounced than they were a year ago. Her scarlet scoop-neck dress reveals hollows beneath her clavicle. Finally she looks down and continues reading.

Etta finds a place to stand at the back of the crowd. She can tell that the reading is nearly over by the way Olivia's voice is building to a crescendo. People lean forward, swallowing her words. For the first time since Etta moved to the row house on Havemeyer in Williamsburg, she worked up the courage to catch the L train into Manhattan. She usually walks across the Williamsburg Bridge and catches cabs, her eyes darting away when she passes the dark subway stairwells.

Tonight she was running late and convinced herself to board the train. But as it rocked back and forth beneath the East

River, she thought of how Olivia's father died, and her throat tightened. She elbowed her way off the train many stops too soon, sprinting up the station steps and gulping in the breezeless July air, as busses and cabs sped up Fourteenth Street.

The metal folding chairs are full; people are squeezed into the aisles, plastered against the shelves, squeezed on every side of Etta. Sweat rolls off Etta's forehead; her hair is damp. But just the thought of Olivia's foreword sends a chill through her. Etta has reread Matthew Lowther's book twice since its cover graced the front page of the *New York Times* on the day of its release last month. And she's read Olivia's foreword so many times she could recite it word for word:

On a drizzly morning last March, I stood on the grounds of the most eminent writing academy in the country in a dilapidated pioneer cemetery watching a team of FBI agents brush dirt from my father's bones. It occurred to me then that my father probably had something in common with the Oregon settlers entombed beside him. You see, before heart rate monitors and embalming made the line between life and death definitive, countless people were most likely unintentionally buried alive.

My father too was buried alive—except what happened to him was no accident.

On a December night in 1985, my father's mouth was sealed with duct tape, his clothes were stripped from his body, and his hands were bound behind his back. Then he was left to asphyxiate in the pitch black of a wooden box six feet beneath the ferns.

Everything I know about my father, I've learned in the last two years. His name was Matthew Lowther. He was an adjunct literature professor at the University of Rochester. He was thirty-two-years-old the summer he moved to Oregon to attend the Buchanan Academy.

Who would want to harm him? What did he do to compel such an act of horror to be inflicted upon him? These questions took me to the Buchanan Academy last June. Eight months later, many of the answers have come to light. Criminal trials have ensued.

Edwin Hardin and Uriah Winston Mills, two of the three people responsible for my father's death, are in prison.

I know one thing for sure: my father was a hero. He gave his life to exposing the truth about Vincent Buchanan, a traitor who masqueraded as a patriot while he shared our secrets with the enemy.

I will probably always have nightmares about the way my father died. They wake me in the middle of the night, leaving me nauseous and sweating, my heart palpating, my chest squeezed so tight I can't catch my breath. I've been prescribed a rainbow of pills—Zoloft, Paxil, Klonopin, Xanax, and propranolol. But I've come to realize that I'll never understand such evil, just as I'll never again be able to sleep in the dark.

That's the part of the foreword where Etta usually has to stop and put the book down to catch her breath. But Olivia is not reading from her foreword this evening; she's reading the part of Matthew Lowther's introduction where he writes about going to Kyoto to research Kitashi Tanaka. Lowther finds Miki, Sakura's youngest sister, living in Tokyo. She is in her sixties and remembers Vincent Buchanan's visits. She tells Lowther that Buchanan visited Kyoto three times when she was a child and stayed with her family each time.

When Lowther is trying to trace Buchanan's movements in Kyoto, he discovers that another American in his twenties named Peter Morrison visited around the same time and attended meetings of the Black Dragon Society in 1932. Lowther recognizes the name Peter Morrison immediately as a minor character in "The End of the River," one of Vincent Buchanan's early short stories, which was published in a posthumous collection.

Lowther returns to the United States and travels to Portland to conduct more research into Buchanan's life. He finds an old article about Tanaka Grocery in the *Oshu Nippo*, Portland's Japanese American newspaper. It lists some of the employees' names, and Lowther tracks down Joe Ochikubo, a Japanese American who was relocated with his family to the

Granada relocation center in Colorado in 1942 and moved to Denver after the war.

Lowther visits Ochikubo in Denver and learns that Kitashi Tanaka and his family returned to Japan in 1929 because they were scared for their daughters' safety as the West Coast became an increasingly hostile place for Japanese Americans. After they left, a white man took over ownership of the store. "We all knew him. He delivered meat to Tanaka Grocery for many years," Ochikubo tells Lowther. It was Vincent Buchanan's brother William.

According to Ochikubo, while the grocery store stopped direct trade with Japan in 1941, they continued a limited exchange of goods through a shipping outfit in Buenos Aires.

That's when Matthew Lowther begins to suspect that Peter Morrison was Vincent Buchanan, and that Buchanan spied for the Japanese by transmitting the sensitive information he learned while researching *The Western Defense* to his friend Kitashi Tanaka, an officer in Japan's secret service Kempeitai. He did it through Tanaka Grocery, now managed by his brother.

But Matthew Lowther needs more proof before he goes public with his theory, and he's eager to look through Buchanan's notoriously inaccessible archives. He decides the only way to do that is to apply for admission to the Buchanan Academy.

Lowther's writing seems to grow darker once he's at the academy, more direct and urgent, almost panicked. Etta can only imagine how terrified he was by the time he delivered a copy of his manuscript to Tanaka Grocery to give Joseph Thompson two weeks to prepare for the storm that was about to descend on his family.

When she thinks about what it must have been like for Lowther the night he was killed, she can almost feel herself suspended in Hardin's office window, the shards of glass under her feet, rain pelting her flesh, nowhere to go but down. But Etta forces it out of her mind, because Olivia is in front of her, leaning on the podium, her face periodically illuminated by camera flashes. Her voice is just as Etta remembered. Etta can almost imagine her friend's face widening into a smile, her voice easing into her loose laughter.

When Olivia finishes the introduction, her eyes pierce the crowd again. Many of the details in the book have trickled out over the past ten months in the international press with headlines like, "American Patriot Outed as Traitor," "Legendary Author Spied for Japan," and "Buchanan Committed Treason." But still the crowd seems to be stunned into silence by the full weight of the revelations.

Etta is sure for a moment that her old roommate is looking at her. Etta brings her hand up to wave. But then Olivia pivots toward a short woman, who's stepping up beside her. People clap. Cameras flash. Olivia smiles and steps from behind the podium.

Etta moves forward, but she is blocked by the circle of bodies tightening around Olivia. A line forms, meandering around tables and shelves, snaking to the stairwell. Etta overhears someone say Vincent Buchanan's name, but she can't focus on the words. All she can think about is how close Olivia is. She half expects to smell the familiar aroma of Olivia's lavender oil.

Olivia doesn't know that it was Etta who pulled off the highway near Jackson and called the police on that rainy October morning ten months ago, the day Director Hardin confessed, divulging the spot where the librarian buried Matthew Lowther, just a few feet away from a crumbling sculpture of an angel. Olivia doesn't know that Etta drove to Portland to visit Joseph Thompson, just as Matthew Lowther had done a week before he died. Olivia doesn't know that it was Etta who sent Matthew Lowther's manuscript to her aunt in an anonymous package with no return address.

The crowd pulsates around Etta. She glances at the book in her hands: *A Traitor in the Trees.* "Foreword by Olivia Saxon," it says in small print under Matthew Lowther's name.

Etta lifts her gaze to the oak bookshelves that soar up on every side of the crowd like the cedars and Douglas firs flanking Roosevelt Lodge, and then she swivels and pushes her way toward the stairs. She emerges onto Broadway and waves for a cab. It's early still, and she has a novel to finish.

Explore the World

of The Garden of Dead Dreams

Thank you for reading *The Garden of Dead Dreams*. Please visit abbyquillen.com/explore to find a book group discussion guide and peek behind the scenes at the making of the book. You can learn about Portland's Japantown and the inspiration for Vincent Buchanan and Roosevelt Lodge. You can also sign up for Abby's newsletter to get the latest updates about her new mystery series.

If you liked this book, please tell a friend and consider writing a short review on the site where you bought it or on your favorite social network. Reviews make a huge difference in helping other readers discover debut authors and new titles.

Connect with Abby online:

Website: http://abbyquillen.com
Newsletter: http://abbyquillen.com/subscribe

About the Author

◆

Abby Quillen is the author of the novel *The Garden of Dead Dreams* and the editor of two anthologies, *Deeper into the Heart of the Rockies* and *Dispatches from the High Country*. Her articles and essays have appeared in *YES! Magazine* and *The Christian Science Monitor* and on *Common Dreams*, *Nation of Change*, *Reader Supported News*, *The Daily Good*, *Truthout*, and *Shareable.net*. She lives with her family in Eugene, Oregon and loves connecting with readers at her website: abbyquillen.com.

Acknowledgments

◆

I am forever grateful to my parents Ed and Martha Quillen, who raised me in a house full of books and shared with me their love of words, history, and literature.

My husband Aaron Thomas has been my most dedicated fan and cheerleader since I first typed "Chapter One" many years ago. His support made this book possible in a dozen different ways.

I'm also thankful to Ezra and Ira, my two sons, who continually remind me of the importance of imagination and storytelling. They will drop nearly anything to hear a good story.

I appreciate everyone who has read parts of this book over the years, including Columbine Quillen and many members of Willamette Writers, including Zahie El Kouri, Shirley West, Jodi Henry, Tamsin Morgan, Deb Mohr, and Linda Clare. Their encouragement was invaluable. And lastly, thank you to Kelly Schaub, Martha Quillen, and Honore Pazdral for their excellent editorial skills.